D0429143

THE MARBLE QUILT

Also by David Leavitt

Family Dancing

The Lost Language of Cranes

Equal Affections

A Place I've Never Been

While England Sleeps

Italian Pleasures
(with Mark Mitchell)

Arkansas

The Page Turner

Martin Bauman; or, A Sure Thing

In Maremma: Life and a
House in Southern Tuscany
(with Mark Mitchell)

The Marble Quilt

· STORIES ·

David Leavitt

Houghton Mifflin Company

Boston · New York

2001

Copyright © 2001 by David Leavitt
All rights reserved

For information about permission to reproduce selections
from this book, write to Permissions, Houghton Mifflin Company,
215 Park Avenue South, New York, New York 10003.

Visit our Web site: www.houghtonmifflinbooks.com.

Library of Congress Cataloging-in-Publication Data
Leavitt, David, date.
The marble quilt : stories / David Leavitt.
p.   cm.
Contents: Crossing St. Gotthard—The infection scene—
Route 80—Black box—Speonk—The scruff of the neck—
The list—Heaped earth—The marble quilt.
ISBN 0-395-90244-4
I. Title.
PS3562.E2618 M36   2001
813'.54—dc21   2001024522

Printed in the United States of America
QUM 10 9 8 7 6 5 4 3 2 1

Book design by Melissa Lotfy
Typeface is Hoefler Text

"Crossing St. Gotthard" originally appeared in *The Paris Review*
and was also included in the anthology *Bright Pages*. The first part of
"Route 80" was broadcast on National Public Radio and included
in the anthology *The Wedding Cake in the Middle of the Road*.
"Speonk" first appeared in *DoubleTake*, "The Scruff of the Neck"
in *The Southwest Review*, and "Heaped Earth" in *Tin House*.

An earlier version of "Crossing St. Gotthard"
was published in a limited edition by Elysium Press.

Contents

For Dad and Jean,
Jim and Diane,
and, always, Mark

The Marble Quilt

CROSSING ST. GOTTHARD

IT WAS THE TUNNEL —its imminence—that all of them were contemplating that afternoon on the train, each in a different way; the tunnel, at nine miles the longest in the world, slicing under the gelid landscape of the St. Gotthard Pass. To Irene it was an object of dread. She feared enclosure in small spaces, had heard from Maisie Withers that during the crossing the carriage heated up to a boiling pitch. "I was as black as a nigger from the soot," Maisie Withers said. "People have died." "Never again," Maisie Withers concluded, pouring lemonade in her sitting room in Hartford, and meaning never again the tunnel but also (Irene knew) never again Italy, never again Europe; for Maisie was a gullible woman, and during her tour had had her pocketbook stolen.

And it was not only Maisie Withers, Irene reflected now (watching, across the way, her son Grady, his nose flat against the glass), but also her own ancient terror of windowless rooms, of corners, that since their docking in Liverpool had brought the prospect of the tunnel looming before her, black as death itself (a being which, as she approached fifty, she was trying to muster the courage to meet eye to eye), until she found herself counting first the weeks, then the days, then the hours leading up to the inevitable reckoning: the train slipping into the dark, into the mountain. (It was half a mile deep, Grady kept reminding her, half a mile of solid rock separating earth from sky.) Irene remembered a ghost story she'd read as a girl—a man believed to be dead wakes in his coffin. Was it too late to hire a carriage, then, to go *over* the pass, as Toby had? But no. Winter had already started up there. Oh, if she'd had her way, they'd have taken a different route; only Grady would have been disappointed, and since his brother's death she dared not disappoint Grady. He longed for the tunnel as ardently as his mother dreaded it.

"Mama, is it coming soon?"

"Yes, dear."

"But you said half an hour."

"Hush, Grady! I'm not a clock."

"But you said—"

"Read your book, Grady," Harold interrupted.

"I finished it."

"Then do your puzzle."

"I finished that, too."

"Then look out the window."

"Or just shut up," added Stephen, his eyes sliding open.

"Stephen, you're not to talk to your brother that way."

"He's a pest. Can't a fellow get some sleep?"

Stephen's eyes slid shut, and Grady turned to examine the view. Though nearly fourteen, he was still a child. His leg shook. With his breath he fogged shapes onto the glass.

"Did I tell you it's the longest in the world? Did I tell you—"

"Yes, Grady. Now please hush."

They didn't understand. They were always telling him to hush. Well, all right, he would hush. He would never again utter a single word, and show them all.

Irene sneezed.

"Excuse me," she said to the red-nosed lady sitting next to her.

"Heavens! You needn't apologize to *me*."

"It's getting cold rather early this year," Irene ventured, relieved beyond measure to discover that her neighbor spoke English.

"Indeed it is. It gets cold earlier every year, I find. Judgment Day must be nigh!"

Irene laughed. They started chatting. She was elegantly got up, this red-nosed lady. She knitted with her gloves on. From her hat extended a fanciful aigrette that danced and bobbed. Grady watched it, watched the moving mountains outside the window. (Some were already capped with snow.) Then the train turned, the sun came blazing into the compartment so sharply that the red-nosed lady murmured, "Goodness me," shielded her eyes, pulled the curtain shut against it.

Well, that did it for Grady. After all, hadn't they just told him to look at the view? No one cared. He had finished his book. He had finished his puzzle. The tunnel would never arrive.

Snorting, he thrust his head behind the curtain.

"Grady, don't be rude."

He didn't answer. And really, behind the curtain it was a different world. He could feel warmth on his face. He could revel in the delicious sensation of apartness that the gold-lit curtain bestowed, and that only the chatter of women interrupted. But it was rude.

"Oh, I know, I know!" (Whose voice was that? The red-nosed lady's?) "Oh yes, I know!" (Women always said that. They always knew.)

Harold had his face in a book. Stephen was a bully.

"Oh dear, yes!"

Whoever was talking, her voice was loud. His mother's voice he could not make out. His mother's voice was high but not loud, unless she shouted, which she tended to do lately. Outside the window an Alpine landscape spread out: fir groves, steep-roofed wooden houses, fields of dead sunflowers to which the stuffy compartment with its scratched mahogany paneling bore no discernible relation. This first-class compartment belonged to the gaslit ambience of stations and station hotels. It was a bubble of metropolitan, semipublic space sent out into the wide world, and from the confines of which its inmates could regard the uncouth spectacle of nature as a kind of *tableau vivant.* Still, the trappings of luxury did little to mask its fundamental discomforts: seats that pained the back, fetid air, dirty carpets.

They were on their way to Italy, Irene told Mrs. Warshaw (for this was the red-nosed lady's name). They were on their way to Italy for a tour—Milan, Venice, Verona, Florence, Rome (Irene counted off on her fingers), then a villa in Naples for the winter months—because her sons ought to see the world, she felt; American boys knew so little; they had studied French but could hardly speak a word. (Mrs. Warshaw, nodding fervently, agreed it was a shame.)

"And this will be your first trip to Italy?"

"The first time I've been abroad, actually, although my brother, Toby, came twenty years ago. He wrote some lovely letters for the *Hartford Evening Post.*"

"Marvelous! And how lucky you are to have three handsome sons as escorts. I myself have only a daughter."

"Oh, but Harold's not my son! Harold's my cousin Millie's boy. He's the tutor."

"How nice." Mrs. Warshaw smiled assessingly at Harold. Yes, she thought, tutor he is, and tutor he will always be. He looked the part of the poor relation, no doubt expected to play the same role in the lady's life abroad that his mother played in her life at home: the companion to whom she could turn when she needed consolation, or someone to torture. (Mrs. Warshaw knew the ways of the world.)

As for the boys, the brothers: the older one looked different. Darker. Different fathers, perhaps?

But Irene thought: She's right. I do—*did*—have three sons.

And Harold tried to hide inside his book. Only he thought: They ought to treat me with more respect. The boys ought to call me Mr. Prescott, not Cousin Hal, for they hardly know me. Also, he smarted at the dismissive tone with which Aunt Irene enunciated the word *tutor,* as if he were something just one step above the level of a servant. He deserved better than that, deserved better than to be at the beck and call of boys in whom art, music, the classical world, inspired boredom at best, outright contempt at worst. For though Uncle George, God rest his soul, had financed his education, it was not Uncle George who had gotten the highest scores in the history of the Classics Department. It was not Uncle George whose translations of Cicero had won a prize. Harold had done all that himself.

On the other hand, goodness knew he could never have afforded Europe on his own. To his charges he owed the blessed image of his mother's backyard in St. Louis, his mother in her gardening gloves and hat, holding her shears over the roses while on the porch the old chair in which he habitually spent his summers reading, or sleeping, or cursing—my God, he wasn't in it! It was empty! To them he owed this miracle.

"And will your husband be joining you in Naples?"

"I'm afraid my husband passed away last winter."

"Ah."

Mrs. Warshaw dropped a stitch.

The overdecorated compartment in which these five people were sitting was small—four feet by six feet. Really, it had the look of a theater stall, Harold decided, with its maroon velvet seats, its window like a stage, its curtain—well, like a curtain. Above the stained headrests wrapped in slipcovers embellished with the crest of the railway hung six prints in reedy frames: three yellowed views of Rome—Trajan's Column (the glass cracked), the Pantheon, the Colosseum (over which Mrs. Warshaw's aigrette danced); and opposite, as if to echo the perpetual contempt with which the Christian world regards the pagan, three views of Florence—Santa Croce, the Duomo, the Palazzo Vecchio guarded by Michelangelo's immense nude David—none of which Harold, who reverenced the classical, could see. Instead, when he glanced up from his book, it was the interior of the Pantheon that met his gaze, the orifice at the center of the dome throwing against its coffered ceiling a coin of light.

He put down his book. (It was Ovid's *Metamorphoses*, in Latin.) Across from him, under the Pantheon, Stephen sprawled, his long legs in their loose flannel trousers spread wide but bent at the knees, because finally they were too long, those legs, for a compartment in which three people were expected to sit facing three people for hours at a time. He was asleep, or pretending to be asleep, so that Harold could drink in his beauty for once with impunity, while Mrs. Warshaw knitted, and Grady's head bobbed behind the curtain, and Aunt Irene said she knew, she knew. Stephen was motionless. Stephen was inscrutable. Still, Harold could tell that he too was alert to the tunnel's imminence; he could tell because every few minutes his eyes slotted open, the way the eyes of a doll do when you tilt back its head: green and gold, those eyes, like the sun-mottled grass beneath a tree.

He rarely spoke, Stephen. His body had the elongated musculature of a harp. His face was elusive in its beauty, like those white masks the Venetians wear at Carnival. Only sometimes he shifted his legs, in those flannel trousers that were a chaos of folds, a mountain landscape, valleys, passes, peaks. Most, Harold knew, if you punched them down, would flatten; but one would grow heavy and warm at his touch.

And now Harold had to put his book on his lap. He had to. He was twenty-two years old, scrawny, with a constitution his doctor described as "delicate"; yet when he closed his eyes, he and Stephen wore togas and stood together in a square filled with rational light. Or Harold was a great warrior, and Stephen the beloved *eremenos* over whose gore-drenched body he scattered kisses at battle's end. Or they were training together, naked, in the gymnasium.

Shameful thoughts! He must cast them out of his mind. He must find a worthier object for his adoration than this stupid, vulgar boy, this boy who, for all his facile handsomeness, would have hardly raised an eyebrow in the age of Socrates.

"Not Captain Warshaw, though! The Captain had a stomach of iron."

What were they talking about? The Channel crossing, no doubt. Aunt Irene never tired of describing her travel woes. She detested boats, detested hotel beds, hated tunnels. Whereas Harold, if anyone had asked him, would have said that he looked forward to the tunnel not as an end in itself, the way Grady did, but because the tunnel meant the south, meant Italy. For though it did not literally link Switzerland

with Italy, on one side the towns had German names—
Göschenen, Andermatt, Hospenthal—while on the other
they had Italian names—Airolo, Ambri, Lurengo—and this
fact in itself was enough to intoxicate him.

Now Stephen stretched; the landscape of his trousers surged,
earthquakes leveled the peaks, the rivers were rerouted and
the crust of the earth churned up. It was as if a capricious
god, unsatisfied with his handiwork, had decided to forge the
world anew.

"Ah, how I envy any traveler his first visit to Italy!" Mrs.
Warshaw said. "Because for you it will be new—what is for
me already faded. Beginning with Airolo, the campanile, as
the train comes out the other end of the tunnel . . ."

Harold's book twitched. He knew all about the campanile.

"Is it splendid?" Irene asked.

"Oh, no." Mrs. Warshaw shook her head decisively. "Not
splendid at all. Quite plain, in fact, especially when you com-
pare it to all those other wonderful Italian towers—in Pisa, in
Bologna. I mustn't forget San Gimignano! Yes, compared to
the towers of San Gimignano, the campanile of Airolo is utterly without distinction or merit. Still, you will never forget
it, because it is the first."

"Well, we shall look forward to it. Grady, be sure to look
out for the tower of . . . just after the tunnel."

The curtain didn't budge.

Irene's smile said: "Sons."

"And where are you traveling, if I might be so bold?"

"To Florence. It's my habit to spend the winter there.
You see, when I lost the Captain, I went abroad intending
to make a six-months tour of Europe. But then six months
turned into a year, and a year into five years, and now it will be

eight years in January since I last walked on native soil. Oh, I think of returning to Toronto sometimes, settling in some little nook. And yet there is still so much to see! I have the travel bug, I fear. I wonder if I shall ever go home." Mrs. Warshaw gazed toward the curtained window. "Ah, beloved Florence!" she exhaled. "How I long once again to take in the view from Bellosguardo."

"How lovely it must be," echoed Irene, though in truth she had no idea where Bellosguardo was, and feared repeating the name lest she should mispronounce it.

"Florence is full of treasures," Mrs. Warshaw continued. "For instance, you must go to the Palazzo della Signoria and look at the Perseus."

Harold's book twitched again. He knew all about the Perseus.

"Of course we shall go and see them straightaway," Irene said. "When do they bloom?"

When do they bloom!

It sometimes seemed to Harold that it was Aunt Irene, and not her sons, who needed the tutor. She was ignorant of everything, and yet she never seemed to care when she made an idiot of herself. In Harold's estimation, this was typical of the Pratt branch of the family. With the exception of dear departed Toby (both of them), no one in that branch of the family possessed the slightest receptivity to what Pater called (and Harold never forgot it) "the poetic passion, the desire of beauty, the love of art for its own sake." Pratts were anti-Paterian. Not for them Pater's "failure is forming habits." To them the formation of habits—healthy habits—was the very essence of success. (It was a subject on which Uncle George, God rest his soul, had taken no end of pleasure in lecturing Harold.)

Still, Harold could not hate them. After all, they had made his education possible. At Thanksgiving and Christmas they always had a place for him at their table (albeit crammed in at a corner in a kitchen chair). "Our little scholarship boy," Aunt Irene called him. "Our little genius, Harold."

Later, after Uncle George had died, and Toby had died, and Toby the Second as well, Irene had come to him. "Harold, would you like to see Europe?" she'd asked, fixing his collar.

"More than anything, Aunt Irene."

"Because I'm planning a little tour this fall with the boys—following my brother's itinerary, you know—and I thought, Wouldn't it be marvelous for them to have a tutor, a scholar like yourself, to tell them what was what. What do you think, Harold? Would your mother mind?"

"I think it's a capital idea."

"Good."

So here he was.

So far, things hadn't gone well at all.

In Paris, Harold had decided to test the boys' receptivity to art by taking them to the Louvre. But Grady wanted only to ride the métro, and got infuriated when Harold explained that there was no need to take the métro: the museum was only a block from their hotel. Then they were standing in front of the Mona Lisa, Harold lecturing, Grady quivering with rage at having been deprived of the métro, Stephen leaning, inscrutable as ever, against a white wall. Harold spoke eloquently about the painting and, as he spoke, he felt the silent pressure of their boredom. They had their long bodies arranged in attitudes of sculptural indifference, as if to say, we have no truck with any of this. Curse our mother for pulling us out of our lives, and curse our father for dying, and our brother for dying, and curse you. To which Harold wanted to answer: Well, do you think I like it any more than you do? Do you think I enjoy babbling like an idiot, and being ignored?

For the truth was, the scrim of their apathy diffused his own sense of wonder. After all, he was seeing this for the first time, too: not a cheap reproduction, but *La Gioconda*. The real thing. How dare they not notice, not care?

Yes, Harold decided that morning, they were normal, these boys. They would never warm to art. (As if to prove his point, they now gravitated away from his lecturing, and toward an old man who had set up an easel and paints to copy a minor annunciation—their curiosity piqued by some low circus element in the proceedings: "Gosh, it looks exactly like the original!" an American man standing nearby said to his wife.) Why Aunt Irene had insisted on bringing them to Europe in the first place Harold still couldn't fathom; what did she think was going to happen, anyway? Did she imagine that upon contact with the sack of Rome, the riches of Venice, some dormant love of beauty would awaken in them, and they would suddenly be transformed into cultured, intellectual boys, the sort upon whom she could rely for flashes of wit at dinner parties, crossword solutions on rainy afternoons? Boys, in other words, like their brother Toby, or their uncle Toby, for that matter, who had kept a portrait of Byron on his desk. Grady, on the other hand, couldn't have cared less about Byron, while Stephen, so far as Harold could tell, liked only to lean against white walls in his flannel trousers, challenging the marble for beauty. Really, he was too much, Stephen: self-absorbed, smug, arrogant. Harold adored him.

There was a rapping on the compartment door.

"*Entrez*," announced Mrs. Warshaw.

The conductor stepped in. Immediately Grady pulled back the curtain, splaying the light. Stephen's eyes slotted open again.

"Permit me to excuse myself," the conductor said in tormented French, "but we are approaching the St. Gotthard tunnel. I shall now light the lamps and make certain that the windows and ventilators are properly closed."

"Bien sûr."

The conductor was Italian, a handsome, sturdy fellow with a thick black mustache, blue eyes, fine lips. Dark hairs curled under his cuffs, rode down the length of his hands to the ends of his thick fingers.

Bowing, he stepped to the front of the compartment, where he got down on his knees and fiddled with the ventilator panel. As he knelt he winked manfully at Grady.

"Oh, I don't like tunnels," Irene said. "I get claustrophobic."

"I hope you don't get seasick!" Mrs. Warshaw laughed. "But never mind. When you've been through the St. Gotthard as often as I have, you shall sleep right through, as I intend to do."

"How long is it again?"

"Nine miles!" Grady shouted. "The longest in the—" He winced. He had broken his vow.

"Nine miles! Dear Lord! And it will take half an hour?"

"More or less."

"Half an hour in the dark!"

"The gas jets will be lit. You needn't worry."

The conductor, having finished with the ventilators, stood to examine the window latches. In securing the one on the right he pressed a wool-covered leg against Harold's knees.

"Va bene," he said next, yanking at the latch for good measure. (It did not give.) Then he turned to face Harold, over whose head the oil lamp protruded; raised his arms into the air to light it, so that his shirt pulled up almost but not quite enough to reveal a glimpse of what was underneath (what *was* underneath?); parted his legs around Harold's knees. Harold had no choice but to stare into the white of that shirt, breathe in its odor of eau de cologne and cigar.

·

Then the lamp was lit. Glancing down, the conductor smiled.

"Merci mesdames," he concluded merrily. And to Harold: *"Grazie, signore."*

Harold muttered, *"Prego,"* kept his eyes out the window. The door shut firmly.

"I shall be so happy to have my first glimpse of Milan," Irene said.

Why French for the women and Italian for him?

They had been traveling forever. They had been traveling for years: Paris, the gaslit platform at the Gare de Lyon, a distant dream; then miles of dull French farmland, flat and blurred; and then the clattery dollhouse architecture of Switzerland, all that grass and those little clusters of chalets with their tilted roofs and knotty shuttered windows, like the window the bird would have flown out on the cuckoo clock . . . if it had ever worked, if Uncle George had ever bothered to fix it. But he had not.

Really, there was nothing to do but read, so Harold read.

Orpheus: having led Eurydice up from the Underworld, he turned to make sure she hadn't tired behind him. He turned even though he had been warned in no uncertain terms not to turn; that turning was the one forbidden thing. And what happened? Exactly what Orpheus should have expected to happen. As if his eyes themselves shot out rays of plague, Eurydice shrank back into the vapors and died a second death, fell back down the dark well. This story of Orpheus and Eurydice Harold had read a hundred times, maybe even five hundred times, and still it frustrated him; still he hoped each time that Orpheus would catch on for once, and not look back. Yet he always looked back. And why? Had love turned Orpheus's head? Harold doubted it. Perhaps the exigencies of story, then: for really, if the episode had ended with the happy couple emerging safely into the dewy morning light, something in every reader would have been left slavering for the expected payoff.

Of course there were other possible explanations. For instance: perhaps Orpheus had found it impossible not to give in to a certain self-destructive impulse; that inability, upon being told "Don't cross that line," not to cross it.

Only God has the power to turn back time.

Or perhaps Orpheus, at the last minute, had changed his mind; decided he didn't want Eurydice back after all. This was a radical interpretation, albeit one to which later events in Orpheus's life lent credence.

Harold remembered something—*Huck Finn,* he thought— you must never look over your shoulder at the moon.

Something made him put his book down. Stephen had woken up. He was rubbing his left eye with the ball of his fist. No, he did not look like his brother, did not look like any Pratt, for that matter. (Mrs. Warshaw was correct about this, though little else.) According to Harold's mother, this was because Aunt Irene, after years of not being able to conceive, had taken him in as a foundling, only wouldn't you know it? The very day the baby arrived she found out she was pregnant. "It's always like that," his mother had said. "Women who take in foundlings always get pregnant the day the foundling arrives."

Nine months later Toby was born—Toby the Second— that marvelous boy who rivaled his adopted brother for athletic skills, outstripped him in book smarts, but was handsome, too, Pratt handsome, with pale skin and small ears. Toby had been a star pupil, whereas Irene had had to plead with the headmaster to keep Stephen from being held back a grade. Not that the boys disliked each other: instead, so far as

Harold could tell, they simply made a point of ignoring each other. (And how was this possible? How was it possible for anyone to ignore either of them?)

"Be kind to your Aunt Irene," his mother had told him at the station in St. Louis. "She's known too much death."

And now she sat opposite him, here on the train, and he could see from her eyes that it was true: she had known too much death.

Harold flipped ahead a few pages.

Throughout this time Orpheus had shrunk from loving any woman, either because of his unhappy experience, or because he had pledged himself not to do so. In spite of this there were many who were fired with a desire to marry the poet, many were indignant to find themselves repulsed. However, Orpheus preferred to center his affection on boys of tender years, and to enjoy the brief spring and early flowering of their youth: he was the first to introduce this custom among the people of Thrace.

Boys of tender years, like Stephen, who, as Harold glanced up, shifted again, opened his eyes, and stared at his cousin malevolently.

And the train rumbled, and Mrs. Warshaw's aigrette fluttered before the Colosseum, and the cracked glass that covered Trajan's Column rattled.

They were starting to climb at a steeper gradient. They were nearing the tunnel at last.

From the *Hartford Evening Post,* November 4, 1878: Letter Six, "Crossing from the Tyrol into Ticino," by Tobias R. Pratt:

As we began the climb over the great mountain of San Gottardo our *mulattiere,* a most affable and friendly fellow within whose Germanic accent one could detect echoes of the imminent South, explained that even as we made our way through the pass, at that very moment men were laboring under our feet to dig a vast railway tunnel that upon completion will be the longest in the world. This tunnel will make Italy an easier destination for those of us who wish always to be idling in her beneficent breezes . . . and yet how far the Palazzo della Signoria seemed to us that morning, as we rose higher and higher into snowy regions! It was difficult to believe that on the other side the lovely music of the Italian voice and the taste of a rich red wine awaited us; still this faith gave us the strength to persevere through what we knew would be three days of hard travel.

To pass the time, we asked our guide his opinion of the new tunnel. His response was ambivalent. Yes, he admitted, the tunnel would bring tourism (and hence money) to his corner of the world. And yet the cost! Had we heard, for instance, that already one hundred men had lost their lives underground? A hint of superstitious worry entered his voice, as if he feared lest the mountain—outraged by such invasions— should one day decide that it had had enough and with one great heave of its breast smash the tunnel and all its occupants to smithereens. . . .

And Irene thought: He never saw it. He had been dead two years already by the time it was finished.

And Grady thought: Finally.

And Mrs. Warshaw thought: I hope the *signora* saved me Room 5, as she promised.

And Harold watched Stephen's trousers hungrily, hungrily. Glimpses, guesses. All he had ever known were glimpses, guesses. Never, God forbid, a touch; never, never the sort of fraternal bond, unsullied by carnal need, to which epic poetry paid homage; never anything—except this ceaseless worrying of a bone from which every scrap of meat had long been chewed, this ceaseless searching for an outline amid the folds of a pair of flannel trousers.

Yes, he thought, leaning back, I should have been born in classical times. For he genuinely believed himself to be the victim of some heavenly imbroglio, the result of which was his being delivered not (as he should have been) into an Athenian boudoir (his mother someone wise and severe, like Plotina), but rather into a bassinet in a back bedroom in St. Louis where the air was wrong, the light was wrong, the milk did not nourish him. No wonder he grew up ugly, ill, ill-tempered! He belonged to a different age. And now he wanted to cry out, so that all of Switzerland could hear him: I belong to a different age!

The train slowed. Behind the curtain Grady watched the signs giving way one to the next, one to the next: GÖ-SCHE-NEN, GÖ-SCHE-NEN. GÖ-SCHE-NEN.

By such songs as these the Thracian poet was drawing the woods and rocks to follow him, charming the creatures of the wild, when suddenly the Ciconian women caught sight of him. Looking down from the crest of a hill, these maddened creatures, with animal skins slung across their breasts, saw Orpheus as he was singing and accompanying himself on the lyre. One of them, tossing her hair till it streamed in the light breeze, cried out: "See! Look here! Here is the man who scorns us!" and flung her spear—

Darkness. Harold shut his book.

As soon as the train entered the tunnel the temperature began to rise. Despite the careful labors of the conductor, smoke was slipping into the compartment: not enough to be discernible at first by anything other than its dry, sharp smell; but then Harold noticed that no sooner had he wiped his spectacles clean, than they were already filmed again with dust; and then a gray fog, almost a mist, occupied the compartment, obscuring his vision; he could no longer distinguish, for instance, which of the three little prints across the way from him represented the Pantheon, which Trajan's Column, which the Colosseum.

Mrs. Warshaw's head slumped. She snored.

And Grady pressed his face up against the glass, even though there was nothing to see outside the window but a bluish black void, which he likened to the sinuous fabric of space itself.

And Irene, a handkerchief balled in her fist, wondered: Do the dead age? Would her little Toby, in heaven, remain forever the child he had been when he had died? Or would he grow, marry, have angel children?

And Toby her brother? Had *he* had angel children?

If Toby was in heaven—and not the other place. She sometimes feared he might be in the other place—every sermon she'd ever heard suggested it—in which case she would probably never get closer to him than she was right now, right here, in this infernal tunnel.

She glanced at Stephen, awake now. God forgive her for thinking it, but it should have been him, repairing the well with George. Only Stephen had been in bed with influenza, so Toby went.

Punishment? But if so, for what? Thoughts?

Could you be punished for thoughts?

Suddenly she could hardly breathe the searing air—as if a hundred men were smoking cigars all at once.

■

Midway—or what Harold assumed was midway—he thought he heard the wheels scrape. So the train would stall, and then what would they do? There wouldn't be enough oxygen to get out on foot without suffocating. The tunnel was too long. Half a mile of rock separated train from sky; half a mile of rock, atop which trees grew, a woman milked her cow, a baker made bread.

The heat abashed; seemed to eat the air. Harold felt the weight of mountains on his lungs.

Think of other things, he told himself, and in his mind undid the glissando of buttons on Stephen's trousers. Yet the smell in his nostrils—that smell of cigars—was the conductor's.

Light scratched the window. The train shuddered to a stop. Someone flung open a door.

They were outside. Dozens of soot-smeared passengers stumbled among the tracks, the visible clouds of smoke, the sloping planes of alpine grass. For they were there now. Through.

The train throbbed. Conductors, stripped to their waist-coats, took buckets and mops and swabbed the filthy windows until cataracts of black water pooled outside the tracks.

People had died. Her brother in Greece, her child and her hus-band in the backyard.

There was no heaven, no hell. The dead did not age be-cause the dead *were not.* (Still, Irene fingered the yellowed newspaper clippings in her purse; looked around for Stephen, who had disappeared.)

And meanwhile Harold had run up the hill from the train, and now stood on a low promontory, wiping ash from his spectacles with a handkerchief.

Where was Stephen? Suddenly she was terrified, con-vinced that something had happened to Stephen on the train, in the tunnel. "Harold!" she called. "Harold, have you seen Stephen?"

But he chose not to hear her. He was gazing at the campanile of Airolo, vivid in the fading light.

In Airolo, Harold looked for signs that the world was becoming Italy. And while it was true that most of the men in the station bar drank beer, one or two were drinking wine; and when he asked for wine in Italian, he was answered in Italian, and given a glass.

"Grady, do you want anything?"

Silence.

"Grady!"

He still wasn't talking to them.

Aunt Irene had gone into the washroom. She was not there to forbid Harold from drinking, so he drank. Around him, at tables, local workers—perhaps the same ones who had dug the tunnel—smoked and played cards. Most of them had pallid, dark blond faces, Germanic faces; but one was reading a newspaper called *Corriere della Sera,* and one boy's skin seemed to have been touched, even in this northernmost outpost, by a finger of Mediterranean sun.

Italy, he thought, and gazing across the room, noticed that Stephen, darker by far than any man in the bar, had come inside. One hand in his pocket, he was leaning against a white wall, drinking beer from a tall glass.

Apart.

He is from here, Harold realized suddenly. But does he even know it?

Then the conductor came into the bar. Harold turned, blushing, to contemplate his wine, wondering when the necessary boldness would come: to look another man straight in the eye, as men do.

∎

Aunt Irene had at last emerged, with Mrs. Warshaw, from the washroom. "Harold, I'm worried about Stephen," she said. "The last time I saw him was when we came out of the—"

"He's over there."

"Oh, Stephen!" his mother cried, and to Harold's surprise she ran to him, embraced him tightly, pressed her face into his chest. "My darling, I've been worried sick about you! Where have you been?"

"Can't a man take a walk?" Stephen asked irritably.

"Yes, of course. Of course he can." Letting him go, she dabbed at her eyes. "You've grown so tall! You're almost a man! No wonder you don't like Mother hugging you anymore. Oh, Stephen, you're such a wonderful son, I hope you know, I hope you'll always know, how much we treasure you."

Stephen grimaced; sipped at his beer.

"Well, we're through it," Mrs. Warshaw said. "Now tell me the truth, it wasn't so bad as all that, was it?"

"How I long for a bed!" Irene said. "Is Milan much further?"

"Just a few hours, dear," Mrs. Warshaw said, patting her hand. "And only short tunnels from now on, I promise you."

THE INFECTION SCENE

Tremendous Friends

LATE IN HIS CHILDHOOD, Lord Alfred (Bosie) Douglas became best friends with a nephew of one of his mother's neighbors, Lady Downshire: a boy with the extraordinary name (at least to our ears) of Wellington Stapleton-Cotton. This was in 1885. The boys went to different schools but spent their holidays together, so when Bosie was sent to Zermatt, in Switzerland, one summer, he made sure to cut his vacation short by a week in order to share the last part of it with Wellington. Though Bosie's mother's house was palatial, Lord Downshire, from whom she let it, had christened it "The Hut," for much the same reason that wealthy Long Island families call their oceanside mansions "cottages." Nearby stood Easthampstead, the *really* big house, where Lord and Lady Downshire held sway, and where Wellington, a frequent visitor, awaited Bosie's arrival. But no sooner had Bosie returned than he came down with the mumps and was quarantined. Illness thus separated the "tremendous friends."

From his sickroom Bosie smuggled a note to Wellington

through the agency of the footman, Harold, suggesting a plan. If Wellington were to contract mumps as well, they could share more than a week; they could share the entirety of their convalescence, in a common bed, and not even go to school.

I don't know what Wellington looked like. I do know what Bosie looked like. Bosie was a sickeningly angelic boy. In a drawing made of him when he was twenty-four, he still has soft blond hair, huge eyes with long lashes, a small, wet mouth that asks to be kissed but might bite. Indeed, so famous would this face become over the years that you might say it established a paradigm: beatific loveliness dissembling a corrupted heart.

As for Wellington, I see him as being both stronger and bigger than Bosie, with dark skin, thin lips, a worried brow. Already he has small tufts of hair under his arms and on his chest. Bosie's body, on the other hand, is covered in a downy fuzz. He is in the last flowering of childhood, whereas Wellington is in the first flush of adolescence, and thus subject, for the first time in his life, to lust. Yet lust is a mystery to him. He has no language for it. He is at the mercy of impulses that his Victorian education insists do not exist. In this regard he differs from Bosie, who possesses an innate familiarity with lust, even though he remains innocent of ejaculation. In other words, what Wellington feels but does not yet understand Bosie understands but does not yet feel. Therefore he can manipulate Wellington, using his girlishness as bait. He wonders: To what lengths can I drive Wellington? Could I persuade him to risk illness, infection, even death, just to be with me?

Yes, apparently, for Wellington readily agrees to the plan.

The next morning a feverish Bosie climbs from his bed and peers out the window. Behind a yew hedge, Wellington is waiting for him. Already Harold has brought the ladder, leaving it, according to Bosie's instructions, propped against the wall. Now he opens the window—the sash screeches loudly—and his friend clambers up and through. Dawn: a late summer breeze freshens the fetid atmosphere with the scent of grass. Wellington hasn't combed his hair. He smells tired. Small clots of what is euphemistically called "sleep" harden in the corners of his eyes. "Hello," Bosie says, then, taking his friend by the hand, leads him toward the bed, which is still warm and slightly moist, as beds tend to become when the ill sleep in them. He sits down before Wellington, guides Wellington's fingers to his swollen salivary glands. He anticipates by a hundred years an age when swollen glands will spell terror for men of his kind. But at that time, in that place, most men who desired each other didn't even think of themselves as a "kind." Not yet. It would take a poem written by Bosie before their love would learn the name it dared not speak.

"Come on," Bosie says. "Let's get in bed."

Wellington hardly has time to pull off his shoes.

"We have to make sure the infection takes," Bosie goes on, pulling the sheets over them.

"How?"

"Like this." And holding Wellington's face between his hot palms, Bosie kisses him. Wellington, who has never been kissed before, is at first surprised, resistant. But he likes the sensation, the silkiness of the sensation, and, giving into it, allows Bosie's tongue to open his lips. It is all for the purpose of being together, after all, of being boys together, *tremendous friends*. Bosie licks Wellington's teeth, licks his tongue, the rough surface of his lips. Wellington returns, repeats each gesture. So much early sexuality is mimicry. *Do to me what I do to you*, we think the other's tongue is telling us. Yet there are some things he would like to do to Bosie that he hopes Bosie wouldn't like to do to him.

"Do you think it's taken yet?"

"Perhaps. Still, we can't be sure."

"Anything else we might try?"

"Yes." And sitting up, Bosie runs his small hot tongue down Wellington's neck, onto his chest; he opens Wellington's shirt and licks the halos of hair around his nipples. Lower down, an erection pokes Wellington's trousers: no surprise. As for Bosie, his nightshirt has ridden up. He turns around, grinds his pinkish behind into Wellington's groin. The heat shocks. Wellington can't help but grind back. Sensation floods him, and he ejaculates, soaking the front of his pants.

Church bells chime. It's six-thirty in the morning. Shadows creep toward the bed. In the hallway, the housekeeper is upbraiding a chambermaid for the way she has folded some towels. Hearing them argue, Wellington and Bosie laugh.

"She'll be coming for us soon."

"Yes."

"Do you feel any swelling?"

Wellington presses his fingers against his neck.

"I think so. I think I do."

Under the bedclothes, he takes Bosie in his arms. They doze. Soon there's a knock on the door, and the housekeeper steps briskly through. "Good morning," she says, then stops in her tracks. "But what's this?"

The boys laugh, pull the sheet over their heads.

"Oh dear," the housekeeper says. "I'll have to fetch Lady Queensberry." And does.

"Wellington!" Lady Queensberry cries, rushing in a few minutes later. "What on earth are you doing here?"

"He's come to get sick so we can spend our holiday together."

"Wellington, get out of that bed right now. What kind of nonsense is this?"

"But, madame," the housekeeper interjects, "if he's already been infected . . ."

Lady Queensberry rubs her temples. Of her four children, she loves Bosie best. She is also starting to have inklings that he will bring her the greatest torment.

"I must consult with Lady Downshire," she concludes, and, leaving the boys to play in the feverish sheets, goes to her dressing room to write that eminence a wearied, apologetic letter.

But the infection doesn't "take," and Wellington returns to Easthampstead. Bosie recovers; the boys head off to their separate schools. Wellington, who should have become the third Viscount Combermere, dies in the Boer Wars. Bosie makes a career of ruin and infection.

Wellington didn't live to learn how narrowly he'd made it out alive.

I base this account on Bosie's own, in *My Friendship with Oscar Wilde*—one of several autobiographies he published later in his life in the hope that he might "set the record straight" concerning his disastrous love affair with Wilde. Here the incident takes up the better part of a paragraph. Bosie explains that he "adored" Wellington, and that he thought Wellington "adored" him. He says that when he came down with the mumps, Wellington climbed through the window, undressed, and got in bed with him. They stayed together half an hour. Then Wellington departed "'as he had come, an undiscerned road,' by the window."

The rest (in particular the arrival of the housekeeper) is speculation, invention, perhaps even impudence on my part, since what I want to show up is the irony that lies behind Bosie's inclusion of this episode in a work intended specifically to *repudiate* charges that he was more than a coincidental homosexual. Indeed, Bosie seems to see the episode with Wellington as yet one more example of the ordinary, virile boyhood he enjoyed before he met Wilde, who corrupted him. No, he says, I am not the rapacious brat whose greed and rage brought down the genius giant. On the contrary, *he* was the devil, *he* seduced *my* greatness. At heart I was just a normal boy.

Of Wellington, he remarks in conclusion, "I look forward to being a boy again with him in Paradise one day not very far off. (When you go to heaven you can be what you like, and I intend to be a child.)"

The Infection Scene

Precedent: in *Philosophy in the Bedroom,* the Marquis de Sade's usual assortment of libertines are having a fine old time buggering and encunting and whipping one another, when Madame de Mistival barges into their playroom. She has come to demand restitution of her daughter Eugénie. The sudden arrival of this righteous interloper cannot, of course, be tolerated, and as punishment Madame de Mistival is raped, both anally and vaginally, the service rendered by a syphilitic valet.

Sequel: San Francisco, the mid-1990s. Two young men—their names are Christopher and Anthony; one is twenty-two, the other nineteen—move in together. They are powerfully in love, each convinced that he has found, in the other, the great, the only true friend he will ever know, the friend without whom his life can have no purpose. They cherish the reading (Dennis Cooper at A Different Light) that brought them together, worship the author under whose dark influence their story began. This was three months ago. In the meantime, because their friends might disapprove of their moving in together after such a brief courtship, they've taken to saying they've been "partners" for more than a year. And why not? They *feel* as if they've known each other for decades. Three months seems too brief a term to contain such abundant happiness. Theirs is the rare, the distinguished thing.

Oh, how they delight in each other! Before they met, neither had much hope for anything. But now a future in which peace and passion go hand in hand seems to be opening out in front of them. In the normal course of events their relations would become fractious, their passion would grow stale, they would cheat on each other, part, not speak for years, meet again and wonder at their rancor and folly. But the normal course of events is not to be followed. Not in this case. There is an interloper present. Both of these boys come from difficult homes; Anthony, the younger of the two, from a disastrous one. When he was sixteen he ran away. An older man took him in, offering shelter and drugs in exchange for sex. The older man begged Anthony to let him fuck him without a condom. On several occasions Anthony, blitzed out on ecstasy, relented. Now he is seropositive. Christopher is not. One will live, the other will die. To Christopher, this condition is intolerable. He will not let his friend die alone. Anthony has no symptoms, nor has Christopher ever witnessed the ravages of the disease. Like many of his age, Christopher is so scorched by despair that for him the prospect of "dying together" takes on romantic connotations, seems pleasant and cozy, like sharing mumps. Anyway, his life so far has given him few other reasons to want to keep living. His abstracted mother, when she isn't working, has her alcoholic boyfriend to deal with, while his father is too busy with a batch of new children to spare time for this unhappy child of an unhappy, unwise, early marriage. All Christopher has is

Anthony, and for Anthony, he decides, he is willing to make any sacrifice.

One evening they go out to dinner. A Mexican place. Chicken mole, enchiladas, greasy tortillas. Christopher makes a proposition to Anthony, who is horrified. "I couldn't," he cries, and Christopher takes his hand.

"Calm down," he says. "Hear me out." And he states his case. He speaks gently, persuasively. He says that he would kill himself if Anthony died, so what does it matter? We all have to go sometime.

Anthony is moved. "You love me that much?" he asks.

"More," Christopher answers. At which point Anthony smiles. This love is the only good thing he's ever known. A flower creeps through the cement of a blasted city, a blasted, postnuclear city: that is how it feels to him.

They fix a date. Next Saturday, they decide, they will have sex. They will not use a condom. Discussing the details, Christopher finds himself becoming surprisingly aroused. Never in his life has anyone fucked him without a condom. In sex, as in all things, he has followed the rules to the letter. But now he suspects the rules to be a lie perpetrated by Dead White Males in order to suppress the freedom of gay people, who threaten patriarchy. Doesn't he too deserve a taste of real abandon, release without restraint? He speaks nostalgically of "Stonewall," even though he wasn't yet born when it happened, even though "Stonewall" exists for him merely as grainy porn flicks, the actors mostly dead. Oh, how young he is! He sees the dead as a glorious fraternity into which he longs to be initiated. But he knows nothing of disease, much less of death.

For the rest of that week Anthony and Christopher lead their lives as always. During the day they go to their jobs (one works at a video store, the other at a coffee bar), at night they walk together up and down Castro Street, or chat with their friends at the Midnight Sun, or watch MTV. By agreement, they do not have sex. They are saving up.

Saturday arrives. Anthony is visibly panicked. "Are you sure you want to go through with this?" he asks Christopher over lunch—sprouts and avocado sandwiches at Café Flore on Market Street.

"Sure as I've ever been about anything," his friend answers, kissing him on the nose.

That evening they cook a good dinner together: spaghetti with a sauce made from a recipe handed down by Anthony's grandmother, who comes from Naples, and whose own mother was rumored to have been a witch. (Inspired by this heritage, he has dabbled in worship of "the Goddess.") Then they have chocolate ice cream. Then they smoke some hash. Neither wants to lose his nerve.

In the bedroom Anthony strips the spread off the futon, lights candles. Christopher has put Enya on the stereo; the songs bleed one into the other with a numbing sameness, like Gregorian chants. Altogether the atmosphere is early or even pre-Christian. The bedroom is a temple, the bed an altar. What is about to take place is ritual sacrifice, to which the pious victim offers himself up willingly. They watch each other undress. Because he knows it excites Christopher, Anthony has put on a jockstrap, letting his penis and balls out the right side. He is dark-haired, beefy, endomorphic. Whereas Christopher is taller, leaner. To be taken by a boy both smaller and stronger than himself excites Christopher inordinately. And now Anthony spreads him open on the bed, lifts his legs in the air. He takes the bottle of lubricant from the bedside table—but Christopher stops his hand.

"Use spit," he whispers.

"Okay." Anthony spits into his palm. *Another rule broken.*

They are doing it now. Anthony is amazed at how much better it feels this way. Without the latex barrier, flesh slides against flesh. For the first time he understands what it was that the older man who infected him had been after: this sensation. This.

As for Christopher, in his stoned state he imagines that his friend is a god hovering over him. Anthony is Apollo laboring in the sky. His voice is distant thunder. Steadily Anthony fucks him, then without warning grits his teeth; deep inside Christopher feels warm wet pulses. He imagines low tide on the Pacific. Waves receding. In the remnant tide pools, hermit crabs with their cargo of dead shells, anemones suctioned to the rocks, spiny mouths that close around his touch.

It's done. *Okay,* he thinks. *This is what I wanted.* And he reaches to embrace Anthony.

But Anthony pulls away. He pulls away, stumbles to the window, opens it. Leans out, not speaking.

Christopher sits up in the bed. *What's wrong?* he wants to ask—and doesn't dare. He knows the answer.

For some reason a strange memory assails Anthony. When he was a child, on the last day of every school year all the kids in his class wrote their names and addresses on cards that they attached to helium balloons. Their teacher then led them outside in a kind of procession, the balloons trailing behind, above her, a leashed bouquet, and when they were all assembled on the playground, she cut the strings. The balloons rose up, masses that separated, as the children, cheering the onslaught of summer, rushed out the open gates to parents, school buses. Only Anthony hesitated. He wanted to wait until he could no longer distinguish his own balloon from the others. He wanted to wait until every last one had disappeared into a dot on the horizon, and the sky was empty again, like a blank page.

Few of the balloons ever made it more than a couple of miles. Instead, for weeks afterward, he'd keep finding shreds of them twisted around the branches of neighborhood trees when he went on bike rides.

Outside the window tonight the moon is bright, not quite full. Rounder than a balloon. Pearl gray. Behind him Christopher puts his hand on Anthony's shoulders.

"Don't worry," he says. "It's what I wanted. More than anything." Kissing his neck.

But Anthony, at the window, is too busy calculating to listen. Six weeks for seroconversion, then the blood test, then a few more days for the results. Oh, the wait! They will wait the way girls wait to see if they are pregnant.

"Of course, it might not take."

Don't let it take, Anthony prays to his great-grandmother's Goddess.

"So just to play it safe, we'll do it every night."

Silence.

"Okay?"

"Okay."

"To play it safe."

"Yes."

Anthony closes the window on the moon.

A Hotel Flirtation

1889. A big hotel on the Côte d'Azur. String quartets, a promenade, parasols. Also a busy network of back hallways in which servants and staff played out their own dramas. No bathrooms, though. In 1889 plumbing was rare, even in the most elegant French hotels. The rich, like the poor, used chamber pots.

When the tutor arrived that afternoon—dragged hither at the behest of his difficult yet enchanting charge—he gave his room a minute and thorough once-over. First he stripped the sheets off the bed and examined the mattress, in the center of which was a largish pink stain. Then he noticed a perfect circle of carpet near the plant stand which, unlike the rest, had not been leached of color by the sun. He should leave well enough alone, he told himself, it was always better to leave well enough alone—yet even as he spoke these words to himself, he was lifting the plant stand to reveal the expected discolorations, stiff to the touch. What had produced them? Various unsavory possibilities sprang to his mind, so that he became nauseated and, putting the plant stand down again, opened both windows and loosened his collar. He was bony, in his early twenties, with thin yellow hair and the sort of constitution doctors of that epoch described as "delicate." From an early age the tutor's mother had warned him not to exert himself too much. He worried excessively (and probably needlessly) about germs. He thought he could smell an evil smell.

The tutor loathes hotels. The hotel is neither public nor private space but some uneasy blending of the two. To live comfortably in a hotel you have to maintain the delusion that the room you occupy is actually your own. And yet this privacy is fictive. The walls are thin. Yes, you carry a key in your pocket, but you also know that somewhere in every hotel, someone else carries a master key.

Hundreds of people sleep on the hotel mattress before it is retired—sleep, or do worse than sleep. The John Bull sweats; the bride spots the sheets with blood; the French doctor does not wipe himself. Some guests have actually had the audacity to die in their beds. Though the tutor doesn't know it, an old Belgian woman died in his bed last March. For six hours her body remained in the fetal lock of sleep, until a maid came in with morning coffee. Screams brought the concierge running. Yet once the corpse had been removed, the hotel manager didn't bother to change the mattress. After all, who would have been the wiser?

At that time, in that place, people settled longer at hotels than they do now. Stays of several weeks or even months were not uncommon. It was never very much time before guests were forging alliances, staking out territories, waging wars. The tutor, having spent a large chunk of his childhood living in hotels, finds the mere prospect of all this wearying. He remembers vividly the hours he had to endure sitting next to his mother in tearooms, longing to run outside, which she forbade. (To some extent he still longs to run outside.) Medieval architecture is his passion. He does not relish intrigues, rumors, cold-shoulderings—the daily bread of hotel life. His charge, on the other hand, thrives in such an atmosphere. With his stalklike body, his pale, delectable features, Bosie might have been one of those white asparagus shoots that grow only in the absence of sun. Natural light did not favor him. His skin burned easily. He required interiority to blossom, the rays of a chandelier.

He was nineteen now, and at the peak of his seraphic beauty.

The tutor checks his watch: it is almost one, the hour at which he and Bosie have agreed to meet. And so, abandoning the mattress, which he would have liked to turn over (but what worse horrors might he have found on the other side?), he leaves his room and heads out to the covered terrace that overlooks the beach. Dressed in a striped jacket, mauve trousers, and broad-brimmed hat, Bosie leans dreamily against the rail, gazing at the promenade, where some old women are strolling. Really, the spectacle of him takes the tutor's breath away. Bosie is narrow-shouldered, with light, wavy hair. His eyes, green and gold, recall the sun-mottled ground beneath a tree. Only his lips are less than classical. Narrow and blood-less, they close into a crooked line. Somehow this imperfection makes him more, not less, desirable to the tutor. Bosie's face might be a girl's face; it is certainly one that girls envy. Yet there is nothing girlish about his carriage—and that is the miraculous thing (and the thing about which everyone comments). Bosie is every inch a boy—albeit one who has to shave only twice in a week. This odd dressing up of essential masculinity in the trappings of feminine loveliness intoxicates the tutor. For the first time in his life, he is in love—a state to which, like most states, he feels unequal. With Bosie he never knows what to do or say. So he stands his ground, peering at Bosie's back, waiting for Bosie to speak, to act, to tell him what to do.

"Oh, Gerald, isn't it beautiful, the sea?" Bosie asks. "I'm so happy we came here. If we'd looked at one more flying buttress, I would have gone mad."

Gerald, who reverences the flying buttress, only nods, and curses his weakness. After all, hasn't he promised Lady Queensberry to divert Bosie's attention from the very temptations the hotel incarnates—the temptations of "society," to which Bosie is already so dangerously susceptible? Yet to this task, alas, he has also proven unequal. Instead of waking Bosie to the uplifting glory of medieval church architecture, he has allowed Bosie to sway his attentions from that holy pursuit. Instead of teaching him to love what he loves, he has let himself be dragged back into an atmosphere he detests, pettish and airless and reeking of eau de cologne.

Gerald is a few years older than Bosie, at present without fixed employment but in future to serve as assistant master at a number of schools, then as a war correspondent. He is also a nephew of one of Bosie's great-aunts. Their pairing up for this journey was the brainchild of Lady Queensberry, who had been worried lest her impatient son should have nothing to occupy him during the interval between Winchester (where he had finished in the spring) and Oxford (to which he would go down in the fall). A continental ramble under Gerald's edifying and stolid management was quickly settled upon as the ideal solution. The trip would have an educative purpose—that is to say, Gerald would ensure that Bosie direct his energies toward the pursuit of cultural enrichment—but at some point the boy got the better of his tutor. Thus the abandonment of cathedrals in favor of esplanades, this hotel, "luncheon."

What the ladies hadn't counted on was Gerald's incipient homosexuality—and Bosie's skills as a seducer.

Most likely it started long before they reached the Côte d'Azur. Indeed, very possibly it was the reason their journey veered from its cultural itinerary in the first place. As I imagine it, early in the trip Bosie picked up on his tutor's sexual anxiety—Gerald's unspoken (and largely subconscious) *looking*. A challenge presented itself. By the end of his Winchester years Bosie had honed the skills he'd practiced so awkwardly on Wellington into an efficient set of strategies for which he might even have written down the rules, much as his hyperactive father wrote (or helped to write) the rules for boxing. To lure his randy schoolmates into bed, however, was by this time becoming old hat; to seduce a relation older than himself, and charged with the responsibility of keeping him out of trouble—now that would be proof of his power!

Here is how I see him working. Though usually they secure two rooms at each hotel in which they stay, occasionally they have to share a double room. Imagine poor Gerald, then, coming in from his washing up, only to find Bosie naked before the looking glass, his very white behind thrust just slightly outward. Gerald stops in his tracks, stares a few sec-

onds, before coughing to announce his embarrassed presence, at which point Bosie turns, laughs, pulls on his dressing
gown.

That night Gerald can't keep the image of Bosie's nakedness out of his mind. His curiosity is heightened in stages.
The Douglas rules: after a first flash of exposure (ideally of
the backside), take care never to show more than a delectable
portion of yourself; only glimpses. One night Bosie's shirt
might flop open, exposing a nipple as red as a pomegranate
seed. Or pulling off his socks, he might caress his own pale
ankles. In his mind, meanwhile, the object of his campaign
struggled to put the pieces together—a struggle made all the
more anxious by the fact that the flash of entire nakedness
with which Bosie had first enticed was even now fading from
memory.

Oh, Bosie is merciless! He is tunneling under, undermin-
ing the foundations of Gerald's already weakened defenses.
Each night poor Gerald suffers agonies of erotic dreamscape
from which he wakes sweating, erection aching, on the brink
of an ecstasy he cannot quite allow. In his dreams he pulses
out phantom orgasms, and feels a consequent phantom relief.
But coming in a dream is like eating or drinking or urinating
in a dream: you wake, and the need is all the greater. Indeed,
the more he suppresses it, the more the urge to uncover
Bosie's sweetly sleeping body intensifies in him, fevers him—
which is just as Bosie intended.

Finally there comes the night when Bosie goes in for the
kill, lets Gerald walk in on him a second time, absolutely naked, but this time lying on his back. There passes a moment
of invitation in which no words are spoken—Can you resist
me? Bosie seems to be asking—and then Gerald, forsaking
decorum, jumps on Bosie, pretends to wrestle him, inhales
greedily his jasminelike scent. Squealing, Bosie rubs hot parts
of himself against his tutor. Gerald thinks: just wrestling;

perfectly acceptable. Only he can't keep from letting his lips brush against Bosie's cheek, he can't keep his erection (mercilessly insistent, restrained only by layers of underlinen) from pushing into Bosie's leg. Boys, boys together! *Tremendous friends.* And then they are looking at each other; the pretense of wrestling falls away; Gerald reaches down, kisses Bosie, wills Bosie's mouth to open to its own devouring.

They grope. Gerald screws his eyes shut, and suddenly sits up. Bosie looks puzzled. Prostitutes are wise to ask for payment before the act. For men sex means a lessening. Disgrace always lurks in afterglow.

Bosie doesn't understand what's happened. He doesn't understand that beneath all those layers, Gerald has just experienced a humiliating, even a defeating orgasm. He doesn't know that among poor Gerald's many woes in life is a predisposition to premature ejaculation, or as it was more often called at that time, "sexual incontinence"—not until Gerald rolls away, and sits on the edge of the bed, and blows his nose. Fear and shame arrest him in equal measure. He cannot say which fact is more painful: that he has committed a criminal offense, or that he has done it so ineptly.

He lifts his head; looks at Bosie. He's braced for the worst: protestations, threats of exposure. His overheated imagination is already thinking blackmail, jail cells, suicide. But Bosie neither teases nor reproaches him. Instead he squeezes Gerald's hand, smiles and winks, before dashing over to the washbasin.

Bosie's nakedness is different now. It encodes no allure as he slips on his dressing gown, climbs into the bed.

"Good night," he says cheerfully.

"Good night," Gerald answers, shivering as he peels sticky cotton from his thigh.

·

The woman, according to Bosie's brief account of the incident, was a cousin of Gerald's; in her early thirties, divorced from her husband and on the run from a lover. In other words, a *mondaine;* an adventuress. That she happened to be staying at the same hotel as Bosie and Gerald was probably a coincidence. Or perhaps it was a coincidence that had been arranged between the cousins. I can't know. I'm making most of this up. For now I'm going to say it was a coincidence, since it would not have been remotely in Gerald's interest to meet up with that particular cousin at that particular moment. Quite the opposite. It seemed to him a case of extremely bad timing.

Bosie gives her no name, and little by way of a description. I shall call her Laura. According to him she was simply "a lady of celebrated beauty, at least twelve years older than myself, the divorced wife of an earl." To me she is elegant, if not exactly beautiful, with small raisin-colored eyes. Her black hair has a sharp, radiant sheen: think of Susan Sontag, Martha Argerich, Tess Gallagher. (Is it cheap of me to offer such comparisons? Probably. And yet this *is* what I am thinking.)

The three of them meet in the hotel lobby. Exclamations of amazement. But what a surprise! Of all the places in the world! Bosie and Laura beam at each other, while Gerald hangs back, pretending enthusiasm even as he struggles to swallow his dread. Of course they must dine together, Laura says; of course Bosie agrees. And quickly, quickly the concierge is flagged down, tables are rearranged; Gerald, upon whose shoulders such masculine business matters seem always to fall, curses both his cousin and himself.

He's never liked her. He's always thought her a tart. Flirting with his brother the way she did. It was positively obscene.

At dinner they drink champagne. Laura and Bosie talk

about society people in whom Gerald hasn't the slightest interest. They talk about royalty. They gossip about Prince Eddy. Laura's heard that Prince Eddy was Jack the Ripper.

"No!" Bosie cries.

"Yes!" Laura says. "They say he's not quite right in the head, and that after the last murder, after he killed that poor girl in her room, the police found him in the vicinity and now he's being secretly held in the palace under the care of doctors. Apparently her majesty is beside herself—absolutely beside herself."

"But that's ridiculous!" Gerald interjects. "Tabloid lies. You shouldn't believe such nonsense."

"Oh, silly," says Laura. "What do you know?"

"I think the murders were really ghastly," Bosie says.

"Ghastly," Laura repeats. "You know, they say he took things—from the bodies. I wouldn't like to say what. You might lose your appetite."

Bosie bursts into laughter. Gerald checks his watch.

"I was chilled when I heard," Laura goes on. "I felt as if it were me he'd gone after. Not that I had anything to worry about, since he only chose—well, you know: *low women*. Still, I had a dream one night. I woke up and there he was, bent over me with his knife. Breathing. I couldn't see his face. I knew I had to switch on the electric light, that if I could switch on the electric light, then he wouldn't kill me. And I reached over for the switch . . . and it wasn't there."

"How awful!" Bosie says.

"Awful!" Gerald repeats, a little mockingly.

He calls for more champagne.

The affair, in Bosie's words, advances along "classic lines." I take this to mean that it becomes a French farce in which Bosie plays the virginal initiate, Laura the sophisticated *châtelaine*. At night there are secret rendezvous; during the day delicious pretenses of innocence.

The second afternoon, neither of them shows up for luncheon. Hot with jealousy, Gerald suffers alone the tedious gaps between the courses, then forgoes coffee to search out the pair, whom he finds soon enough in the hotel gardens, sitting in a sort of bower, under a cascade of roses, holding hands and laughing over what he presumes to be some inanity, while Laura's unpleasant little Bedlington terrier—sculpted to resemble a lamb—growls at their feet. They don't see Gerald. He lurks undetected among the trees. They kiss, and he cannot move. A debased yearning to see Bosie made love to by his cousin roots him to the spot. Cautiously Bosie slips his hand into Laura's dress, cups her pear-shaped breast. Gerald thinks: I'm no match for her. Then he thinks: What am I, to put myself in competition with a woman?

Disgusted, he flees his hiding place and returns to the hotel. In the brocade and velvet sitting room, some outraged old ladies are deploring the scandalous behavior of a "certain woman" who has come to the hotel and seduced a boy nearly young enough to be her son. Gerald, his eyes in a book, listens avidly.

Eventually the old women get up to take a walk along the promenade. He doesn't notice. By now he's lost himself in the book—Winckelmann—soothing prose about Greek things. What he tries not to think about, what he knows from his own tutors, is that Winckelmann was murdered in a Trieste hotel room by a Tuscan cook. A bad end, but he was a sodomite.

At around three Bosie strolls into the sitting room. "Hello, Gerald," he says.

Gerald doesn't answer. Bosie takes the armchair opposite his. "Oh, Gerald, Gerald," he says—and still Gerald doesn't answer. So Bosie picks up a magazine from the table between the chairs and starts flipping through it. *"The Women's World,"* he reads aloud, "edited by Oscar Wilde. Oh, look at this, an article by Mrs. Wilde! About *muffs*. Well, I doubt she ever would have got that published if she hadn't been married to the editor, do you think?"

"If you wouldn't mind, I'm trying to read."

"What are you reading?"

"Winckelmann."

"Ah, Winckelmann. But I suppose Pater isn't quite your thing, is he?"

"Too subjective," Gerald says.

"Subjective!" Bosie puts down his magazine. "The trouble with you, Gerald, is that you're so . . ."

He quiets. Then: "She's very nice, your cousin."

A deeper silence. Confidingly, Bosie leans across the little table that separates him from his tutor. "Gerald, may I tell you something?"

"What?"

"I think I'm in love."

Gerald puts down his book. "Do you mean with my cousin?"

"Yes. With Laura."

"That's nonsense. She's a grown woman. You're a boy."

"Ah, but does age really matter, to the heart?"

"Your mother would not approve," Gerald says. "I was supposed to take you on a tour so that you might learn something, not lounge around some boring hotel all day flirting with my damned cousin." He sneezes. "No, this settles it. Tomorrow we leave."

"We shall not leave," says Bosie.

"I say we leave, and we shall leave."

"And I say we shall not. Or you may. You may do what you like."

"I would suggest your mother—"

"I would suggest there are some things I might tell my mother."

Gerald stands. His face has gone pale. "What are you saying?" he asks stiffly.

Then Bosie laughs. He laughs and laughs. "Oh, come now, Gerald!" he says, stands himself, and pats his tutor manfully on the back. "Must you worry so? You always worry! Don't! If you'd let yourself, you could have a perfectly good time here. Why not let yourself?"

"This is not what your mother had in mind."

"So what? Must she know?"

Gerald shakes his head. Excusing himself, he returns to his room. The bed assaults him: the knowledge of that stain. He must come up with a plan, he decides, and comes up with one. It is not a bad plan. Certainly it doesn't lack for courage.

A Piece of Bad News

"The doom room," the counselor called his office; or "the fate gate"; or "the torture chamber." Never to the faces of his clients, of course. To his clients it was "the consulting room," and nothing else. Perhaps all of us use a different language in our heads than in the world; and certainly among his colleagues the counselor would never have admitted to amusing himself with such cynical word games. Still, so long as the brain's private monologue cannot be wiretapped, he will not be fired for his thoughts; he will not be fired for thinking of his office as "the torture chamber," or for dividing his clients into the doomed (positive) and the saved (negative): terrible, archaic locutions that go against every principle of his train-

ing, which is in large part why he takes such malicious pleasure in their use.

At the moment the counselor is standing outside his office, by the water cooler. In his right hand he holds a fragile
cone filled with purified water, in his left a piece of paper on
which the future of a young man he has never met is spelled
out. About five feet from him stands a door, behind which
the young man sits, waiting, having no idea that the counselor, who is not in the least thirsty, has decided to drink another coneful of water instead of going in and ending the ag-
ony of his suspense. And why? Because he can. Nor will
anyone (his colleagues, for instance) ever know that this little
cruelty is intentional. That's the pleasure of the thing. He is
palpating, caressing his own power. For a few minutes, the
young man is his slave, and as in certain sadomasochistic sex
rituals in which the counselor has also taken part, he's not going to be allowed relief until his master is good and ready.

After he finishes his third cup of water, the counselor
checks his watch. Five minutes. Yes, he decides, probably
he's kept the kid sweating long enough—to do so any longer
would be to cross the border into detectable sadism—and
dashing his paper cone into a recycling bin, he opens the door
and strolls casually inside. The young man, in his seat opposite the empty desk, flinches. No surprise. His terror is so
visceral it can be smelled.

"Hello," the counselor says, offering his hand, all smiles
and affability and cool skin. "Christopher, right?"

"Right."

"Good to meet you."

The counselor sits down. How odd! He recognizes the boy.
But where from? Christopher is brown-haired, handsome in a
rough way, and according to the report the counselor spreads
out before him, just twenty-two. But why does he look so familiar? Something about the eyes . . .

Then, quite suddenly and horribly, the counselor remembers: he and Christopher have had sex. Not slept together, just had sex, standing up, at a club a few blocks down Market Street. Maybe six months earlier. If he recalls correctly, he gave Christopher a blowjob.

The counselor coughs. Suddenly he is as sweaty as Christopher. Punishment, he thinks, punishment for having taken pleasure in making the boy wait . . . meanwhile he dreads actually looking at the report. (Oh, what cavalier arrogance, not to have checked, before entering, whether the news he has to dispatch was bad or good!) And now, he asks himself, what if the boy turns out to be positive? The result, for him personally, will be several very hairy days, as he awaits his own test results. Did he swallow? He can't remember if he swallowed. Probably not. Was there a lot of pre-cum? The counselor has bad gums, and therefore ought not to be in the business of giving blowjobs in the first place. Still, it's a habit of which, despite logic and remonstrance, he has failed, over the years, to break himself. For though he would never suck off a man he knew to be HIV-positive, he feels no compunction in sucking off men (witness Christopher) whose names he hasn't even learned. Ignorance, in the end, really may be bliss, or at least a prerequisite for bliss, just as safety may be less a condition than a boundary, the exact location of which we can only guess at, measuring a little with science, a little with hunches. Why listen to statistics when common sense—which tells him what he wants to hear—is so much more congenial a guide?

"Well," he says now, "let's cut to the chase, shall we?" And glancing down at the piece of paper in front of him, he prays very quickly. Blinks. "You've tested negative," he says, before he himself can even absorb the fact of it.

"Sorry?" Christopher says.

"You've tested negative."

"But that can't be."

"Why not?"

"Because . . ." The boy leans closer. "Listen, are you sure you haven't mixed up my results with someone else's?"

"We triple-screen to avoid that."

"But can't the results be wrong?"

"There are occasional false positives. Never false negatives."

"But they have to be wrong."

"Why?"

Christopher doesn't answer. Nor is the counselor—his own heartbeat decelerating with relief—in any mood to probe the matter further. Instead he goes into his negative drill, hands a rather shell-shocked Christopher a copy of *The Gay Men's Guide to Safer Sex,* and shoos him out of the office.

Through the waiting room, Christopher stumbles. Like the counselor's office itself, the waiting room has been designed by a local architect who, after his lover's death, decided to devote himself to the science of creating spaces that "minimize panic, maximize tranquility." This architect is now rich from a practice dedicated exclusively to clinics, testing centers, hospices—rooms in which bad news is given, painful treatments administered. Yet to all that yellow and blue carefulness, Christopher is oblivious, immune. How can he be negative? Before he left, Anthony fucked him six times without a condom. He shouldn't be negative. The news strikes him as a kind of curse.

Out on Market Street, in brisker air, he goes into a phone booth, drops in coins, punches buttons.

Two rings. "Hello?" Anthony says.

"Hi."

A short silence. "Christopher, I told you not to call me. I don't want to talk to you."

"I got the results."

"And?"

"Come meet me and I'll tell you."

"No. I just told you, I don't want—"

"Then I won't tell you."

"Oh, man! You're crazy, you know that? I can't believe I ever got caught up in this shit . . ."

"Anthony, please."

"How could I have been such an idiot—"

"You know what? The counselor was someone I tricked with."

"I don't care. I don't give a fuck."

"Anthony, if you'll just listen to me—all I want is to see you. Like old times. You owe me that."

"Why? You scare me, you know that? You're dangerous."

Christopher laughs. "For Christ's sake, man, I'd never hurt you. I love you."

"You love me like a suicide loves pills."

"But it's not about dying, it's about solidarity! That's the point, to prove—"

"It doesn't prove anything."

"Why don't you understand? You understood before."

"Before I was crazy too, a little bit." On the other end of the line, Anthony beats his fingers against the phone. "Now I'm going to ask you just one more time. What happened?"

"If you'll meet me, I'll tell you."

"That's blackmail."

"But if it's the only way I'll get to see you, what choice do I have? I mean, Anthony, you're all that matters."

"Is that supposed to make me feel better?"

"Yes. Why not?"

"You're the one who doesn't understand."

"I understand more than you think. If you'd just agree to see me, to sit down with me, you'd realize that."

Another silence. Then, "All right. Café Flore in fifteen

minutes. But just to get the results, you hear me? Nothing else."

"Thank you, Anthony. I can't wait—"

Anthony hangs up.

"Well, goodbye," Christopher says to the dial tone. And hangs up himself.

Gerald Takes Matters in Hand

That evening, with an assurance the brazenness of which will later stun him, Gerald puts his plan into action. To begin with, he decides to enlist the aid of the old women in the lounge who have been gossiping about Laura's misbehavior. To lure two or three of them into conversation after dinner, to express to them, "in strictest confidence," his anxiety over his charge—not to mention his serious doubts as to the moral fiber of his cousin—turns out to be easy; after all, Gerald has spent most of his life in the company of old women. Unctuous and meek, he knows how to earn their allegiance. In many ways he is an old woman himself. A little confiding, a few whispered words of anxiety, and the entire female population of the hotel is set against Laura.

At around ten o'clock, he returns to his room, where he spends a gratifying half-hour with Winckelmann. Then he steps into the corridor, walks to Bosie's room, knocks at the door. As expected, no answer. Bracing himself, he heads down the hall, to the room his cousin occupies. Once again, with great deliberateness, he knocks at a door.

Loud barks from that ersatz lamb, the Bedlington terrier.

"Laura, this is Gerald," he announces manfully. "I ask you to open the door."

Again, only barks.

"I know that Bosie's there with you. Now please answer the door, else I shall have to fetch the management."

A sound of rustling. Then the door cracks, Laura's scowling face greets his. "What are you talking about? Are you mad? He's not here."

"He is there, and I demand that you open the door."

"You're mad! I'm alone, in bed."

"Laura, for the last time . . . I do not wish this scene to become public. Need I remind you that Bosie is a minor? Send him out to me at once."

The door closes in his face. The dog barks. A few seconds later, it opens again, and a teary-eyed Bosie emerges. Worse than that, a transvestite Bosie, dressed in one of Laura's gallooned nightdresses.

Some of Gerald's ladies, coming down the hall, stop in their tracks, stare in horror at the gauzy apparition.

"You shall come with me," Gerald says. And yanking Bosie roughly by the arm, he drags the boy back to his own room; shuts the door behind them. "Now get out of those ridiculous clothes."

Obediently Bosie pulls the nightdress over his head.

"You should not have done this, Gerald," he says. "I call it most unfair."

"Put this on," Gerald says, thrusting a dressing gown at Bosie, trying not to notice his nakedness. For once, Bosie does as he is told.

"Tomorrow we leave," Gerald goes on. "I expect to see you packed and ready in the lobby at seven. Nor would I like to hear that you have visited my cousin in the night."

Bosie, subdued, watches with surprise and pleasure as Gerald moves toward the door.

▪

Perhaps the scariest thing about Bosie, particularly in his middle years: his malignant, even obsessive litigiousness. And not merely where Wilde was concerned. For though the degree to which he singularly compelled Wilde to take legal action against his father is debatable, what is a matter of public record is that after Wilde's death, Bosie himself was involved in no less than ten libel actions. He himself brought libel actions against: the Reverend R. F. Horton, who had called a newspaper Bosie was editing, *The Academy,* "an organ of Catholic propaganda"; Wilde's first biographer, Arthur Ransome, after he described Bosie as a man "to whom Wilde felt that he owed some, at least, of the circumstances of his public disgrace"; the *Morning Post,* after it accused Bosie of anti-Semitism; and the *Evening News,* which in 1921 falsely reported his death and described the Douglas bloodline as showing "many marked signs of degeneracy." (In rebuttal, Bosie argued that even though in his youth he might have exhibited "symptoms of wickedness," he was by no means a degenerate: "I am a horseman," he declared proudly, "a good shot, a manly man, able to hold my own with other people.")

In addition, Bosie was himself sued for libel on three occasions: once by Wilde's friend Robert Ross, once by his father-in-law, Colonel Custance, and once—amazingly enough—by Winston Churchill, whom Bosie had accused publicly and repeatedly of entering into a Jewish-led conspiracy to lower the value of government stock. Churchill had no choice but to bring an action against Bosie, who lost, and was jailed for six months at Wormwood Scrubs. (While in prison, as Wilde had written *De Profundis,* he wrote *In Excelsis,* a sonnet sequence containing anti-Semitic slurs of a more than usually repellent aspect.)

The case against the *Evening News* Bosie actually won, which is probably why he crows about it in his autobiography—yet what is curious is the moment when he chooses to crow about it. The reference comes just after Bosie's seduction by Gerald Armstrong's cousin. Like his rendering of the episode with Wellington, the account he gives here is brief—only a few paragraphs—and seems to be offered in order to challenge "the accusation which has been made against me of being what is called abnormal and degenerate from a sexual point of view. (By the way, the last time this accusation of being 'degenerate' was made against me was by *The Evening News* in 1921, and it cost that enterprising journal £1000 in damages to me and a good many more thousands in costs.)"

Now that is an alarming parenthetical—alarming because its import seems to be, in essence, "Don't fuck with me": a warning even to the reader himself, who has presumably put down money to purchase Bosie's book, that he would do well to avoid offending its author.

It is the only instance I can think of, either in literature or that species of writing that purports to be literature, in which a writer has overtly threatened his reader.

As for the details: what is striking to me about Bosie's account is the degree to which it undercuts his putative intention, which is to establish once and for all his heterosexual vitality. Thus when Gerald decides he has had enough and knocks at his cousin's bedroom door "demanding restitution of his ravished ewe-lamb," the "ewe-lamb, reduced to tears and dressed in one of the lady's much-beribboned nightgowns," is delivered to his keeper "to the accompaniment of loud barks from the lady's pet dog." Hardly the paragon of boyish swagger, that description. Also, no explanation is given of why Gerald has come to think of Bosie in the first place as *his* "ravished ewe-lamb."

No, the transvestite frills in which the episode is dressed make it difficult to take seriously Bosie's pouting claim that had well enough been left alone, "my lady love would at any rate have kept me away from baser promiscuities"—presumably those committed in the company of Wilde. Indeed, one has to ask why, if Bosie's intention here is to prove his manliness, he chose to include the episode in his autobiography in the first place.

The only surprise was that in the end, Gerald did find it in himself to challenge Bosie; to wrest him from his cousin; to drag him from that hotel on the Côte d'Azur.

Courage. Perhaps it is not so surprising after all that timid Gerald grew up to be a war correspondent.

On the Edge of the Abyss

Where does it come from, this story? I'm still not certain. Probably it began with a newspaper article, something glimpsed three or four years back on the West Coast. According to this article, a San Francisco psychiatrist was noticing a dangerous trend among very young gay men: in essence, they were starting to abandon those very rules of "safer sex" that their elders had struggled so hard to instill and publicize. And this just at a moment when those rules were finally becoming second nature (and when as a consequence the rate of HIV infection was going down).

What had happened? No one seemed sure. Certainly that generalized anomie of which so many young people complained in the early 1990s could not be ignored as a contributing factor: ours is an age of suicide, and what is unprotected sex anyway but—to borrow a phrase from Wilde—"a long, lovely suicide"?

As for the gay teenagers themselves, the ones interviewed

spoke not only of despair, but of exclusion; solitude; loneliness. Think about it: when everyone you know is HIV-positive, when everywhere you look HIV-positive men and women are banding together to form not merely families but a society—to serve the needs of which whole industries have cropped up—how can you not feel that you have been left behind? Bear in mind that this condition was unique to a few urban centers, San Francisco chief among them: cities in which the HIV-positive had their own magazines, rites, habits and philosophies and language; to weary further an already wearied word, their own culture. More potently, with one another (or so felt several of the boys interviewed) the HIV-positive could flout the totemic restraints of "safer sex." Infection threw them free from caution, and so they could throw caution to the wind, and with one another do what they wanted, as much as they wanted, while on the outskirts the seronegative watched meekly, enviously, nursing their fear.

It is hard for me—a child of a different (and perhaps more life-loving) age—to imagine a world where early death is the norm, and where therefore life itself may begin to seem like a death sentence.

I thought about this article for months after I read it. Then I read a biography of Bosie, and the present and past did their alchemy. Out of the flames Anthony and Christopher stepped forth, naked, almost fully formed.

As for the counselor, he is a character about whom, in my mind, an aureole of profound uncertainty hangs, perhaps because his private cowardices and hypocrisies reflect my own.

I leave him now, to follow Christopher down Market Street to the Café Flore, where at a sunny table Anthony awaits him. Passing these boys, and being told that one was HIV-negative and the other HIV-positive, you might very well confuse which was which, since Anthony looks flushed and vigorous, while Christopher is haggard, thin, his chin pimpled, his elbows scaly with psoriasis. Across from Anthony, who drinks an iced cappuccino, he sits down shyly. "You look great," he says. "Did you get your hair cut?"

"Christopher, don't waste my time. Tell me."

"How long has it been since you moved out?"

"I don't know—two weeks."

"Two weeks and three days." Christopher smiles. "So I hear you have a new lover."

"Man, do we have to talk about this now? Can't you see I'm sweating this out? I have to know. I deserve to know."

"Why?"

"Because if you're positive, I did it to you. And that's something, if I'm going to have to live with, I need to start coping with."

"If I'm positive would you stay with me? Take care of me?"

"No."

"That's blunt."

"I have to be blunt. Like I said, you scare me."

"Or I could sue you . . . like what's-his-name with Rock Hudson. Say you lied and told me you were negative."

"As if I have any money for you to get."

"Oh, I wouldn't do it for money."

Anthony stands. "I don't have to listen to this," he says. "I want to know, but not that much."

"I'm sorry. Sit down. Please sit down. I'm speaking from grief, can't you see? I'm angry because I love you, because I grieve losing you, can't you see that?"

Anthony is silent. He sits down. Then he says, "If you loved me, you wouldn't have asked me to do it. You wouldn't have burdened me with—as if I don't have trouble enough already."

"But you didn't have to agree."

"You have more power than you realize. That's why you're dangerous. You act like you're this innocent little thing, why me, why me, when all the time—"

Christopher buries his face in his hands. "How did it come to this?" he asks. "We loved each other. Three weeks ago, a month ago, we would have sworn we were together forever."

"Not anymore."

"So you're saying you don't love me?"

"No, I don't, if that's what you have to hear." Anthony scratches the back of his head. "You know what? I feel like you're trying to rope me back into a relationship with you. That this whole meeting, it's all been a pretense. I wouldn't be surprised to learn you hadn't even had the fucking test."

"Oh, no, I had it. And this morning I got the results."

"The results you won't tell me."

For a few hopeless seconds Christopher looks at the table. Then he lies. Why he lies, he'll never, for the life of him (and it will be a long one), be sure.

He says, "I'm positive."

All at once Anthony is on his feet, the table is toppling, cold mud-colored coffee streaming onto Christopher's lap. He leaps away from it. "Goddamn you!" Anthony cries, and pushes at Christopher, who pushes back. Around them strangers stand and gawk and whisper. "Odors from the abyss," one man says to another, while at the next table a woman gives her lover a look that is supposed to say, *Thank God for our more peaceable relations.* The lover, however, thinks, *We are closer than we believe. We are all closer to the edge than we believe.*

The seizure has passed. Self-consciousness revives, and with it vanity, which causes Christopher to mop halfheartedly at his ruined shirt. In the interval fighting appears to have

THE MARBLE QUILT · 56

taken place—hitting too—for blood now drips from Anthony's mouth.

"Are you okay?" a waiter asks, handing him a wad of paper
towels.

"I'm okay. Thanks. I'm okay."

"Anthony, I'm sorry."

"Stay away from me."

"If you'd just let me—"

"Stay away from me. Don't follow me," says Anthony, hurrying out of the café. Of course Christopher follows. At that
dangerous asterisk where Market Street intersects Noe and
Twenty-third, the light is red. "Wait!" he calls. But Anthony
doesn't wait. Instead he hurls himself onto Market Street,
threads his way through six lanes of traffic, alights on the
other side. He will die and Christopher will live. He will die
and Christopher will die . . . At last the light turns green. And
Christopher, who loves life more than he is willing to admit,
crosses cautiously, as his mother taught him; looks both ways,
as his mother taught him. Then he steps up onto the curb.
Glances down Noe. (No Anthony.) Glances down Market.
(No Anthony.) Where has he gone?

Only the pavement knows, and the pavement isn't talking.

The Ruins of Another's Fame

In the spring of 1901, a few months after Oscar Wilde's death
in Paris, Bosie received a fan letter from a twenty-seven-year-
old poetess named Olive Custance. Olive's first book of verse,
Opals, had been published the previous year by John Lane; she
loved opals; her friends called her Opal. Bosie, on the other
hand—perhaps because opals were thought to bring bad luck
to those not born in October—insisted on calling her Olive.

They entered almost immediately into a love affair. Olive, though lacking Bosie's pedigree, was considered a great beauty, and came from money. As a poet she was dismal—worse even than Bosie, which was perhaps why they admired each other's work. That spring, in Paris with her mother, she had flirted with the famous lesbian Natalie Barney, going so far as to write Natalie a poem about how "Love walks with delicate feet afraid / 'Twixt maid and maid." Besotted, Natalie proposed that she (Natalie) ought to marry Bosie, after which the three of them could live together in a *ménage à trois*. Olive demurred. Later, in a letter, Natalie made the same proposal to Bosie, who also demurred.

Like his love affair with Laura, Bosie's romance with Olive seems to have involved a certain amount of transvestitism, albeit in this case on Olive's part rather than his own. For instance, in a note to Olive written shortly before he embarked on a trip for America—where, he joked, he hoped to find a rich heiress to marry—Bosie suggests that she dress as a boy and accompany him. In letters, Olive refers to herself as Bosie's "little Page": "Write to me soon and tell me that you love your little Page, and that one day you will come back to 'him,' my Prince, my Prince." His princess Olive is not: "*She* will be very beautiful. But meanwhile love me a little please . . ."

On March 4, 1902, they marry; their son, Raymond, is born on November 17. The marriage does not go well, however, according to Bosie, because Olive loves only "the feminine part" of him: the "more manly" he became, the less attractive he was to his wife. To make matters worse, Bosie and his father-in-law, Colonel Custance, took an instant dislike to each other. An upright Christian gentleman, the Colonel—eager for an heir, and unhappy with the way that his daughter and son-in-law (flighty and irresponsible poets both) were raising his grandson—decided that it was his duty to wrest custody of Raymond from them, toward which end he duped Olive into signing away her inheritance so that she would fall into a position of financial dependence upon her parents. Enraged, Bosie barraged the Colonel with vituperative letters, and when the Colonel stopped opening them, with postcards and telegrams—the e-mail of his age. He called the Colonel "a despicable scoundrel and a thoroughly dishonest and dishonorable man," and promised to send accusatory letters to his clubs, his bank, and the tenants of his estate. Later, after the Colonel threatened to cut her off without a penny if she did not hand Raymond over, Olive left Bosie for a time, and he added his wife's name to his list of enemies. "My father is angry all the time because I love Bosie still," she wrote to Lady Queensberry. "But would it do Bosie any good if I am turned out to starve? I am helpless since I made those settlements . . . I only wish I had the courage to kill myself!"

Custance was not the only person Bosie hated at this stage of his life. He also hated Mr. Asquith, the prime minister. He hated Asquith's wife, Margot, and Winston Churchill. He hated Robert Ross, Wilde's younger friend and literary executor, and he hated Ross's solicitor, Sir George Lewis, son of the same Sir George Lewis who had been Wilde's great advocate, and who in 1892, at Wilde's behest, had extricated Bosie (then an Oxford undergraduate) from the intimidations of a blackmailer. The second Sir George (no coincidence, in Bosie's view) numbered *both* Colonel Custance and Robbie Ross among his clients.

Where did all this hate come from? Wilde seemed to think it was linked to Bosie's "terrible lack of imagination, the one really fatal defect of your character." Hate, in Wilde's words to Bosie, "gnawed at your nature, as the lichen bites at the root of some sallow plant."

Hate, then, as disease; infection.

·

Wilde's gravest error—some might say his fatal error—was that he chose Bosie instead of Robbie Ross to be his lover. In making such a decision, he allied himself decisively with risk, volatility, and passion (Bosie) instead of prudence, circumspection, and restraint (Robbie). For Robbie, unlike Bosie, was reliable. When he met Wilde, he was a young man of slight build and no great beauty, with a delicate mouth set rather low on his face, a weak chin, wide, wet eyes. Scholars generally concur that he was "the first boy Oscar ever had." But then Bosie came along, and Robbie was demoted to the capacity of advisor and confidante, the friend into whose ears Oscar poured his passion when the affair was going well and his misery when it was going badly; none of which stopped him from supporting Oscar steadfastly throughout the years, even when it was both unpopular and unprofitable to do so. It was Robbie who took care of him after he got out of prison; Robbie who tried to dissuade him from reconciling with Bosie; Robbie who, in the decade following Wilde's death, managed more or less single-handedly to bring his estate out of bankruptcy and get his work back into print.

How Bosie despised him! Years before, they had quarreled over a boy called Alfred, whom Robbie had seduced, and whom Bosie had then seduced away from him. Now the prey over which they fought was Wilde's corpse and, more specifically, the manuscript of Wilde's prison letter *De Profundis,* which Robbie had given to the British Museum and which Bosie would have liked to see burned. Increasingly he was becoming aware that Wilde's resurrection (of which Robbie was the chief architect) was going to necessitate his own depiction as the instigator of the great writer's downfall. This he could not bear, and so sometime around December 1, 1909, he begins to rail in print against the cult of Wilde, whom he calls a "filthy swine . . . the greatest force for evil that has appeared in Europe during the last 350 years." Robbie, along the same lines, is "a filthy bugger and blackmailer . . . an unspeakable skunk." As for Bosie himself, he is merely a "normal" husband and father who only wants the world to know that despite youthful wickedness, he has reformed: toward this end, he transforms *The Academy* into an organ of rightwing propaganda.

There is a touch of the Victorian spinster in Robbie, a disquieting mixture of quaintness, cowardice, and spite. On the surface he is the classic nineties aesthete, quietly flouting even the creed of nationalism that ushered in the Great War by painting the walls of his rooms on Half Moon Street a tone of weary gold: an evocation of France, of "abroad." Nor does he lack for pugnacity: indeed, in his role as Wilde's literary executor he sued so many bookstores and publishers that in *Who's Who* he lists litigation as one of his hobbies. Like Bosie, he enjoys winning battles. By the teens he has grown into a small, tidy, mustached man of middle age who wears a turquoise blue scarab ring and carries a jade cigarette holder. When he entertains friends at his flat—its decor "half Italian and half Oriental," according to Siegfried Sassoon, and featuring a devotional panel of Saint Sebastian and Saint Fabian over the mantelpiece—he dons a black silk skullcap, serves Turkish delight, hands out boxes of Egyptian cigarettes. Yet *quietly.* This is the key to Robbie, the factor that distinguishes him from Bosie: the open warfare Wilde invited he makes certain always to avoid. When he takes the poet Wilfred Owen to dinner (and then home after dinner) he introduces him into a world of well-bred, refined homosexuals for whom Wilde's flamboyance is a quality at once to be admired and regretted, for though Wilde is their hero, nonetheless his breaking of the rules—it cannot be denied—has made life more difficult for them. Much better to have one's say slyly, even anonymously, and without pointing any fingers.

Robbie's diligence, the earnestness with which he undertakes his labors on Wilde's behalf, suggests the degree to which he embodies that very work ethic against which Wilde, in his witty defenses of idleness, strove to rebel. For Wilde was bad: he fouled the sheets of decent hotels, went into debt, drank. Robbie, on the other hand, conducted all his affairs—even his amorous ones—with tact. Had Wilde chosen him instead of Bosie, he might have grown into an honored old man of letters, with his sons at his knee, his wife at his side, his "companion" quiet in the background. Instead of which Wilde chose Bosie—pouting, spendthrift, malicious Bosie—and died a bankrupt.

On December 1, 1908, the eighth anniversary of Wilde's death, a dinner was held in Robert Ross's honor at the Ritz Hotel in London. The purpose of this dinner was twofold: first, to announce the publication of the final two volumes of Wilde's collected works (which Robbie had midwifed); second, to celebrate the emergence of the Wilde estate into solvency (which Robbie had negotiated). One hundred sixty people—among them Somerset Maugham, the Duchess of Sutherland and Wilde's two sons, Cyril and Vyvyan—attended. Not Bosie, however. He declined his invitation, writing that in his view the dinner was "absurd."

After Frank Harris and H. G. Wells, among others, had toasted Robbie, he himself stepped up to the dais, where he described all that he had had to undergo while resurrecting Wilde's reputation. Then—in ironic reference to himself—he quoted a fragment from an eighteenth-century poem:

I hate the man who builds his name
On the ruins of another's fame.

He could just as easily have been talking about Bosie. Though probably he would have sued anyone who dared link this couplet with his career, nonetheless Bosie must have recognized the degree to which his fate was becoming yoked to that of his dead lover. For Wilde's resurgence threatened not merely his campaign against vice, but his very identity, his new idea of himself as a reformed libertine. More and more it must have been evident to him that his success would actually require Robbie's failure, and with it the preservation of Wilde's image as an unregenerate sodomite.

They are now more intimate, Bosie and Oscar, even than in the days when they scandalized London society by taking rent boys out to dinner at the Savoy. The object of the game is Robbie's ruin, which Bosie begins to seek aggressively. In letters, he threatens to horsewhip Robbie: "You have corrupted hundreds of boys and young men in your life, and have gone on doing it right up to the present time." His intention seems to be to goad Robbie into initiating an action against him, as once his own father, goaded by Bosie, goaded Wilde. Yet Robbie refuses to answer, even when Bosie writes to the prime minister demanding that Robbie be fired from his post as assessor of picture valuations to the Board of Trade (and promising to let off a stink if Mr. Asquith continues to receive "this horrible man" in his house). Later he sends another letter, "nailing" Robbie, to two judges, the recorder of London, the prime minister, the public prosecutor, Mr. Basil Thompson of Scotland Yard, the publisher John Lane, Sir George Lewis, and the master of St. Paul's School (as once he promised to mail his defense of homosexuality to every judge, lawyer, and legislator in England), and makes sure that Robbie is informed of the fact. Already T.W.H. Crosland, his coeditor at *The Academy,* has labeled Robbie's efforts to resuscitate "the maligned and greatly suffering Wilde" merely "one dirty Sodomite bestowing whitewash upon another." Now he makes his point plain: "If these letters do not contain the truth about you, there can be little question that you would have taken a certain and obvious legal remedy."

Matters come to a head for Bosie in the spring of 1913, with a spate of lawsuits. On April 18 he initiates a libel action against Arthur Ransome before the High Court. Then on April 24 Colonel Custance initiates a libel action against Bosie before a Magistrate's Court. (At that time, in that place, libel was a criminal, not a civil, offense.) Then in early May, Bosie has to go to the Chancery Court to argue with his father-in-law over the matter of Raymond's custody.

Colonel Custance's was the only lawsuit Bosie ever backed off from; it was also the only lawsuit in which his outrage can be construed as being even remotely justified. After all, Custance really had written to Olive, "The moment he (Bosie) takes the boy away all payments to you cease."

At the Chancery Court, Bosie was granted custody of his son for two-fifths — and Colonel Custance for three-fifths — of Raymond's vacation time; Bosie was told to pay the boy's tuition.

The Dark Grey Man

One evening a few weeks after his last conversation with Anthony, Christopher is standing near the magazine rack at A Different Light, thumbing through a copy of *The Advocate*. Every evening, now, he comes here, to this place where his great love was born, and waits patiently. For if he keeps faith, he believes, and if he shows his faith by returning here, piously, every night, then soon enough Anthony will feel its radiance, and come through the door. Perhaps he won't realize why he's coming through the door, perhaps he'll think he's here just to look at magazines, or buy a book, or hear a lecture. But Christopher will know.

If you saw Christopher today, you might not recognize him as the boy who was waiting at Café Flore a few weeks earlier. This is mostly because of his hair: last week he got a buzzcut. Tonight he's wearing a black T-shirt, combat boots, and a fatigue jacket, an outfit that worries some members of the bookstore staff, who fear he might be packing artillery in the bulging pockets of his pants. Not that they need be concerned: in fact, Christopher poses no danger to anyone but himself. If you looked inside the sleeve of his T-shirt you would find, on his right biceps, a healing tattoo (his first), an old-fashioned heart of the sort that sailors used to favor, except that instead of saying "Mother," the ribbon that bisects it says "Anthony."

Anthony. No one else is allowed to see the tattoo. Even the men Christopher sometimes permits to pick him up and take him home are not permitted to take off his T-shirt, for if they did, then they would see it, and the spell would be broken; Anthony would never come to his senses; he would never come home. Yet if the tattoo remains secret—somehow Christopher knows this—then he *will* come, drawn as if by a talisman, if not tonight then tomorrow, if not tomorrow then next week. Nor will Christopher ever have to admit that he lied at Café Flore, for by then, if he plays his cards right, the lie will have come true. More and more, people are doing it, he's heard. *Bareback,* they call it. *No glove. Skin to skin.*

At the moment, next to where Christopher is browsing, there stands a bearded man with a beer gut, alternately glancing at the pictures in the latest issue of *Bound & Gagged,* giving Christopher the eye, and attending to the back of the store, where a lecture has started—nothing as exciting as that mobbed reading at which Christopher met Anthony (Dennis Cooper, the dark lord of American gay literature); no, this is just another Dead White Male, or nearly. At least eighty. At present he's standing before the lectern and two dozen folding chairs, of which two-thirds are empty. On and on he drones, his coughy voice no match for the claque of strong-lunged young lesbians who have just started a conversation about Jodie Foster near the cash register. Their oblivious disregard offends one of the listeners, who turns, glowers, says, "Will you please be quiet, girls?" Christopher starts. It's the counselor! For a nanosecond their eyes meet; the counselor's lips contort. Then he returns his attention to the lecturer.

By now the bearded man has taken his copy of *Bound & Gagged* to the cash register and is paying for it. Should he follow him? Christopher wonders. After all, older guys are more likely to have it; if he does enough of them, it'll be a sure thing . . . only this one looks like he might be psycho. He offers a last glance of entreaty, then leaves. Putting down *The Advocate,* Christopher listens for a moment to the speaker. He explains that he is here to eulogize a friend of his, a poet who died of AIDS sometime back in the dark ages. "The vivid influence of Cavafy," the old man says about the poet, and points to a poster set up on an easel behind the lectern: two skinny boys with golden hair, posed before a severe arrangement of cactuses. "As Roger used to put it, if only for the sake of the forty-seven people in the world who still read poetry," he goes on, and suddenly Christopher recognizes — the idea rather floors him — that *he,* the old man, is one of the boys in the poster. (The other must be the poet.) And what a mind-blowing idea that is! To grow, to grow old . . . (*Not if I can help it!*)

The audience, what little there is of it, is becoming restless. The old man's voice is monotonous and harsh. He is a bore. A fat, weary-looking youth gets up to leave. The bag lady who comes to all these readings, to sit alone in a corner chair amid her shreds of blanket, ceaselessly opening and closing the top of a plastic water bottle, starts humming to herself. Again the counselor turns, levels a glance at Christopher that makes him smile.

Gravy train, Christopher thinks.

"What Henry James called 'the air-blown grain . . . Byron in Thessalonica . . . The muse of history." History! Well, Christopher has *really* had it now. For he hates history, which for him means his high school teacher, Mrs. Helfgott, chattering nasally about the War Between the States. Earlier, when the lesbians were being so rude, he felt sorry for the old man. But now, by invoking history's muse, he has proven himself merely to be another dumbass fart. Part of the status quo. What good will history do us in nuclear winter? Christopher thinks as the lecture ends, and a thin runnel of applause rises from the folding chairs, out of which most of the few listeners immediately bolt. As for the bag lady, she opens her water bottle and closes it, opens her water bottle and closes it. Hums.

"Does anyone have any questions?"

Silence. The counselor raises his hand.

"Yes, John?"

"Professor McMaster, forgive me if this sounds gossipy—"

"The best kind of question. Go on."

"Thank you. Well, when I was a graduate student at Berkeley I remember a rumor went around that Roger Hinton—"

"Many rumors have circulated about Roger, most of them true."

"Very likely. Anyway, according to this rumor, when he was on leave from the Marine Corps near the end of the Second

World War, he went to Brighton to seduce Lord Alfred Douglas, so that he could say he'd slept with someone who'd slept with Oscar Wilde."

A low murmur of surprise now rises from the hinterlands of the bookstore. Indeed, such is the magnetism of Wilde's name that even the lesbians cease talking and turn toward the lectern.

"Ah yes," the old man says. "Unfortunately, that one I've never been able to corroborate. There is evidence that Roger was in England in 1944, the year before Douglas died. There's even evidence that he went to Brighton. Beyond that, though, I haven't been able to prove anything except—you see, Roger learned early on that the best way to keep people interested in him was to keep them guessing. So whenever anyone asked him about that particular rumor—or any rumor—he'd make a point of sort of dancing around the question without actually answering it, just the sort of maneuver our political leaders have become so adept at lately. Still, if one is, as I am, a literary critic—which amounts, in essence, to being a snoop—then it's hard to resist the impulse to dig around in the poetry for clues, even though, as we all know, the purpose of poetry is never merely to render up autobiographical ore. Perhaps, John, you will recall an odd little ballad of Roger's called 'The Dark Grey Man.'"

The counselor (John) smiles at the name, recites: "'I remember him treading dark water, / The dark-souled, dark grey man.'"

"Very good, very good. Yes, it's a puzzle, that one. For years I couldn't work it out, which surprised me, because as we all know, Roger's poetry is usually fairly *un*opaque—at least by design. He used to say that he was a novelist manqué. And yet that poem always struck me as being, in certain ways—well, very *unlike* the rest of his work. Intentionally obscurist. I always thought of it as a puzzle or riddle for which you had to find the key . . . and then one day, while I was researching my biography, I happened upon an extraordinary fact." From the lectern he picks up his book. "According to Rupert Hart-Davis in his biography of Bosie, the name Douglas derives from the Gaelic *dubh glas,* and means 'dark water' . . . which Walter Scott rendered in *The Abbot* as 'dark grey.' In that novel an eighteenth-century Douglas, a warrior, is 'the Dark-Grey man.'"

The old man clears his throat; quotes: "'As if fishing for Neptune's daughter / In the dark grey, roiling water, / Or perhaps he'd already caught her, / That dark-souled, dark grey man.'

"Well, and what, after all, is the most obvious synonym for 'roiling'?"

John raises his hand. "You," the old man says—suddenly a professor again, as John is suddenly a student.

"Wild," John says.

"Wild. Exactly. Exactly."

He smiles. The bag lady hums.

Campden Hill, or the Abyss

Now we enter into what is perhaps the most difficult period in Bosie's life to make out. The problem is not lack of information. On the contrary, documents abound, too many of them: police reports, trial transcripts, lurid coverage in the tabloid press. (Excessive paper is a side effect of the litigious life.) These documents ensnare and obfuscate, they are a jungle of innuendo and error. Under their canopy details meld: one forgets at which trial Freddie Smith, Robbie Ross's erstwhile thespian lover, admitted to wearing powder and paint not only on stage, but in church. (And is Freddie Smith in any way related to F. E. Smith? No, *he* was Robbie's counsel . . . though only in the first of the trials.)

The sheer quantity of actions in which Bosie was involved means that even *he* has difficulty keeping them in order, with the result that when he is arrested upon his arrival at Folkestone in 1914 (for the last few months he had been hiding out in France) he has no idea on which warrant he is being charged: is it Colonel Custance's bench warrant, revived after Bosie wrote a letter to King George V complaining of the "foul way" he was being treated by his father-in-law? No, that one appears to have escaped the officer's attention. Is it a warrant left over from Robbie's earlier action against Crosland, then, the one in which he asserted that Crosland, "being concerned with Lord Alfred Douglas, did, on September 17, 1913, and on diverse other dates between September 17 and February 14 last, unlawfully and wickedly conspire, combine, confederate, and agree together, and with diverse other persons unknown, unlawfully, falsely, and corruptly to charge Robert Baldwin Ross with having committed certain acts with one Charles Garratt?" No, that case Robbie has already lost.

Instead the warrant turns out to be new, issued by Robbie, and accusing Bosie of "falsely and maliciously publishing a defamatory libel" about him. Bosie only finds this out when he gets to London, though; already his cousin Sholto Douglas, along with an Anglican parson called Mills, is standing in the courtroom, waiting to bail him out. But hold on! At the last minute, Sir George Lewis stalks in dramatically from the wings, declaring that as long as a warrant still exists for Bosie's arrest regarding "certain other charges of which he has been convicted"—charges involving a gentleman who just happens to be another client of his, Colonel Frederic Hambledon Custance—bail cannot be granted! So Bosie is shipped off to jail for five days, an experience no doubt intended to provoke second thoughts in him but from which he emerges more rather than less determined to ruin Robbie.

Provocation is seduction. In the atmosphere of panic that took hold just before the Great War, even Bosie's most ludicrous delusions take on the heft of reality. Reviewing the coverage, one begins to believe that there actually was a sodomitical conspiracy afoot, the intention of which was to depose the king of England and put Robert Ross—as heir to dear dead Oscar—onto the throne. Nor do Bosie's ravings about Robbie—whom he calls "the High Priest of all the sodomites of London"—lack their equivalent in public life. More and more, the language of infection (and disinfection) seeps into the national discourse. Thus it is reported that German *agents provocateurs* have begun circulating among the healthy ranks of the military, handing out venereal diseases like candy. (According to the article, these Germans are sexual kamikazes, motivated by duty instead of lust—which elides the trickier question of why Albion's sons are so susceptible to their charms.) Foreigners are "parasites who live on the blood of fighting men." War is "the sovereign disinfectant," Robbie's friend Edmund Gosse writes, "its red stream of blood . . . the Condy's fluid that cleans out the stagnant pools and clotted channels of the intellect." A few years later, in Wormwood Scrubs prison for libeling Churchill, Bosie himself declares in verse:

> *The leprous spawn of scattered Israel*
> *Spreads its contagion in your English blood . . .*

Of course, he was playing to the gallery here, to that philistine majority from whose ranks jurymen were selected, and for whom homosexuality, artistic talent, and pacifism necessarily went hand in hand with pro-hun and pro-Jewish sentiment (and possibly espionage). For the downside of

Bosie's anti-Oscar stance is that it puts him in the awkward position of having to rely for support upon a "public" toward which, as a snob and an aristocrat, he feels only contempt. This was where Crosland became invaluable. Crosland—it cannot be denied—had a certain prescient genius; he could smell the xenophobic terror of the middle classes, to which war had not yet given a voice. He also understood that above all else, a prophet must be a good public speaker, someone who can transform inchoate rage into eloquent diatribe. And who better to play the part of prophet than Bosie? Because he is not *of* them, then maybe he can win them, convince them that far from Oscar Wilde's boy, he is their savior, sent from heaven to crusade against sin, sodomy, socialism, Judaism, and all foreigners who have chosen to make their home in England.

By now Bosie is forty-three years old. He is no longer beautiful. The fate of men who resemble Renaissance seraphim in their twenties is that as they age their handsomeness does not mature. Thus Bosie, in a photograph taken of him in 1919, looks exactly the same as Bosie in a photograph taken in the 1890s—same glossy dark blond hair, same high cheekbones and wide eyes, same slim torso—except that (how else to put it?) he is no longer young. Instead of weathering his features, time has let Bosie rot, leaving us with this circus spectacle, the prematurely elderly child.

Whenever he writes, odors rise from the page. His hatred—his "lack of imagination"—is boundless. For example, one day in 1913 he reads in the *Reynolds* newspaper that a male prostitute called Charles Garratt has been arrested upon leaving the flat of one Christopher Millard. Millard, as Bosie well knows, is Robbie Ross's secretary, and Wilde's bibliographer; might the boy, then, count Robbie among his clients too? (Very likely; from experience Bosie knows the sodomite's habit of trading boys like recipes.) There is no time to lose, and promptly he sends a solicitor to speak to Garratt, who admits that he knows of Robbie but refuses to say more until he is let free. Next Crosland visits Garratt's mother, a charwoman in Lincolnshire, stands her a drink at a pub and says that if she speaks up, the men who corrupted her son will be punished. She is alarmed, and takes him to meet her daughter, a Mrs. Flude, to whom he explains that recently two men named Millard and Ross got her brother so drunk that he passed out, only to awaken the next morning dressed as a woman and smelling of perfume. All of this is invention—as Garratt will later testify, he's never even met Ross—which does nothing to stop the fantasy from taking a fierce hold on the national imagination. For such a scenario—the boy seduced, drugged, and quite literally emasculated—speaks to the very fear that Crosland wants to exploit: the fear of foreignness, contamination, contagion. No doubt the Germans are behind it all . . . and haven't we heard plenty already about the sorts of things that go on in Berlin?

Provocation is seduction. When Robbie Ross, in 1914, finally sued Bosie for criminal libel, he seemed at last to be taking some action; in fact he was merely submitting to a prostitute's wiles. "Come on," Bosie had beckoned—for years— "climb into this warm, close bed." So at last Robbie climbed into that warm, close bed, as Oscar had; as Gerald and Wellington had. And Bosie pounced.

As soon as he's released from jail, he sets about seeking evidence with which to condemn Robbie. The stakes in the game are high. Given his record, if Bosie loses, he will probably go to prison. On the other hand, if he wins, then Robbie will probably be tried on charges of "gross indecency," found guilty, and sentenced, as Wilde was, to hard labor. A lurid spectacle, this: one spiteful queen attempting to use an unjust law to "out" (and thereby destroy) another. Nor are Robbie's own belligerent tendencies to be overlooked in the matter. For if he had simply ignored Bosie's threats, then very probably by his silence he would have done his enemy far greater damage than he did by providing him with the soapbox of a trial. After all, Bosie's diatribes in the gutter press posed no danger so far as Robbie's high-ranking friends were concerned. On the contrary, so greatly did his treatment by the police incense Margot Asquith, the prime minister's (lesbian) wife, that she went to Scotland Yard to have it out herself with the director of public prosecutions. Later, Edmund Gosse persuaded more than three hundred people, including Sir James Barrie, Thomas Hardy, H. G. Wells, and Bernard Shaw, to sign a testimonial to Robbie, which was presented to him along with a "purse" that he used to endow a scholarship "for *male* students only" at the Slade School of Art. None of this, needless to say, went down particularly well with Bosie, but then again it wasn't intended to.

Bosie's campaign to ruin Robbie begins deep in the past. He brings out the old scandal of the schoolboy called Alfred whom Robbie was supposed to have seduced in 1893; the problem here is that later Bosie had lured Alfred away from Robbie (and written him love letters). Then he tries to persuade Garratt (again) to testify that Robbie was one of his clients. Garratt refuses. Then he tries to dig up evidence to substantiate a rumor that three years earlier Robbie attended a New Year's Eve party at which men danced with other men. He fails. Finally he goes after Freddie Smith, Robbie's former boyfriend and putative secretary. Here he has more success. A fellow member of Freddie's dramatic society, Emma Rooker, agrees to state in court that she once saw Robbie embrace Freddie and call him "my darling," while the Reverend Andrew Bowring—the same pastor who had dismissed Freddie in his capacity as an acolyte after he was found to be wearing

make-up and powder to church—expresses his grave doubts
as to Freddie's qualifications for the position of secretary to
"a man of literature." And that would have been it, the entirety of Bosie's plea of justification, had not, in his own
words, a "miracle" occurred.

Having just returned from a fruitless trip to Guernsey and
several other places where Robbie was supposed to have got
up to no good, Bosie received a tip that during the years just
after Wilde's death, while he was living in Campden Hill,
Robbie had "victimized" sixteen-year-old William Edwards,
who subsequently went off to South Africa and died. *Go to
Campden Hill,* a tipster told him, *go to a certain address and ask
for Mr. Edwards. He will tell you what you need to know.* So Bosie
went. His hope was to persuade the boy's father to testify
against Robbie at his trial. But when he knocked at the door
of the address given, he was told not only that no Mr. Edwards lived there, but that no Mr. Edwards had ever lived
there.

At an utter loss, looking up and down a street lined by "at
least 150 houses"—this was probably Campden Hill Road,
near Holland Park, now one of London's most notorious
cruising grounds—Bosie sent up a prayer to Saint Anthony of
Padua (the patron saint of lost objects) and waited. It was
then that a little boy strode up to him and asked him if he
needed help. Bosie stated his dilemma; the little boy smiled
and explained that all the numbers in the street had recently
been changed. Then he took Bosie by the hand and led him
to the right house.

"I firmly believe," Bosie wrote later, "that the child was an
angel . . . He was a most beautiful little boy, and he had an angelic face and smile." Just as Bosie did.

*When you go to heaven you can be what you like, and I intend to
be a child.*

■

At the trial Mr. Edwards testified that in 1908 his son William had come home wearing a shirt with the name "Ross" printed on its collar. His older son, a soldier, testified that after William's disappearance he had gone to a bar on Copthall Avenue in search of Robbie, who had tried to buy his silence and then, when he refused the bribe, threatened to accuse him of blackmail. (I am sorry to say that such a tactic sounds just like Robbie.) Emma Rooker testified, as did the Reverend Andrew Bowring, and Vyvyan Holland (his mother had changed their name), and Bosie. Robbie himself testified — not very well, apparently, for in his summing up the judge complained that his performance had been inadequate. "I waited and waited, but I waited in vain for any moral expression of horror at the practice of sodomitical vices . . . It was certainly not so emphatic a denial as you would expect from a man with no leprosy on him."

After three hours the foreman of the jury announced that it had failed to reach a verdict. The judge sent them back. The foreman returned with the same news. Later it was revealed that they were split eleven to one in favor of acquittal — yet the holdout refused to budge. In future ravings, Bosie would insist that this gentleman — who robbed him of complete victory — was a plant, a vassal of the nefarious Sir George Lewis.

Not long after, Robbie died. He did not live to be old. Bosie lived to be old.

A Link in a Chain

"You've got more books than the bookstore," Christopher says, slinging his backpack off his shoulder and sitting down on John's (the counselor's) sofa.

From across the room, where he's opening a bottle of wine, John looks at him cautiously. Is there reproach in Christopher's voice? he wonders, the reproach of youth, of a generation that disdains history? Or is *he* too much of a skeptic? Perhaps, he thinks, Christopher is expressing simple wonder. This is closer to the truth. The fact of the matter is that John's apartment—in which there are only books, buckling shelves full of books, books piled on either side of the sofa— somewhat intimidates Christopher. From near where he's sitting he picks one up, turns to the title page. *Real Presences,* he reads, *Is There Anything in What We Say?* He puts the book down as if it's bitten him, picks up another. *Roger Hinton: A Life,* by Jack McMaster. "Oh, the old guy who was lecturing," he says, glancing neutrally at the photograph on the back of the jacket. (It is the same photograph that was on the lectern.)

"Do you read much?" John asks, sitting down next to him, handing him a glass of red wine.

"I like to read."

"Who do you like?"

Who, not *what.* What embarrasses Christopher now is that he can't remember the names of any authors. It's as if the question itself has expunged them from his brain.

"Dennis Cooper," he says after a moment, grateful at least to have successfully grasped at something. "I heard him at A Different Light, too."

"Anyone else?"

"Those vampire books."

"Oh, Anne Rice? Yes, I like the early ones."

Slyly John throws an arm around the back of the sofa, behind Christopher's neck. It may be the very immorality of what he's doing—the fact that by inviting a client home he's breached both the written and unwritten ethics of his profession—that excites him tonight, even more than the simple miracle of having convinced Christopher to come to his apartment. For he's not used—has never been used—to attracting. Unlike Jack McMaster, for instance (and Roger, for that matter; and *Bosie,* for that matter), John was not good-looking as a boy. *They* had that ironic loveliness of the ephebe, that delicate beauty to which the imminence of manhood lends an erotic flush. For such a beauty there has always been, will always be, a market. John, on the other hand, was at twenty both geeky and spotty; all limbs; none of the parts seemed to fit.

The irony (he sees it clearly tonight) is that while Roger aged wretchedly—Jack too—he has, as it were, grown into his body. At thirty-seven, he is a handsome man.

Now, on the sofa, he puts down his wineglass; scoots closer to Christopher, who's gazing rather vacantly at the disarranged books, the groaning shelves. "As you may have surmised," he says, "I haven't always been a social worker."

"No?"

John shakes his head. "I used to be an English professor. Well, an *assistant* English professor. Jack—the fellow who gave the lecture—was my mentor. My teacher."

"Yeah?"

"I wrote my dissertation on Oscar Wilde."

"Oh, I know about him," says Christopher. "He was, like, the first faggot, right?"

"More or less."

"And that guy Jack—that teacher of yours—when you were his student, did he fuck you?"

The question rather takes John aback; it also arouses him.

"Well, yes, actually," he admits after a moment.

"So that means that if he fucked you, and that poet he was talking about fucked him, and what's his name—Oscar

Wilde's boyfriend—fucked the poet, then if you fuck me to-night it'll be like I got fucked by the first faggot."

"I guess so," John says, laughing.

"Cool."

"You like the idea?"

"I like the idea of your fucking me," Christopher says, and looks John steadily in the eye. "Will you? I really need it."

John blushes. Suddenly Christopher is lunging at him, kissing him, kneading his erection.

"But I haven't got any condoms! I meant to buy some, only—"

"It's okay," Christopher whispers urgently, "it's okay—"

"I could run out and—"

"Feel in my back pocket."

John does. Slipping his hand inside, he paws Christopher's buttock for a moment, then withdraws a single condom in its tidy plastic wrapper.

"You think of everything."

"There's lube in my backpack."

"That I've got in the bathroom."

"So where do you want to do it? Here? In the bedroom?"

"Bedroom's more comfortable." And standing—how terrible and thrilling is this boy's eagerness—Christopher takes John's hand and yanks him to his feet.

A Stroll on the Beach

In his later years, Bosie makes it his habit, on sunny days, to take a morning walk along the sea. Bypassing all the rubbish in Brighton, the promenade and the tearooms and holiday camps, he heads south, to where the rocky beach is emptier.

Taking off his shoes, he lets the cold water run over his feet, which churn up tiny whirlpools around them before collapsing into the dense, wet life of the rocks.

It is 1944. Springtime. Though he doesn't know it, in a little less than a year he will be dead. Yet he is not a dying man. Instead he is simply an old man, one of hundreds who stroll each morning along the promenade and the beach of this seaside town, this town of pensioners. Most of his neighbors know perfectly well who he is. "The one who ruined Wilde," they say; or else, "The one Wilde ruined." Such whispering and staring, even when overtly hostile, he accepts more placidly today than he might have in the past, letting it roll over his ego as gently as the water now rolling over his feet. For time has diminished the rage that once coruscated his eyes and corroded his hours. It's not that anything has changed in the world; the change was in his soul. This is why he can regard this war—the second one—with so much more composure than he did its predecessor. Cynicism is an old man's prerogative. *You should have listened to me,* he can say; *the hun must be squelched utterly, else he will re-emerge, time and again, with greater awfulness.* Indeed, as of today only a single blemish clouds Bosie's conscience, and that is the fact that the modern German's loathing of the Jews has rendered the anti-Semitism of Bosie's earlier poetry not only unfashionable but faintly scandalous. Without disclaiming the greatness of *In Excelsis,* Bosie cannot help but regret such lines as

> *Your Jew-kept politicians buy and sell*
> *In markets redolent of Jewish mud . . .*

Yet he was never one to shrink from unpopular positions.

A few weeks earlier Olive, who had been ill for several years, finally died. This was both a sorrow and a relief for Bosie. True, they had not lived together for decades; still, with the coming of war their once acrimonious relations had at least resolved themselves into a state of ceasefire that did not disallow the possibility of friendship. Often they dined or took tea together—sometimes in Bosie's modest ground-floor flat at St. Ann's Court, more often at Olive's much grander digs at Viceroy Lodge, which looked onto the sea. For Colonel Custance's death had left Olive a rich woman—a fact that she sometimes lorded over her estranged husband, as for years he had lorded over her his self-proclaimed spiritual and poetic superiority. (No one admired Bosie's poetry more than he did; by the same token, he admired no one else's poetry—with the possible exception of Shakespeare's—more than his own.)

In Brighton, though, the tables were turned. Now it was Bosie who, as a consequence of his poverty, had to apply to Olive for money. She made him an allowance that she was not above occasionally threatening to suspend. No doubt the disparity in their circumstances—which, by keeping Bosie's income low, she could be certain to maintain—pleased his wife. In her will she left to her husband an opal necklace (rather ironic, considering his dislike of opals), all the money in her bank account, and an allowance of £500 per annum. (All this, however, went into receivership, as Bosie had never discharged an earlier bankruptcy.) To their son, Raymond, she left her flat at Viceroy Lodge, which did not prevent Bosie from moving in almost instantly upon her death. For a few months he lived there quite happily, until Raymond, who had for many years been an inmate at St. Andrew's Hospital, decided that he wanted to give "life outside" a try, and evicted his father. At the time Raymond was in his early forties—the same age that Bosie was when he took on Robbie Ross in court. In 1926 Raymond had been diagnosed as schizophrenic and admitted to an asylum for "electroconvulsive therapy and narcosis." (Not incidentally, that same year he had fallen in love with a grocer's daughter named Gladys Lacey, but his parents and grandparents had disapproved of the match, and kept him from marrying her.)

Let us now say that the morning of which I am writing—the morning when Bosie takes a walk along the beach—is the same morning on which Raymond is scheduled to arrive in Hove and displace his father. It is still early; Raymond's train won't pull in for hours. As Bosie strolls up and down the beach, I imagine that he is trying to suppress the rather petulant displeasure that Raymond's decision to come to Hove has provoked in him. After all, as he well knows, his son's release from the hospital where he has been living, on and off, for twenty years is—has to be looked at as—a good thing. It means that Raymond is getting well, with which Bosie has no argument. And yet must his getting well require turning his father onto the street? On the surface, at least, Raymond has been nothing but cordial to Bosie, has even vowed to give him an extra £300 pounds per year as soon as Olive's will has gone through probate. Even so, it *does* seem hard. (All right. Let's just say it.) Bosie's weeks at Viceroy Lodge, under the capable management of Olive's maid Eileen, have been happy ones. There he has entertained, among others, his old friend Lord Tredegar and his wife, Olga, the former Princess Dolgorouki, as well as several members of the younger literary generation (by younger I mean those in their fifties), invited for elaborate teas featuring toast, scones, cream cakes, jam puffs, tarts, and other schoolboyish treats with which their middle-aged stomachs proved unable to cope. The juvenile character of these gatherings, though bewildering to Bosie's guests (after all, he was now in his seventies), delighted the host, who still looks upon his childhood years as the best of his life. His old friend Wellington, for instance, he often thinks about these nights, as he thinks about Alfred, the schoolboy he seduced away from Robbie Ross, and the boy at Oxford who blackmailed him, and the rent boys with whom, sometimes in Oscar's company and sometimes out of it, he was able to revive, for a moment, a lost dream of laddish camaraderie: *tremendous friends*. This is something he's realized only lately: when he was a wicked young man, what he was really after wasn't sex; it was those innocent attachments of boyhood to which sex—alas—only sometimes took him back. For though the route from childhood to manhood is a clear, straight path, to return, he has learned, one has to take back roads, stumble up rocky paths, try to make sense of deceptive and illegible signs. You rarely get where you want to be, and when you do, the magic place is never as you remembered.

Of course, Raymond is the worst wrong turn of all. Where his son is concerned Bosie cannot, no matter how hard he tries, shirk off the unpleasant suspicion that if the boy has grown into an ill and fragile man, it is largely Bosie's own fault. For Raymond was, in many ways, the most beloved of the many boys with whom he tried to recapture his lost adolescence. Even more than Wellington, *he* was Bosie's tremendous friend, especially during the summer when Raymond was thirteen, and Bosie—enraged by what he saw as the iniquity of a court determined to favor the claims of his vindictive father-in-law—picked him up at his school and without telling anyone spirited him to Scotland, which was outside the Chancery Court's jurisdiction. There he rented a house near the southern end of Loch Ness, and enrolled Raymond at the Benedictine Monastery and College of Fort Augustus. Every afternoon they went swimming, or fishing, or took exploratory gambols through forests in which generations of Douglases had roamed and hunted. For Bosie was Scottish, he was a Scottish laird, and Raymond—though half

Custance—needed to be reminded that in his veins there ran also the blood of the dark grey man.

His point may have been to persuade Raymond that the trip amounted to a Boys' Adventure, something out of Robert Louis Stevenson, and not a traumatic kidnapping from which Raymond would never recover. Nor, apparently, did Bosie fail in this objective. Indeed, Raymond's credulous acceptance of his father's fantasy was the very thing that would do them both in.

One day, after barely a term at his new school, Raymond went fishing in Loch Ness and never came back. Fearing that he had drowned, for almost a week, day and night, his father and the monks trawled the lake's waters. Then, rather out of the blue, Bosie received a telegram from Olive informing him that Raymond was safely back at Weston, his grandfather's estate. It seems that Colonel Custance, perhaps in collusion with George Lewis, had set up a secret means of communication with the boy, whom he had then enticed to embark on an even grander adventure than the one on which his father had taken him. It would work like this: Raymond, on the pretense of wanting to fish, would take a boat and row to the opposite side of Loch Ness. There a private detective would be waiting to carry him away in a car. All very thrilling, especially the car, which in 1915 must really have seemed, to an impressionable boy, the *pièce de résistance,* with its promise of speed and stealth and spy novel glamour. The detective drove Raymond across the border into England, where his mother and grandfather met him. Only once he was safely ensconced again did Olive inform Bosie of what had happened. Bosie, who had had to endure almost a week of tormented uncertainty, could not forgive her for what she had put him through. Nor could he forgive Raymond, of whom he washed his hands; he would never again have anything to do with his treacherous son, he vowed—forgetting, perhaps, that the treacherous son was at the time only thirteen years old.

The tide is running out. Turning around, again like a child, Bosie walks backward, as if fitting his feet into his own footsteps, so as not to leave a trace of having made a return journey, so as to suggest that this morning he walked, and walked, and then simply disappeared.

An instant later he notices that he's not alone.

He raises his eyebrows. Not far off, shoes in his hand, stands a soldier. An unfamiliar uniform . . . Canadian, perhaps? American? From where he hovers at the water's edge, the soldier gazes out at the sea in a way that seems to Bosie both provocative and touchingly naive. For though he is old now, he was once beautiful, and so has some experience of the tactics to which nervous admirers resort in order to avoid being caught out in their curiosity.

Stopping, for the moment, Bosie watches the soldier. What does he want? Is he here by chance? Very unlikely. The soldier's presence amuses him, if for no other reason than that it is exemplary of something that has become, in recent years, so commonplace. He never expected to grow into a monument, a human equivalent of Trafalgar Square, or the Tomb of the Unknown Soldier. Yet this, as a consequence of Wilde's ever increasing fame (Robbie did a good job, in the end), has turned out to be his fate. More and more young men come to Hove for one reason only: to seek him out; to gaze at him. On those rare occasions when they muster the courage to approach him, he is never less than perfectly polite. Instead he listens quietly, smiling, as they make their elegant speeches.

If they're good-looking, he invites them home for tea, and sometimes to bed.

Now the soldier turns; approaches. Bosie straightens his

back. He is, he knows, no longer attractive. Not that it isn't possible for an old man to be beautiful. Toscanini, for instance, is a beautiful old man. In his case, age preserved the thick hair, the athletic arms and limbs. In Bosie's, only the worst features seem to have emerged unscathed from the holocaust of time—the crooked mouth, the eyes with their startled rabbit's look.

Not that it matters. He has something else. In the end, Wilde gave Bosie more than he bargained for.

I hate the man who builds his name
On the ruins of another's fame.

"Mr. Douglas?"

Yes, he *is* American. Otherwise he'd have called him Lord Alfred.

"Yes?"

"I hope I'm not bothering you. I—" Sheepishly the soldier puts down his shoes, takes off his hat. His beauty startles Bosie in that it is exactly the same sort of beauty he himself possessed once.

"Yes?"

"My name is Roger Hinton. Private Roger Hinton, of the United States Marine Corps. And I just wanted to say . . . I'm a poet, and a great admirer of your work. I'm here on leave. Especially *In Excelsis* . . . Such a marvelous poem!"

Bosie allows his lips to turn up in a slight smile. What rot! he thinks. Later, when they're at Olive's flat, he'll tease the boy, try to taunt him into admitting that he's never even read *In Excelsis*. Not that it matters. Once it would have. Once he would have hoped that when young men stared at him in admiration, they'd be thinking, "Douglas at Wormswood Scrubs," not "Wilde at Reading Gaol."

"So you're a poet. How interesting. Do you write sonnets?"

"I've written a few."

"Shakespearean, or—"

"No, Petrarchan, like yours."

"What a charming coincidence, to meet a young son-neteer on the beach. And tell me, Mr. Hinson, will you be sojourning long in Hove?"

"Hinton. Only forty-eight hours. As I said, I'm on leave."

"You must take tea with me. I'm afraid it will have to be today. This evening my son arrives. If that's possible for you . . . I imagine your schedule—"

"No, I'm utterly free." (The *utterly* takes Bosie aback. Perhaps the soldier really *is* a poet.) "I don't know anyone in Hove, or Brighton, for that matter. I've only come here to see you."

"How charming. And which way are you heading, if I might ask?"

"Whichever way you are, Mr. Douglas."

"Please call me Bosie."

The young man blushes. "Bosie. And you must call me Roger."

"Very well, then. Roger."

Together they begin walking back, toward the prome-nade.

Sabotage

Middle of the night. While John snores in bed, Christopher, in his black T-shirt, switches on the light; fumbles in the bathroom with his backpack. So far only once, but if he plays his cards right he'll be able to get at least two more out of him before they part . . . After all, even though the guy's old, he's horny; has no trouble keeping it up, unlike some of those other sorry bastards. Opening the backpack (the fact that he is stoned—John gave him some good pot—makes the operation all the harder to perform), he extracts a fresh box of condoms, still sealed in plastic, which he tries (and fails) to tear open with his thumbnail. Finally he bites into the box; the plastic gives; little tooth marks puncture the cardboard. Tearing it open, he extracts the condoms, strung together like Christmas lights, divided by little lines of perforation. He rips until one comes loose. Dropping the others to the ground, he picks up the condom, holds it to the light. How innocent it looks, all rolled and thickened like his grandmother's aproned stomach, not the sort of thing you would expect to be capable (if you didn't already know) of smothering or saving a life! Yet there it is. The condom, his friend, his enemy . . . Anthony will die and Christopher will live. (*Not if I can help it.*) Anthony will die and Christopher will die. And now, from his backpack, he extracts a box of pins; takes one out; stabs the condom fleetly through its heart. Metal emerges out the other side. Withdrawing the pin, he holds the condom a second time to the light. Yes, there it is (though too tiny for any but a trained eye to recognize). That's the beauty of it. He will slip it into the pocket of his T-shirt now, wake John, and compel him to further acts of lust; John will not resist. Then without even being aware of it he'll do his duty to Christopher, the ironic duty of his profession, and never guess that the powdered sheath on which he is staking all the future bears beside its guarantee the harrowed and minute signature of the saboteur.

Bosie to Olive, from Loch Ness (1915): "Raymond is well and happy. He loves Scotland . . . He has given me the mumps and I have had it for the last 5 days."

Sources Consulted

Maureen Borland, *Wilde's Devoted Friend: A Life of Robert Ross,* Oxford, 1990.

Lord Alfred Douglas, *Oscar Wilde and Myself,* London, 1914. *The Complete Poems of Lord Alfred Douglas,* London, 1928. *The Autobiography of Lord Alfred Douglas,* London, 1929. *My Friendship with Oscar Wilde,* London, 1932.

Without Apology, 1938.

Oscar Wilde, A Summing-Up, 1938.

Richard Ellmann, *Oscar Wilde,* London, 1987.

Rupert Croft-Cooke, *Bosie: Lord Alfred Douglas, His Friends and Enemies,* New York, 1963.

Philip Hoare, *Wilde's Last Stand,* London, 1997.

H. Montgomery Hyde, *Lord Alfred Douglas,* London, 1984.

Douglas Murray, *Bosie: A Biography of Lord Alfred Douglas,* London, 2000.

The Marquess of Queensberry and Percy Colson, *Oscar Wilde and the Black Douglas,* London, 1949.

Timothy d'Arch Smith, *Love in Earnest,* London, 1970.

ROUTE 80

B Movie

JOSH AND I are leaving each other. These last few weeks we've spent together, at "our" house, trying to see what, if anything, we could salvage from five sometimes good years. At first things went badly; then we started gardening. Josh has always been an avid gardener, while I couldn't tell a lily from a rose. How roughly my vacant acknowledgments of his work rubbed up against all the effort he put in, all those springs and summers of labor and delicacy! And did my not caring about the garden mean that I didn't care about him? After he left, naturally, the flowers turned to weeds.

The therapists in our heads told us that this was something we could do together, a way beyond talking (which meant, for us, fighting), like the trip my mother and father took to watch the sea elephants mate. Kneeling in the dirt, holding the querulous little buds in their nursery six-packs, there was another language for us to speak with each other, as virgin as the leafy basil plants we patted into the soil. Our old, gnarled, tortuous relations were rude and hideous weeds we ripped out by the roots.

I made up dramas as I planted, horticultural B movies in which I was the hero defending the valiant rose from the villainous weed. Or I was the valiant rose, and Josh the villainous weed, and the hero was someone I was hoping to meet someday. Or I was the villainous weed.

Digging, I came upon little plastic stakes from past seasons, buried deep, unbiodegraded, bearing photographs and descriptions of annuals Josh had planted in more innocent, if not happier, times, and which had long since passed into compost.

There is the top of a wedding cake in our freezer. It is frosted white, and covered with white, orange, and peach-colored frosting roses. It was left there by the young newlyweds who sublet the house when Josh and I, unable to decide who should stay and who should go, both went. Jenny and Brian are saving this wedding cake to eat on their first anniversary, which is apparently a tradition for good luck. When I came back, they moved into an apartment where the freezer was too small; the cake stayed behind.

There is a road, too. I don't like roads, the way they run through everywhere on the way to somewhere else. The road is where we lose dogs and children, the way we take when we leave each other.

This road, in my mind at least, is Route 80. Josh and I used to say that our lives and destinies were strung out along Route 80, which runs from New York, where we lived for years, through New Jersey, where he grew up, through the town where he went to school and on to San Francisco, where I grew up. Even though our house is nowhere near Route 80 — and perhaps this was the first mistake — it is Route 80 I imagine when I imagine the wedding cake, like a pie in the face, being thrown.

I was driving down the highway, this long and painfully

lovely July day, when I saw the orange lilies bursting from their green sheaths. Until two weeks ago, when I finally asked and Josh told me, I wouldn't have noticed them, and I certainly wouldn't have known they were lilies. Now I know not only lily, but fuchsia, alyssum, nicotiana, dahlia, marigold. Basil needs sun, impatiens loves shade. At night I read tulip catalogues, color by color, easing gradually toward the blackest of them all, Queen of the Night.

All of this I have finally let Josh teach me—but (of course, of course) too late.

The lilies shut their petals, at dusk, over the road. And don't they become frosting flowers, freezer annuals, with their sly, false promise of good luck? I can feel them smearing under the wheels, sugar and butter, a white streak like guano where a bridegroom is racing away from his bride.

With my parents, going to watch the sea elephants became a tradition. Josh and I joined them once. The huge males shimmied along the rocks toward their waiting harems, and the hands of my parents, in spite of all that had passed between them, reached toward each other like flowers reaching toward the sun. My parents' hands were brown; there was dirt under their nails.

Who can claim that our love does not endure, less like flowers than like the little stakes with the photographs of flowers, stubborn beneath the soil?

Perennial.

Full Disclosure (*A Decade Later*)

Mark told me this story:

Years ago, he loved a cellist whom we shall call Gary. Gary loved Mark a lot, but his cello more. This was because Gary's mother had sold her own mother's wedding ring to buy him the cello. Not that she had to; she and her husband were affluent, and could easily have afforded it. No, she wanted the gift to connote sacrifice. She wanted Gary, every time he touched his bow to the strings, to know that for his sake his mother had given up something that she loved.

I understand this woman.

"Fostering dependency," the therapists call what she did, and according to them it is a real no-no. Yet it is exactly what I, too, have done. And at the heart of the matter is the fear of being alone, which makes Gary's mother the scariest person I know. So, a reasonable voice inquires, why shouldn't a child want to get away from someone so scary?

I remember another story, about my ex-boyfriend, whose name really was Gary. The ingredients in this story were: a wedding cake in the middle of the road (required by National Public Radio, which had asked a lot of writers to write stories on this theme); some elephant seals; and the little stakes with photographs of flowers on them that turn up each spring when, with shovel or spade, one reopens the soil. In that story, I called Gary Josh.

Here is the coincidence: the real Gary, the cellist, is named Josh.

So this is not a story at all, but a *tableau vivant:* a garden party, a cocktail party, at which the guests are me, Mark, Gary, Josh, the mother, and all of our fictive equivalents. Oh, and the cellist hired to provide the entertainment. Her face is shrouded. We shall call her Need. And the little air she plays, the little phrase, if we could translate music into words, would enter our ears as "Never leave me, never leave me, never leave me."

BLACK BOX

IN THE LATE 1980S, in New York, if a homosexual man died of anything other than AIDS, people generally reacted with skepticism. Especially if the officially listed cause of death was a disease with which AIDS might have been complicit—cancer, pneumonia, some mysterious infection of the heart—it would be taken for granted that the deceased's loved ones were trying to protect his reputation, or their own.

More troubling still were those occasions when the cause of death was one to which AIDS, even in the most extreme scenario, could not be linked. This was considered bad plotting—as if in a novel a character at whose head a specific piece of ammunition, for pages, had been steadily aimed, were to be killed not by his expected assassin, but by a stray bullet, fired from a direction in which no one would have thought of looking.

Such was the case with Ralph Davenport, the noted interior designer, who had the misfortune of being one of the passengers on that London-bound plane that blew up off the coast of Newfoundland one balmy summer evening in 1988.

No one felt the irony of his death more acutely than Bob Bookman, with whom he had lived for the past fifteen years. This was because the afternoon before Ralph had boarded the ill-fated Flight 20, he and Bob had had a fight over his refusal to get an HIV test. Generally speaking, in those years, men like Bob, who could count their sexual partners on two hands, were eager to get tested; Bob had been tested four times. Men like Ralph, on the other hand, whose sexual histories had been more volatile, avoided the test, arguing that it would do them no good whatsoever. As Ralph saw it, to learn that he was definitely HIV-positive (as opposed to merely *probably* HIV-positive) would be to let go the one slender reed of hope on which his sanity depended. Better to live in a cloud of unknowing, he believed, than submit to the dread of certainty. To which Bob replied, "But what if you're negative? I am."

"It wouldn't change my life."

"You could breathe a sigh of relief."

Ralph shook his head. "The waiting would kill me faster than any virus," he said, then zipped up his Travelpro, kissed Bob on the cheek, and went off to die. For days, weeks after that, fishing boats trawled the coastline over which his plane—a cursor blinking across the screen of night—had blossomed into a fireball, a parrot tulip, before raining down in pieces. They were looking for bodies. They were looking for the black box.

Bob was a literary man. With his name, what choice did he have? Small-boned and bespectacled, he looked good in the sort of interiors that were Ralph's specialty: cluttered, English-y spaces, enlivened by mad fabric mixes, chintz with checks, brocade with hot pink Indian sari silk. Not to mention, of course, the books. Books—in corners, on the staircase, piled next to sofas as an alternative to side tables (sometimes he even put lamps on them)—were Ralph's decorative calling card. He used to joke that he had chosen Bob only because Bob, with his argyle sweaters and bow ties, left just the right authenticating imprint on the pair of leather library chairs in their living room. No one accessorized these interiors more perfectly than Bob.

It was a look to which Ralph's clients, few of whom were readers, took avidly. Under his aegis, they bought old books from a dealer who sold them by the yard, and told their maids to leave the chair cushions attractively rumpled: the idea was to create the illusion of a space where people *thought*. Ralph, who read only design magazines, profited from his vision, which had gotten him twice onto the cover of *Architectural Digest*. Toward the end he was just starting to win the corporate commissions that are the bread and butter of any serious design firm; the night he died he was on his way to England to buy furniture for a downtown advertising agency that wanted to "soften its image." Then the plane went down. That was how Ralph's sister, Kitty, put it when she called. "A plane went down near Newfoundland," she said. "I'm only a little worried because I know Ralphie was planning a trip to London sometime soon. Make me feel better and tell me he didn't go today."

But of course he had. "I wouldn't be too concerned," Bob said. "Dozens of flights leave every day for London. What's the chance he was on that one?"

Still, to play it safe, he called Ralph's assistant, Brenda, to find out which airline he'd taken: Ralph traveled so much that Bob no longer bothered to keep track of the arrangements. She was crying when she picked up the phone. "The thing is, he usually flew American," she said, "because that's where he had his frequent flyer miles. But then the last time they wouldn't give him an upgrade to business class, and he got furious. He swore he'd never fly American again, and you know how Ralph is. Once he makes up his mind, he'll never change it."

Bob hung up immediately. He lowered himself into one of the library chairs and switched on the television, which was hidden inside an eighteenth-century Tuscan bread chest. News of the crash filled every channel. On CNN, a pale boy stood in front of his mother, who was stroking his hair. "We were having a clambake," the boy said, "and I was watching the stars, when suddenly there was this explosion. The plane broke up and fell into the water."

On another channel, a second witness—a woman with sunken cheeks, her glasses taped at the right temple—insisted that before the plane had blown up, something was heading for it. "I can't be sure," she told the reporter, "but I'd swear it was a missile."

"Do you think it's likely there were survivors?" the reporter asked.

"An explosion like that? Let's put it this way, if there were survivors, I'd feel more sorry for them than the ones that died."

At that moment, just as Bob expected, the telephone rang.

The next morning Kitty, who had a therapeutic personality, flew with her husband to Newfoundland. Because Ralph's parents were both dead, she qualified as next of kin. "You should come, Bob," she told him over the phone. "At first I was dreading it, but now that we're here, with all the other families . . . I don't know, it helps, somehow."

"I'd really rather not," said Bob, who could not, in any case, envision quite how he'd explain his relationship with Ralph to the airline. After all, it had no official designation. It did not matter that they had shared an apartment for fifteen years, or that Ralph had put up the money with which Bob opened his bookstore. That was business. He wasn't in any legal sense "kin."

"But it's healing!" Kitty said. "For instance, just this morning, when I woke up, I looked out at the water—our rooms all overlook the water, the counselors insisted on that—and it seemed so placid. Such a lovely, soothing scene."

"How long are you planning to stay?"

"Until they find Ralph. Or the black box."

"Ah, the black box," Bob repeated. For once that was pulled up from the bottom of the ocean, the television assured him, all speculation about the cause of the crash—bomb, missile, pilot error—could be put to rest. Much hung in the balance, including lawsuits. In that black box, Kitty told him, were stored the voices of the pilots in the moments just before the plane blew up. "Although it's not really black," she added. "It's orange."

"How long will it take to find it?"

"We hope only a few more days, depending on the weather. It's supposed to give off a signal. Please come," she concluded, her voice almost seductive in its entreaty. "We need you here."

But he didn't go. Instead he stayed at the bookstore. He liked the bookstore—which Ralph had also designed—far more than the apartment. Here, at least, Ralph's signature made sense, since books were the place's *raison d'être,* as opposed to merely a decorative device. During the day Bob sat at the cash register, ringing up purchases and giving advice to customers, much to the bewilderment of his employees, two girls from NYU, and to the chagrin of Ralph's friends, who kept dropping by to offer their condolences.

"Are you sure you want to be here?" asked Brenda.

"Why don't you come over for dinner?" suggested Gwyneth, Ralph's lawyer. "You look pale, like you need a home-cooked meal."

"I'd really rather not," Bob answered, as he had answered Kitty's pleas that he fly up to Newfoundland. In the end, he even took to sleeping in the bookstore, on a foam rubber pad dragged up from the basement. Soon the dismay of Ralph's friends ripened into a kind of scandalized horror, as if in choosing this particular method of grief Bob was throwing in their faces certain conventions on which their own ability to cope, even to be distracted from death, somehow depended.

Strange people—acquaintances of Ralph's he'd met only briefly, or never at all—started coming into the store. Four days after the crash a woman with gray hair and owlish glasses approached Bob and asked him if he was himself. When he affirmed that he was, she peered at him almost clinically, as if she were a zoologist and he the only surviving specimen of some rare genus: the disaster widow, a piece of human wreckage.

"Oh, I'm sorry, I imagined you looking quite different," the woman said, pulling a shapeless, nubbly sweater down over her hips. "I'm Veronica Feinbaum. I'm sure Ralph told you about me."

Ralph had. Of his regular clients, she was the one he had found the most trying. As Bob recalled from dinner talk, Veronica lived in a vast Park Avenue apartment, and was married to an entertainment lawyer whose wealth had bought her seats on the boards of several charitable organizations. Yet her lot in life did not satisfy her, and so she had recently gone back to school, to Columbia, where she was studying Classics.

"It's a pleasure to meet you," Bob said.

She clasped his hand in hers. "I'm so sorry," she said, then, lowering her voice, added: "Still, it must have come as a relief."

He frowned. Her face, arcaded by columns of ill-brushed hair, was fleshy with health. A curious mixture of solicitude and challenge enlivened her unctuous smile.

"A relief?" he repeated.

"Of course. Otherwise, think of all the suffering you both would have had to endure. Wasting, dementia. At least this way it was quick."

Bob let go of her hand. "Thank you for your concern," he said.

"Ralph would have told you, I'm not one to mince words. My husband always says to me, 'Ronnie, shut your yap, it'll get you into trouble.' But I say, why beat around the bush when everyone knows it's nonsense? Much better to be frank and open. Fellows like Ralph, they're basically under a death sentence, just because they lived where they did and when they did. I don't know if he mentioned it, but I sit on the board of the Gay Men's Health Crisis. It's taught me to hold with the Greek view of death—you know, that it's better for a man to be taken at his peak."

"No, he didn't."

"Well, I'm glad we've had this talk," she said, and pressed a card into Bob's palm. "I doubt there are many people you can be this open with, so please, if you need to vent, call me *any* time."

She left, floating out the door in a hazy effulgence of perfume. Bob looked at the card. GEORGE AXELROD, DDS, it read. And on the back: TUESDAY, 3/7, 2:30 PM.

That afternoon a small man with pale blond hair came into the bookstore. "So I've found you at last," he said when Lizzie, the taller and shyer of Bob's employees, led him to the front desk. "It's so important that we talk. Could we go somewhere?"

Bob was ruffled, bemused. He almost laughed. When the

man spoke, his voice was oddly honeyed, as if he were making an inept attempt at a come-on. He was in his mid-thirties, Bob guessed, with watery blue eyes and the kind of boyish good looks that have a way of cracking as a person gets older. Close up, Bob could see minute lines around his eyes. His hair was thinning. He wore a beige trench coat over his suit, which was black, a white shirt, a red-and-blue-striped tie. In his right hand he carried a briefcase.

"Excuse me?" Bob asked.

The man laughed. "Oh, I haven't said who I am yet. Sorry. My name is Ezra Hartley. I'm . . ."

He glanced furtively over his shoulder, as if to make sure that no one else in the shop—neither of Bob's employees, nor the lone customer browsing in the alternative medicine section—was listening. Then he leaned across the counter, so that Bob caught a whiff of his milky breath.

"I met Kitty in Newfoundland. She told me about you."

Bob's lips tightened. What was this? Some perverse effort of Kitty's to fix him up with the only other homo among the crash relations? He wouldn't have put it past her.

"So Kitty sent you?" he asked.

"Oh, no. I'm here completely on my own initiative. She just . . . told me about you. We got to be rather close, Kitty and I. Everyone did, in Newfoundland."

"Yes, I'm sorry I wasn't there. It just didn't quite—well, feel right."

"I understand. I tell you, it took a lot of courage for me to call up the airline, and say, 'Look, I have a right to—you know—be there.' But I did, and I'm glad I did."

"So I assume you . . . lost someone?"

"I'm connected, if that's the right word, to the children. The ones from upstate, who were going to Edinburgh. You know, the school trip."

Of course Bob knew. For days, both on television and in the newspapers, he'd been hearing about the children—about how they had raised the money for the trip themselves, by holding bake sales and car washes; about how, in this enterprise, they had been encouraged both by their parents, several of whom had also died in the crash, and their teacher, whom Peter Jennings had just named "Person of the Week"; about the eagerness with which they had anticipated the flight, which for many of them was both their first and last journey on an airplane.

Exactly what Ezra's "connection" to the children was, however, he appeared reluctant, at least in the bookstore, to divulge. "It's curious how hungry, almost lustful, people get for details," he whispered over the cash register. "Especially if there's some horrible irony, like the person had just missed another plane. Or if he was famous in some way. Your Ralph, for instance—forgive me for using his first name, but I feel as if I know him—he was probably the most famous person on board. Or that woman who won the lottery. Imagine." Ezra scratched his upper lip, on which there was a mustache so pale as to be almost invisible. "You win a hundred thousand dollars in the lottery, and then . . . But I'd really rather not keep on talking here. Couldn't we go somewhere?"

"Yes, of course. Debbie!"

His second employee, a languid girl with a nose ring and a rose tattoo on her left wrist, now separated herself from the stack of books she was shelving and drifted over to the register.

"Could you take over? I have to go out for a while."

"Sure, whatever," Debbie said, and replaced him on his little stool. He and Ezra stepped out onto the sidewalk. A wind had come up. Across the street a bulky man with a crewcut was walking into a bar that happened to be the oldest gay bar in the village. "We could go there, if you want," Bob said, pointing.

"Oh, I'd really rather not. I'd really rather go to your apartment."

"My apartment? Why?"

"Well, it's just . . . I mean, we're bound to end up there anyway, aren't we?" Ezra smiled.

"But why are we bound to end up there?"

"Because of what I have to show you." He indicated his briefcase. "It's not something I can show you in public."

Bob stalled. Behind Ezra's guileless lack of discretion, he was sure he could detect Kitty's interfering hand. It all seemed a bit demented to him, this propositioning, no doubt an offshoot of the enforced intimacy that had been the apparent leitmotif of Newfoundland. Or perhaps he was wrong to assume that Ezra was propositioning him; perhaps, on the contrary, he was reading into this brusque request an impulse that could not have been further from Ezra's intentions. For it went without saying that Ezra, as he stood there staring at Bob, appeared not only guileless, but childlike. Normally Bob was not, by his own admission, a libidinous man; in that department Ralph had always been the more high-octane of the two, which explained at least in part his habitual infidelities, to which he rarely owned up, but which Bob always learned about anyway, through Ralph's habit of leaving little clues everywhere: condom wrappers in the bathroom, scraps of paper with strangers' phone numbers on the kitchen counter. Men called late at night, then, learning that Ralph was out of town, hung up without leaving their names. And through it all, Bob had never gone looking for someone else, as Ralph regularly did. It had become a source of pride to him, his ability to resist the very impulses to which Ralph, time and again, proved so susceptible; only now, poised in this standoff with

Ezra, something about the very oddness of the situation, their shared and mysterious link to the plane crash, skewed his perspective, made him suspicious . . . and curious.

A moment of silence passed, during which Ezra looked up the block toward Seventh Avenue, across the street at the bar—anywhere but into Bob's eyes. Finally he coughed, stuffed his left hand into his coat pocket. "Well?" he asked.

"All right, we'll go to my apartment," Bob said. "Why not?" And he started off—walking fast, as was his habit.

"I appreciate this. Listen, shall we take a taxi? My treat."

"It's not far enough for a taxi."

The wind had picked up. Ezra buttoned the collar of his coat tight around his throat. "I should tell you, I've seen your apartment already," he shouted after Bob, with whom he was having trouble keeping up. "I'm not ashamed to admit that I'm an avid reader of design magazines. So I'd heard of Ralph Davenport long before the crash. He was very talented, wasn't he?"

"They say he had a way with books." They had arrived at Bob's stolid brownstone, up the stairs of which Ezra now trotted after him, to the second-floor landing. The apartment, when they stepped inside, was stuffy, overwarm. All the curtains were drawn. "I haven't been here for a few days," Bob said, pulling up a blind.

Dust flew. "Wow," said Ezra, gazing at an English Arts and Crafts card table that Ralph had bought in London the year before. "This is beautiful. May I?" He took off his coat, sat down on one of the library chairs. "You know, there was one woman on the plane—this isn't generally known, because the family doesn't want the publicity—and she was on her way to Switzerland, where her brother—I'm not making this up—had just been killed in a plane crash. A private plane." He settled his briefcase in his lap. "Pretty extraordinary, that. In

Newfoundland it became a kind of game, thinking up parallels. You know, a surgeon is performing open-heart surgery . . . when he has a heart attack. Or an ambulance is on the way back from a car accident . . . when a car rear-ends it."

"I get the drift. Oh, would you like anything to drink?"

"Just water, thanks."

Bob fetched a glass from the kitchen, then sat down across from Ezra, in the second library chair. Ezra was smiling at him. He had his legs spread in what might have been a lewd way.

"So," Bob said.

"So," Ezra said.

There was a moment of silence, almost of helplessness, during which Ezra's fingers worked the combination lock on the briefcase.

"You said you were connected to the children?" Bob prodded.

"Yes, well, to their teacher, actually. The heroic history teacher, who taught them all semester about Scotland, and was taking them to Edinburgh."

At last he opened the briefcase, producing a newspaper clipping, which he handed to Bob. A heavyset man with a gray beard—the sort of man who always wears a cap with a brim, and was wearing one—smiled out broadly from a landscape of snow and trees.

"Of course living as we did in rural New York State," Ezra went on, "we couldn't be as open as you and Ralph were. We couldn't, for instance, have lived together. You see, Larry was divorced. He might have lost visitation rights with his kids, if anyone found out." Ezra reclaimed the clipping. "I teach at the high school too, incidentally. Journalism. So that just made things more complicated."

He closed, but did not relock, the briefcase.

"Well, I'm sorry," Bob said after a moment. "I mean, about Larry."

"I appreciate that, although as I've said about a million times this week, there's really not much point to 'Sorry,' when we're all in the same boat."

"True."

"I mean, Larry and I were together seven years. I moved to an apartment near his place just so I could walk over there. We couldn't risk anyone seeing my car parked in his driveway at night. And then in the mornings, I'd sneak out early. We'd drive to school separately, always make sure to arrive at least ten minutes apart. When we took vacations, we lied about where we were going, we flew on separate planes and met at the other end. Seven years like that."

"It must have been difficult."

"It was. But let's skip all that, because I didn't just come here to get sympathy. What I came about—it's the footage. I need some help deciding what to do with the footage."

"Footage?"

Ezra nodded. As at the bookstore, he looked over his shoulder, perhaps to make sure that no unexpected stranger, no friend or domestic, was about to step into the room. Then he reopened the briefcase and took out a videotape. "To be honest, I haven't looked at it myself," he said, handing it to Bob. "I couldn't at first, and now . . . I don't know, I'd just rather not. Would you mind if I wait in another room while you watch it?"

"But what is it?"

"You'll see. Where's the bathroom?"

"On the left."

"I'll wait there." He got up. "Call me when you're finished. It shouldn't take more than ten minutes or so."

Patting Bob on the shoulder, Ezra walked to the bathroom

and closed himself in. The lock clicked. Through the crack at the bottom of the door, Bob saw a light switch on; he heard the fan starting to whir.

He glanced at what he held in his hands: an ordinary videotape, it seemed. Maxell. Sixty minutes. Although an adhesive tag had been affixed to its front, nothing was written on it. Did that mean that it contained what Bob, at that moment, suspected it might contain, that is to say, pornography, probably homemade, perhaps images of Ezra's friend, the dead history teacher? No, not likely. Really, he thought, he was sinking further and further into salaciousness—had been, ever since Ezra had walked into the store.

Finally he switched on the television, and loaded the tape into the VCR. Colors appeared—a Mondrian rainbow—and then a voice (Ezra's) said, "Testing, one-two-three, testing, one-two-three." A blur of motion filled the screen, before clarifying into a corridor. Whoever held the camera was walking in the midst of a crowd, everyone wearing red. "Here we are boarding the bus," the voice declaimed, "on our way to watch Mr. Dowd's history club embark on its historic voyage to bonny Scotland. This is Ezra Hartley reporting for PVTV: Porter Valley Regional High School Television."

Then grass. A parking lot. A school bus, teenagers posed in pairs and clusters, some drinking Cokes. Inside the bus, more children mugged before the camera. "Hey, I hear those guys don't wear anything under their kilts!"

"Now, kids, no more of that—"

A huge face filled the screen. "Tigers rule!"

"Approaching the airport, you can see the excitement building on these kids' faces. Let's see, who shall we interview first? Nadine Kazanjian, class of 1988 valedictorian, how are you doing today?"

A dark-eyed girl smiled. "Fine."

"Is this your first trip to Europe?"

"Yeah."

"And you're excited?"

"Yeah."

"What are you most excited about seeing?"

She looked pensive. "Well, I guess probably it would have to be the Tower of London, when we stop in London. Or Edinburgh Castle."

"And what are your future plans, after you get back from Scotland?"

"Well, in the fall, I'll be enrolling as a freshman at SUNY New Paltz."

"Tigers rule!"

"Shut up, please, Peter, I'm conducting an interview. Have you decided on your major yet?"

"I was thinking history."

"Is that thanks to Mr. Dowd?"

"Yeah, I guess."

"You like Mr. Dowd?"

"Uh-huh, he's a great teacher."

"Tigers rule!"

"Peter, I told you—"

A sudden break, then, almost a rupture. In the next scene the kids were at the airport, checking their bags. Ezra's camera panned back, and suddenly all the red made sense: the children were wearing identical sweatshirts, red sweatshirts, that said PORTER VALLEY REGIONAL HIGH SCHOOL CLASS TRIP, 1988. Underneath was a drawing of a tiger wearing a kilt.

On to the gate. "Everybody together, I want a group shot!" Ezra shouted, and the man with the cap (Mr. Dowd; Larry) gathered them in, along with three pairs of parents. Thirty people, more or less. One girl was very beautiful, red-haired, with intense green eyes. Behind her the boy who had shouted "Tigers rule!" once again shouted "Tigers rule!" He had pim-

ples on his cheeks. To the left, nearer Mr. Dowd, Nadine
Kazanjian (already, on the news, Bob had heard about Nadine
Kazanjian) put an arm around the shoulders of a short black
boy whom Bob also recognized, for there had been a feature
about him on CBS: he had suffered from a congenital heart
defect.

Bob did not close his eyes. He did not flinch. He was hor-
ror-stricken, yes—it went without saying—yet he could not
have turned away even if . . . even if at that moment Ralph
had come storming through the door, dripping wet, as he had
in one of Bob's dreams a few nights earlier. For these faces—
he felt as if he needed to study them, if for no other reason
than to see if there was anything besides innocence in them,
some knowledge, some foreshadowing of their fate. It occurred to him dimly that when he had wondered if Ezra were
peddling pornography, he hadn't been so far off the mark;
only this was pornography of a scarier and more insidious
kind; this was closer to a snuff film.

It was then that he saw Ralph. At first he wasn't sure—just
a figure passing in the background. Immediately he aimed the
remote control, rewound, moved forward again, this time in
slow motion. Behind the mob of children and parents a figure
moved, wearing a jacket Bob would have recognized anywhere, for it was Ralph's favorite jacket, a brown leather
jacket he'd bought years ago, when he was still a student, and
that was now patched on both elbows. With the hypnotic
grace of a dancer, Ralph crossed behind the students, glanced
briefly at them, then sat down. He carried two bottles of
water.

Two.

Someone was sitting next to him.

Again, Bob rewound. The figure to Ralph's left was blurry.
Bob couldn't even tell if it was male or female; only that
Ralph—very distinctly—took one of the water bottles and

handed it to . . . whom? This friend. This unsuspected companion.

Again, a break in the footage. The children were now
handing in their boarding passes, waving wild goodbyes as
they headed toward the gate. One by one they disappeared,
as into a pair of jaws. "Well, that about wraps it up," Ezra
said. "In two weeks time, we'll be back to record the great
homecoming. In the meantime, for PVTV, I'm Ezra Hartley.
Goodbye, kids, and good luck."

The footage broke off. Hissing confetti filled the screen.
Like a wakened dreamer, Bob started; stood; turned off the
VCR. In the bathroom the fan still whirred, though the light
had been switched off.

He knocked on the door. "Are you finished?" Ezra called
from inside.

"Yes, I'm finished."

The lock clicked open, and he stepped out. "Well?"

"Well . . . yes."

Bob returned to his chair. Ezra followed him. "So what did
you think?"

"To tell you the truth, I'm not exactly sure what I think."

"But did you find it disturbing?"

"What kind of question is that? Of course I did."

Ezra sat down. "I'm sorry, I didn't mean to put it that way
. . . I'm incredibly nervous just now, as you can imagine. My
heart's racing, I'm sweating like a pig—"

"Well, I suppose at the very least I ought to be grateful to
you . . . you know, for giving me a last glimpse of the loved one
and all."

"That's why I can't look at it myself. A last glimpse of the
loved one would be more than I could bear."

"But how can you not have looked at it? Someone must
have—Kitty, for instance—otherwise—"

"No, you're the only one."

Bob looked up. "But then how did you know about Ralph?"

"What about him?"

"His being on the tape."

"Ralph is on the tape?" Ezra's hands flew to his face. "Oh, I'm so sorry! If I'd . . . Ralph is on the tape? But you must think I'm monstrous! To spring something like that on you without any warning . . . Believe me, if I'd known, I'd never—"

"Hold on. Then why were you so keen for me to watch it?"

"I told you, because I need your advice about what to do with it. Where to sell it."

"Sell it!"

"That's the whole point of my coming to New York. I want to sell it to one of those scandal programs—you know, *Hard Copy*, or something. Hadn't you guessed?"

"But why?"

"For the money, of course! I thought I'd begin by asking fifty thousand. Do you think that's reasonable? Too much? Too little?"

"Wait a second, are you actually saying you think people will pay money for this?"

"Of course—but only if I act fast. I know how journalism works. People eat this stuff up. My hope is that if I can get a bidding war going, get them foaming at the mouth, the price will really climb. Only I don't have the right contacts, and if I did it myself, I might end up being sold short."

"But you'll hurt people. The parents of those kids—"

"Oh, I know people will be hurt. Only when you think about, when you consider the sort of indescribable hell they're already going through, honestly, what difference will ten minutes of footage make? It might even be a comfort, seeing their children one last time."

"You'll be cashing in on their suffering."

"Correction. My suffering, too. After all, who's front and center in that video? Larry. 'Person of the Week.' And anyway, everyone else is going to make money, a lot of money, off this thing. I mean, confidentially—it's not public yet—they're pretty sure now that the crash was due to an electrical failure—not a missile, not a bomb. There was an engine part the airline hadn't got around to replacing even though they were supposed to. And if that's the case, there are going to be lawsuits—big lawsuits—and big settlements. Everyone who's next of kin will be compensated, all the parents of all those kids, and Larry's kids, and Kitty. Has she talked to you about it, by the way? About money?"

"No."

"She'll probably give you some. Kitty's a decent sort. And yet when you think about it, why should Kitty be getting anything? I mean, is she *really* next of kin? Only legally. In every real sense, you are . . . just as I am."

Bob said nothing. Almost triumphantly, Ezra crossed his arms. "You see? Now the whole picture looks different. What's fifty thousand, after all, compared to what *they're* going to get? And of course I'll give you a percentage for your help. Twenty-five percent, I was thinking."

"But what on earth makes you think I can help you?"

"You can get me contacts. Living here in New York, you must know people in television."

"I don't know anyone in television."

"Well, then you must know someone who knows someone. Or someone who can represent me . . . us. Someone who can sell the tape for us."

The "us" stung. "I feel very strange about this. I'm not sure I want to get involved in something so . . . frankly, so questionable."

"But all you have to do is give me an introduction! I'll do

the rest. And anyway"—here Ezra touched Bob's arm, which made him flinch—"it's as much for your sake as mine. You're obviously a decent guy, Bob. Still, a bookstore can't rake in a fortune, and Ralph had a big career ahead of him, didn't he? If he hadn't been killed, you would have had things to look forward to, money to look forward to, which now you'll never see. And so if everyone else is going to be compensated, why should you get left out in the cold?" He smiled. "Yes, I can see it now. His being on the tape, Ralph's being on the tape . . . that's really the icing on the cake. For that I think we can jump to seventy-five K, don't you?"

Bob moved away from Ezra's touch. "Look, I can't think right now. You'll have to give me some time."

"But there isn't any time! Every minute we waste, we lose money."

"Just until tomorrow morning?" He checked his watch. "It's nearly five now. Nothing's going to happen between now and tomorrow."

"I wish I could be sure. Still, I suppose I don't really have much choice, do I, other than to pick a lawyer at random from the phone book." He stood up. "All right. Tomorrow. Early, though."

"I'll call you by eight."

With a gesture of impatience, Ezra put on his coat, re-locked his briefcase. Bob followed him to the door.

"Ezra," he said, when they got there, "you wouldn't by any chance be willing to leave the videotape with me, would you? Just for tonight. I give you my word, I won't show it to any-one."

Ezra grinned. "I never doubted for a minute that I could trust you," he said, then opened the briefcase, took the tape out, and handed it to Bob.

"Thank you."

"Besides, this isn't the only copy."

"Somehow I suspected that."

"Like I said, I know how journalism works. Well, good night. Think carefully about what I've told you. Oh, and if you need to reach me—even if you just want to talk—I'm at the Sheraton on Broadway. Room 2223."

"Okay."

"Call any time. Even the middle of the night. Or just come over . . ."

Again, he smiled—this time a bit tartishly, Bob thought. They shook hands, and Ezra left.

Almost as soon as Ezra was out the door, Bob locked it. He went into the bathroom. An unfamiliar smell of lemons hung in the air—Ezra's cologne, perhaps, or his shampoo. Bob switched the fan back on, shut the door behind him. Then he carried the tape over to the bread chest and loaded it, once again, into the VCR.

He fast-forwarded through the first scenes—the bus, the interview with the doomed valedictorian, the checking of the bags—and let the button go only once the young travelers were at the gate, gathering for their farewell. Nothing had changed in fifteen minutes. "Tigers rule!" Peter with the pimples shouted, as Ralph, still in his leather jacket, glided past with his two water bottles. How his hair was thinning! He had a birthday coming up, his thirty-ninth. Rather dispassionately, he regarded the children—was he worrying that they might make noise during the flight?—then sat down, as before, next to his shadowy companion, to whom he passed a bottle. Here Bob pressed the pause button; stepped closer to the television, so that the tip of his nose brushed the screen. Yet he was no more able to identify Ralph's blurry friend now than he had been twenty minutes earlier.

He stopped the tape. A dim idea seized him, and he stumbled to the bedroom, to Ralph's closet, which he hadn't opened since the crash. Was it possible the leather jacket might still be there? . . . but it was gone. Where it had hung, only an empty hanger dangled. Other clothes pressed in on the vacancy, like flesh crowding to close a wound: pants and belts, a hank of ties, a new wool blazer Ralph had bought the winter before but not yet worn. And how faint—yet how distinct—his smell was! It lingered in his shoes, rose up from the hamper. Still, nothing about the closet provoked the slightest nostalgia in Bob. He didn't want to bury his face in the shirts. He wanted to haul them away, have the place aired and fumigated. As swiftly as he had opened it, he shut the closet door.

The next step was to search Ralph's desk, an early-twentieth-century rolltop, positioned at the far end of the bedroom. In the past, it had never occurred to him to rifle through the trove of documents Ralph kept there, if for no other reason than because he had always felt so secure in their companionable coupledom that even when he knew Ralph was having sex with other men, the matter hadn't seemed important enough to warrant prowling; the stability of their bond, not to mention the zeal with which Ralph loved him, were givens, and if over the years sex had ceased to be a crucial part of their relationship—well, what of it? The truth was, Bob didn't care all that much about sex. To him there was nothing wrong with a man going elsewhere to seek out those gratifications with which his home—a place of safety and retreat—had never been meant to provide him in the first place. So why was it that today, in the wake of a death that rendered jealousy moot, nonetheless jealousy, for the first time in years, was rearing in him? Was it Ezra's presence that had induced this unlikely response? Or was jealousy merely one of the many cloaks in which grief costumed itself?

With a weirdly furtive anxiety, as if he feared Ralph might

come striding through the door at any moment and catch him in the act, he opened all the drawers of the desk and emptied their contents onto the floor. Key rings, bookmarks, computer disks, an extra knob from the kitchen cabinets, fabric swatches, pages torn from design magazines, sketches of sofas and coffee tables and naked boys, earplugs, snapshots from a Halloween party, some old Corgi cars, a monogrammed leather passport holder that had been a Christmas gift from Kitty, extra Filofax pages, packets of tissue and gum, scissors, paper clips, a stapler, pens and pencils and pads stolen from various hotels: all this detritus, this flotsam of a life being lived at full throttle, fell in heaps on the Tabriz carpet. It made Bob think of the things Ralph had taken with him, and that had gone down with the plane: his datebook, his briefcase, the toothbrush now so conspicuously absent from the bathroom sink. A few days earlier, Kitty said, a dog's collar had washed up on the beach near her hotel. Nothing, however, of Ralph's; nor Ralph himself.

For a few moments, Bob sifted through this heap of valueless objects. Then, as nothing in it illuminated the identity of Ralph's companion, he moved on to the files. "Letters and Postcards"—from clients, from Kitty, from Brenda on her honeymoon—proved unrevealing, as did "Apartment," "Taxes," and "Insurance." The contents of the next file, "Credit Card Bills," he scanned with greater avidity, in the hope that there, at least, he might happen upon some clue, some shred of evidence pointing to an affair. Yet aside from an order for flowers, which Ralph would have normally charged through his office, nothing in the file shed light upon or even verified the stranger's existence. No extra plane tickets had been purchased in Ralph's name. Nor had he used the card to pay for any of the typical expenses of an affair: motel rooms, sex toys. Did this mean that he was being careful, taking the sort of precautions that in the past he hadn't deemed necessary? And if so, why? Because for once he had gotten caught up in something serious enough to merit deception? Yet if this was the case, nothing in his behavior, in the weeks before he'd boarded the plane, had given him away.

Kicking aside the papers, Bob lay down on the bed. What he was feeling was a maddened curiosity, a rage directed not at Ralph himself but at whatever forces were conspiring to make available only this clue, this fleeting image of a water bottle being passed into a stranger's hand. Nothing at all would have been better, he decided, or short of that, something he could work with, from which he could at least derive a lead or two. Perhaps if he scanned the lists of the dead, called the airline and demanded to know next to whom Ralph was sitting, then he might find something out . . . only wouldn't making such calls be to presuppose a prior "arrangement" of which he had no evidence? What if, on the other hand, the friend was someone Ralph had picked up in the men's room? Or better yet, just a fellow passenger he'd started chatting with, and for whom he'd offered to fetch some water? An old lady, even. Someone who couldn't walk very well.

He closed his eyes. The mistrust in which he had been wallowing since Ezra's visit horrified him. It did not fit the profile of a man who wore argyle sweaters, and owned a bookstore, and prided himself on the civility of his domestic arrangements. For his life with Ralph had always been the very model of civility. There was no surprise here: a craving for the refinements in which their childhoods—Bob's in a Dallas suburb, Ralph's on a series of military bases in California, Korea, and Germany—had been so singularly lacking was what had attracted them to each other in the first place. Thus their courtship had taken place in antiques shops. The first purchase they had made together was a set of Sèvres porcelain dessert plates. Even when they were young and poor, and lived in an East Village walk-up, they always had good furniture, Persian rugs, old hotel silver. For these things, above all others, mattered to Ralph, and if, on occasion, an urge came upon him to go out searching for sex of the seamier variety— an urge utterly out of keeping with his otherwise scrupulous habits—well, what did it matter? Squabbling was tawdry, like paper napkins. Much better to show a bit of tolerance, to laugh the matter off, to remain, at all costs, *civilized*.

Only once before had jealousy gotten the better of Bob. This was in the early eighties, when for a few months Ralph had entered into a sort of carnal tailspin. Every night he'd gone out at around eleven (they were still living in the East Village then), only to return at dawn, reeking of cigarette fumes and sweat and poppers. Then he would shower, while Bob lay quiet in their bed with its upholstered headboard, its four-hundred-thread-count sheets, its canopy of English glazed chintz (Roses and Pansies), pretending to be asleep but really listening for the water to shut off. Eventually Ralph, moist in his cotton pajamas, would climb in next to him, lie still for a few moments, then, with great caution, wrap his arms around Bob's chest and nuzzle his neck.

One morning during this period, as they were fixing breakfast in their tiny kitchen, Ralph started washing an orange. Where cleanliness was concerned, he could be excessively fastidious—when he ate french fries, he would leave the tips on the plate, like cigarette butts, rather than put anything his fingers had touched into his mouth—and now, watching him wash his orange, which he was going to peel anyway, Bob giggled. "What is it?" Ralph asked.

"It's just . . . you'll lick some stranger's asshole through a hole in the wall, but you won't eat an orange without washing it."

Ralph put the orange down. Almost angrily he glared at Bob; he swallowed, as if swallowing back an impulse to lash out. And then he, too, laughed. He laughed and laughed.

Bob opened his eyes again, sat up. Had he fallen asleep? Behind the pillows in their beige cases, the headboard, made from a pair of Venetian gilt and painted gesso doors, creaked in reaction to his weight. Although he was alone, he was lying on the left side of the bed; he had always slept on the left, just as Ralph had always slept on the right. Each had his own table, his own drawer, Bob's containing disorder (earplugs and magazine clippings and buttons and handkerchiefs and cufflinks), Ralph's only a first-aid kit, a flashlight, matches, and a few candles. On top of each table sat a red tole lamp hand-stenciled with fritillaries. To the left was the window draped in the beige linen *toile de Jouy* it had taken Ralph so many months to settle upon, and next to the window was the dresser, and across from the dresser was the desk, its drawers pulled open, its contents spread all over the carpet, as if a thief had been searching fruitlessly for jewels . . . Getting up, Bob quickly put everything back.

Streetlamps came on; instinctively he shut the curtains against them. In the morning, he knew, he would have to answer Ezra's scandalous proposition. And what would he say? From a financial perspective, it was true, Ralph's death had left him in a precarious position. The import of his will was no secret; it was identical to Bob's, both of them stating that if one should predecease the other, the survivor would inherit the apartment, whatever money was in the dead partner's bank account, and the cash value of his business. Yet so far— just as Ezra had guessed—Ralph's business hadn't earned much in the way of profit; the big money was supposed to come next year, when he completed the first of his corporate commissions. Nor was the bookstore alone likely to generate

the kind of income necessary to keep up the mortgage payments on a large Manhattan co-op, purchased at the height
of an economic boom. Their whole life, when you thought
about it, had been provisional, based on the assumption that
Ralph wasn't going to die—and this was odd, for in recent
years his health had become for both of them a chronic, if
largely private, worry. Ralph, for instance, was always feeling
his glands. Whenever he got a cold, an expression of grim sto-
icism claimed his face, only to give way, once he had recov-
ered, to a kind of euphoria, as if getting over the cold meant
that he was utterly safe: exactly the sort of reassurance the
HIV test was supposed to provide.

No, Bob reflected, the problem with Veronica Feinbaum's
ill-mannered remarks wasn't that they had been so off the
mark; the problem was that in her contempt for the niceties,
her devotion to the unvarnished truth, she had given voice to
the very cynicism that the rest of their friends, out of respect
for the dead, had left unspoken. Not an if, but a when: all of
them—Bob too—took it for granted that one day soon Ralph
would get sick. For the orange had its price. And though
in recent years Ralph had made it his habit, when engaging
in what he called his "extracurricular activities," always to
practice the safe sex that Veronica's beloved GMHC pro-
pounded, even so, the residue of those early debauches could
not so easily be leached from the blood. Every morning when
they woke up, Bob wondered, *Will this be the day?* He'd never
admitted it before, but he had. He had kept his eyes averted
from the future, grateful only for what didn't happen, for
every blessed deferral.

Not far away church bells rang: six o'clock. This was the
hour when flights to Europe made their departures, when
taxis mobbed the terminals at JFK, and travelers in whom the
mere prospect of the abbreviated transatlantic night had al-

ready incited a state of proleptic weariness and disorientation dragged their luggage through the snaky line to the check-in. Then would come the journey itself—he knew it well—the mask and the earplugs, labored sleep, a too early dawn. Under the closed eyelid of the window, light would creep, heralding jet lag and the stumbling weirdness of arrival. Many times Bob and Ralph had made that trip together. He recalled with a certain tenderness early mornings in Paris, dropping off their bags at the hotel and then, because the room wasn't ready, wandering red-eyed and unwashed through the half-asleep city, stopping at a bar for coffee and a warm croissant and gazing at the brisk, freshly shaven Frenchmen as if they were members of another species . . . And had Ralph, in the same way, been looking forward to his first morning in London? Was he envisioning, just before the plane blew up, the monuments and museums through which he would lead his wide-eyed companion, or the restaurants he would take him to? The sushi bar at Harrod's? Or that Thai place on Frith Street he liked so much?

It didn't matter. His hotel room—long reserved—had gone unclaimed. Oh, no doubt the flight had begun as flights always do, with a stewardess standing at the front of the cabin and explaining the use of the life jacket and the oxygen masks. More inured to flying than his companion, Ralph would have ignored her implorations to consult the little plastic card mapping the emergency exits. But the companion—for some reason Bob was certain of this—would have studied it assiduously. "In the event of a water landing," he would have heard her intone, all the while attending to the cartoonish plane, conveniently submerged just to the level of its doors; the passengers, resembling figures from a first-grade primer, making their orderly progress onto the slides; the slides themselves detaching, floating tranquilly out onto tranquil water, as if not only people, but fate could be trusted to behave, to follow the playground rules . . . yet when you thought about it, who had ever heard of a "water landing"? When in the entire history of commercial aviation had one taken place? In the world, planes blew up. People died. Their bodies were incinerated, or eaten by sharks. And though, for the first few days after the crash, newscasters would persist in avowing that divers were still "hopeful of locating survivors," well, everyone knew that this was just a gesture, made in deference to some outmoded protocol. You knew better than to believe that someone might actually be out there, clinging to a piece of wreckage, held aloft by a life jacket when in truth there hadn't been time even to put on a life jacket.

The apartment was now so dark that Bob could hardly see the furniture. Switching on the lights, he reached for his jacket, then hurried out onto the street and hailed a taxi. Past warehouses and department stores he rode, white brick apartment blocks and condemned tenements, until the taxi dropped him off amid the headachy neon of Broadway at night. The lobby of the Sheraton, when he stepped into it, was filled with airline pilots and cocktail music, overtired children, a chaos of perfumes and accents through which he pushed his way to the elevator. Up to the twenty-second floor he rode, then walked down a long corridor to a door marked 2223, on which he knocked.

Within seconds, Ezra answered. He had taken off his jacket and tie. His cheeks glowed, as if he had just been washing his face.

Seeing Bob, he smiled without surprise. "I'm glad you came," he said.

"I wanted to return the tape," Bob said, "only I seem to have forgotten it . . ."

"Never mind about the tape," Ezra said, and, leading him through the door, closed it behind them.

▪

After that Bob gave in to strangeness. He accepted that the terms of his life had been altered radically, perhaps irrevocably, that from now on he was going to be a citizen not of the familiar world, but of an off-kilter landscape rather resembling the villains' hideouts in the old *Batman* series, shot with the camera atilt so that children would believe the Catwoman and the Joker and the Riddler actually lived in lopsided buildings, urban Towers of Pisa, where the floors slanted up or down or swayed like a seesaw. At least the past, for all its coarseness and sorrow, had been part of a fluid traffic, enviably unremarkable and thus passed over by television's greedy eye. Here, on the other hand, dog collars washed up on Newfoundland beaches. He lived not in his own apartment, but with Ezra, on the twenty-second floor of the Sheraton. They had their dinner naked, room service club sandwiches the crumbs of which got between the sheets, all the while observing with a certain detached wonderment a battle to purchase the videotape every bit as fevered as Ezra had predicted, with Bruce Feinbaum, Veronica's husband, acting as referee.

Only forty-eight hours had passed since they had taken the tape to Veronica. While Ezra hid, once again, in the bathroom, Bob watched it through with her, the two of them perched on leather library chairs exactly like the ones in his own living room, although here the television was hidden in a Shaker cupboard instead of a Tuscan bread chest. This go-round, the children's death march did not appall him as it had before; even Ralph's brief apparition did not appall him. Instead he watched, fascinated, as an apprehension of the tape's import gradually stole over Veronica's face, opening her mouth and pulling her eyebrows taut and painting her skin first scarlet and then a dyspeptic gray. If she noticed Ralph at all, she chose not to mention it. Instead, as the tape broke off, she seemed to be struggling to compose a response in keeping with her self-appointed role as a woman immune to sentimentality.

Later, at her husband's office, she told Bob and Ezra about a legend she had recently encountered in her Greek class, in the hope that sharing it would allay any feelings of guilt they might be suffering. "Cleobis and Biton," she began, "were the sons of Hera's priestess at Argos. And one day when she was supposed to perform the rites of the goddess, the oxen that usually took her to the temple didn't show, so her sons harnessed themselves to the chariot and dragged her there themselves. Five miles. Into the mountains. When they got to the temple, the priestess was so grateful to the boys that she prayed to Hera to grant them the best gift possible. And what did Hera do? Knocked them off. Killed them, in the prime of life. That's the Greek view of death."

"Funny," her husband said. "When you got to the end, I thought you were going to say that Hera killed the mother so the boys wouldn't have to drag her all the way back. Which is, I guess, the Jewish view of death." And he picked up the phone.

Afterward Bob and Ezra went back to the Sheraton, where they spent most of the day having sex. Intermittently they would take breaks to eat, or watch television, or answer Bruce's phone calls. Progress reports came about once an hour. "We've got an offer of sixty K," Bob said at five, "but I can tell from her voice, they're prepared to go higher."

By six they had gone higher. Ezra ordered champagne with the club sandwiches. Because the windows did not open, their room had begun to stink. When the bellhop brought the food, his nose twitched. Ezra only laughed. Gratification made him giddy. He could not seem to get fucked enough. As for Bob, never in his life had he felt so horny; it was as if Ezra had tapped into some cache of libido he hadn't ever sus-

pected himself of harboring. He was a tiny man, Ezra. He had
tiny feet, a tiny penis. He was in no way Bob's type. Still,
when Bob fucked him, he felt as if he were breaking through
the shell of the known universe. Somewhere near the ceiling
there floated an undiluted pleasure, toward which the vessel
of his body flew unpiloted.

When they weren't having sex, they talked about the future. It went without saying that Ezra would never return
to Porter Valley. Instead, he said, his plan was to settle in
Manhattan, using the money from the sale of the tape to buy
himself an apartment. Once he was fixed up, he would look
for a job teaching at a private school. Then he would live quietly, his phone number unlisted, in case anyone from Porter
Valley should ever decide to hunt him down and shoot him.

"And in the meantime?" Bob asked.

"In the meantime I'll stay at your place."

His place! Not a question, a declaration. "Come to think
of it, what are we doing here?" Ezra went on. "This room
costs a fortune. And your apartment would be so much more
comfortable."

"I can't go back there yet," Bob replied, for he was thinking of the bed: he had never slept in it with anyone except
Ralph.

"Why not?"

"I'm having the place exterminated."

"Exterminated!"

"I mean, I'm having the exterminators in."

Ezra frowned. They stayed on at the Sheraton. In the
mornings, when the maid came to clean the crumbs out of
the bed and spray room freshener, they put on their jack-
ets and took a walk through the theater district. Generally
speaking, the half hour the maid needed to clean the room
was the only time they got out. "I'd love to see *Cats*," Ezra

said, gazing up at a marquee. "Let's go see *Cats*. I've never been to a Broadway musical."

"We'll get tickets this afternoon," Bob promised. And yet, by the time the afternoon rolled around, they were already in bed, the club sandwiches had been ordered, the television was on.

Now the phone rang every half an hour. "We're up to a hundred twenty-five K," Bruce told them at four. Then, at four-thirty: "*Hard Copy*'s come in ten thousand higher." After hanging up, Bob aimed the remote control at the screen, unmuting whatever was on. As a rule they watched only the programs that were at war to win the rights to the tape. If two were on at the same time, they'd switch back and forth between channels. All these programs had thrusting names, and alternated the gruesome (kidnap victims buried alive) with the heartwarming (a two-year-old dialing 911 to save his grandmother). On one, a dachshund kept an alligator at bay just long enough for its master, whose arm had been bitten off, to crawl out onto the street and scream for help. In this instance, the report was accompanied by a "dramatic re-enactment" of everything that had occurred, including the arm's reattachment.

At Bruce's office, negotiations continued well into the night. Already the price had climbed far beyond what Ezra had hoped for. "This thing is smoldering," Bruce said over the phone. "It's hotter than I ever could have guessed." By morning, only two contenders remained. By three that afternoon a show called *The Real Story* had finally won, with a bid of $150,000. This meant that once Bruce had deducted his percentage, Bob would clear $30,000 and Ezra $90,000.

To celebrate, they went out to dinner at a sushi bar on Park Avenue that had just gotten three stars from the *New York Times*. It was posh and quiet. The chefs were tall for Japanese, with faces and hands as gleaming as the slabs of salmon and halibut they sliced so expertly. One of them, Bob noticed after a few minutes, was missing his right thumb.

"If they're really planning to air the tape tomorrow, we'll have to get out of the hotel in the morning," Ezra said. "The last thing I want right now is to be chased down by reporters."

Bob glanced up at him. "Do you honestly think they'd find you?"

"They might."

"But there are hundreds of hotels in New York. Anyway, you told me you registered under an assumed name."

"Still, I'd rather not risk it. At your place I'll feel safer."

"All right," Bob said, gulping sake, "but you'll have to sleep on the sofa. Just until I get a new mattress."

"What's wrong with the old one? Don't tell me bedbugs, because you said you just had the exterminators in."

"No, not that . . . It's just that it was Ralph's mattress. Ralph's and mine."

Ezra's mouth narrowed; he was quiet. "Really, Bob," he said after a moment, "considering all we've been through, don't you think that attitude's a little—well—sentimental?"

"But you must understand. No one else besides Ralph and me has ever been in that bed."

"Are you sure?"

"Of course."

"But you must have gone out of town sometimes by yourself. How can you know what Ralph got up to while you were away?"

"He might have gotten up to all sorts of things. Just not in the bed."

Ezra raised his eyebrows.

"What? You're doubting me?"

"I just think that maybe you're being a tad bit naive."

"It doesn't matter," Bob said finally. "What Ralph did doesn't matter. The point is, *I* never slept with anyone else in that bed."

"Is that really what this is about? Or is the truth that you just don't want to share that bed with—you know—some scoundrel, the kind of person who'd sell a tape of innocent children to a scandal show?"

"I never said anything to suggest that."

"Still, I can read between the lines. In the anonymity of a hotel room, that's one thing . . . but to have the horrible Ezra in your precious marriage bed, oh no!"

"The tape has nothing to do with it."

The bill arrived. Ezra paid—he insisted—after which they walked back to the hotel. Most of the way they didn't speak; Ezra had his fists buried in the pockets of his trenchcoat, kept his head bent, seemed at once ruminative and cross. Every few minutes Bob would try to introduce a neutral topic of conversation, only to have it shooed away like an insect. Finally he gave up. They arrived at the hotel, went up to the room, where Ezra threw off his coat, sat down at the little desk across from the bed, and frowned at the window. It took Bob a few seconds to realize that he was frowning at his own reflection.

Finally he turned to Bob, and said, "I haven't been straight with you. There are things I haven't told you—and other things I have told you that, well . . . aren't true."

"Oh?"

"Yes." He gazed at his own hands. Then he said, "Larry Dowd was never my lover. He wasn't even queer."

"What do you mean, wasn't queer?"

"We were colleagues, that's all—who sometimes ate lunch together. Oh, I admit, I had the hots for him, a little. But I never said anything. I wouldn't have dared. So far as I know, he had no idea that *I* was queer."

"You mean you made up the whole story?"

Ezra nodded.

"But what about the tape?"

"That was for the kids. You're years out of high school, you think that journalism class means a newspaper. Remember, we're living in the age of video! The kids wanted video, so I just . . . invented this idea of PVTV. And then the plane went down, and suddenly it seemed like I was being offered an opportunity."

"To make money?"

"Not only that! Also to commemorate—what might have been, what would have been, if conditions had been different, if Larry had been different . . . And then when I got to Newfoundland, and heard about Ralph, and met Kitty—well, things just fell into place. It seemed predestined that I should come to New York. That I should find you. That we should—"

"But you said it was a question of justice. *You* don't deserve justice."

"I deserve this chance. How else was I ever going to get to New York? Stuck out in Hicksville, a closet case teaching high school journalism."

"So you decided to pay for your freedom with the corpses of dead children."

"No! It was for you, too . . . for us."

Bob turned away. "If I'd known what you were up to, I'd never have helped you."

"That was why it was imperative you not know what I was up to."

"Then why are you telling me now?"

"Because you wouldn't let me sleep in Ralph's bed. Because

you made me feel like shit, like my very presence was defiling. And then I thought about it, and you know what I decided? You're right."

Bob moved toward the door. "I'm sorry," he said, "I have to digest all of this. I have to figure out what I feel."

"Of course." Suddenly Ezra turned. "Only please remember, no matter how much you hate me, you'll still get the money. Thirty thousand dollars. For that, at the very least, you ought to be—"

Bob ran. At the elevator, he pressed the call button twice, focused his eyes on striped wallpaper, listened for the ringing of a bell.

"Grateful," Ezra murmured in the distance.

The elevator doors opened, admitting Bob—irony of ironies—into a throng of uniformed stewardesses.

The day after the tape aired, Kitty called to deplore Ezra's "disloyalty." Veronica called to reassure Bob that he had no reason to feel guilty. Only Ezra did not call. Every day, at the bookstore, Bob watched for him, at first with fear, then with worry. At home he waited for a message on his answering machine. None came. Perhaps Ezra had gone back to Porter Valley. Perhaps, in a fit of guilt, he had done himself in. As for whatever little storm the screening of his tape had drummed up, it took place too far outside the arena of Bob's daily life for him ever to hear about it. He was Bob Bookman, owner of Bookman's Books. What happened on programs like *The Real Story* had nothing to do with him.

One afternoon a few weeks after the airing, Kitty called to say that an umbrella monogrammed with Ralph's initials had washed up on a Maine beach. "They're bringing it to me for identification," she added, "and I wondered . . . well, if you wanted to come. If you wanted to be here when it arrived."

Bob wasn't sure how to answer. Was he sorry? Relieved? Sorry—and relieved—that it hadn't been Ralph's body that had washed up?

"I think I can trust you to handle this," he said after a moment.

"Well, I just wanted to be up front about everything," Kitty asserted, in a voice suggesting that up until now she hadn't been.

"By the way, any word on the black box?"

"Not yet. My suspicion is that if they were going to find it, they'd have found it."

"But they're still looking."

"They're still looking."

They hung up. Bob sat down in one of the library chairs. Once more, that odd feeling of dislocation had claimed him, the world suddenly tilting so acutely he feared Ralph's piles of books might come tumbling to the floor. Then the sensation passed. Opening the Tuscan bread chest, he took out Ezra's videotape—the copy he had never given back—and loaded it into the VCR. He hadn't watched it in weeks, not since the afternoon he and Ezra had taken it to Veronica. Now, however, he was on that bus again, the dressing habits of Scotsmen were being debated, Nadine Kazanjian was expressing her wish to see the Tower of London. "Tigers rule!" Peter with the pimples cried, as the members of Mr. Dowd's history club gathered for their farewell. To Bob they looked wearier than on previous viewings, as if the effort of repeating the scene so many times had exhausted them. Nadine put her arm around the black boy who had a heart condition, the beautiful girl with the green eyes brushed back her hair . . . and then Mr. Dowd (Larry) smiled, and Peter yelled "Tigers rule!" again, and a bearish man wearing an Atlanta Braves T-shirt stumbled past, carrying two bottles of water. One of them he handed to a woman who was dividing up the sections of *USA Today.* She wore her long hair piled on top of her head, like Marjorie Main in the old Ma and Pa Kettle movies. Next to her was a dachshund, asleep in its carrier.

Bob stopped the tape. He rewound it. He watched it again. Not that he expected anything to have changed: the change had already happened. Ralph was gone—if he had ever been there in the first place, ever been more than a hope, or a hallucination. Need alone had kept him there those few extra days, kept him as vivid as his companion was murky; but that was all. A sleight of hand, a trick of the imagination, or nature, the way a chicken's body will flail even after its head has been cut off. Motion without life.

"Oh, those poor children," Bob said, putting his head on his knees. And in a softer voice: "Oh, my poor Ralph." Let Veronica rejoice in the death of the young! He would never join her, just as he would never take comfort in the knowledge that if Ralph had survived, it might have been only to suffer a worse fate later on. For though the loss of those we love might cure our fear of losing them, loss, as he now knew, was worse than fear. No matter what Ezra claimed, there would be no "compensation." Yes, he would come and go from the bookstore, he would once again be Bob, and lead Bob's life, but with this difference: from now on that life would contain an element of punishment.

He took the tape out of the VCR; held it for a moment; then, with his fingers and wrists, broke it in half. How delicately the celluloid unspooled, gray-black ribbon stretching to the floor! Without its precious contents it was nothing, just another black box lost in seaweed-stained waters, in depths no human voice could hope to penetrate.

SPEONK

I'VE NEVER BEEN to Speonk. To me it is just a stop on the train, a dot on a map. For all I know, it might be "Llanview," or "Pine Valley," or "Genoa City"—one of those imaginary towns that come to life an hour a day on soap operas. Probably, however, Speonk isn't like any of those places. Probably it is a town full of satellite dishes.

This begins in traffic, on a summer Sunday evening on Long Island. After a comatose weekend spent in crowded houses on the wrong side of the Montauk Highway, three people are making their sleepy way back to New York. I am in the car, along with Naomi and her friend Jonathan, an actor who for the past two years has played Evan Malloy (dubbed "Evil Evan") on *The Light of Day*. Recently Jonathan decided he'd had enough of rape, blackmail, drug peddling, larceny, and the like, and gave the producers of the show six weeks' notice: just enough time for Evan to commit a murder, frame his good-as-gold brother, Julian, and at the eleventh hour get found out. Evan went to prison, and Jonathan, on the heels of his final taping, went to Penn Station, where he caught a train to Bridgehampton, relieved that their paths had finally diverged. He spent the weekend sleeping on the beach, and now, two days later, is sitting languid in the back seat of Naomi's car, still looking a bit like the tough he's become famous for playing, in a baseball cap and dirty white T-shirt.

"Even with this traffic, I think we should be back in the city by ten," Naomi says.

He laughs. "That'll still be less time than it took me to get out here."

"You came by train, didn't you?" I ask.

"Jonathan had a little trouble getting to Bridgehampton," Naomi says. "It took him—how long was it, Jonathan? Six, seven hours?"

"Seven and a half."

"What happened?"

He stretches his arms over his head, so that when I look over my shoulder, I catch a glimpse of the hair in his armpits. "Well, you know how in Jamaica you have to change trains," he says. "I got on the train across the platform, and asked the conductor if it was going to Bridgehampton, and he said it was. So then I settled back and fell asleep, and when I woke up, a different conductor was shaking my shoulder, and saying, 'Last stop, last stop.' Only we weren't in Montauk. We were in Speonk."

"Speonk?"

"The lousy conductor in Jamaica lied to me. He put me on the wrong train."

"I think," Naomi interjects, "the conductor must have recognized you from the show and decided this was a perfect opportunity to get back at you for all the rotten things you did. Or rather, the rotten things Evan did. A woman spat at him once."

"No."

"Yes. She walked right up to him in the middle of Lincoln Center and spat in his face. Isn't that right, Jonathan?"

He shrugs. "God knows why. The show is crap. God knows why people take it seriously."

"But go on with your story," I say. "So you were in Speonk. What did you do?"

"Well, I found a pay phone and called Ben Brandt, who I was supposed to be staying with. I had no idea where I was, and I wanted to ask how far Speonk was from Bridge-hampton."

"You should have called me, Jonathan," Naomi says. "I would have picked you up."

"I know, but I didn't think to. So anyway, Ben answers the phone, and he goes, 'Speonk! Where's that?' And I go, 'No-where.'"

"Can you believe Ben didn't offer to go get him? Some friend."

"It was, like, one-thirty in the morning, and there weren't any trains. But I read in the schedule that there was a train I could catch at four from Hampton Bays. Hampton Bays isn't that far from Speonk. So I called Ben back, and said, 'What should I do?' and he goes, 'Hitchhike.' So I hitchhiked."

"And someone picked you up."

"A truck picked me up. Finally. This great big hulk of a guy, with tattoos, and this smaller guy. They were cousins. They recognized me from the show. They said they'd take me to Hampton Bays, provided I came home with them first so the big guy could show me to his wife."

"Get out."

"Can you believe it?"

Jonathan shrugs. "It was just stupid. It was the middle of the fucking night. The guy called his wife on his cell phone, he must have gotten her out of bed. She was in her bathrobe when we got there."

"So what happened then? What did she say?"

"The usual. She wanted to know what it was like behind the scenes, if any of the couples on the show were couples in real life. She seemed sort of confused. I don't think she quite understood that we were just actors, that this was just a lousy job. So I told her what I could, and she made me some coffee, and then her husband and his cousin drove me to Hampton Bays and I caught the train."

"It was five by the time he pulled into Bridgehampton," Naomi adds. "At least Ben had the decency to pick him up *then*."

In the back seat, Jonathan yawns, stretches his legs. "It was just stupid," he says. "A stupid waste of time."

The traffic grinds to a halt.

I don't know where we were then. We might have been anywhere. We might have been in Speonk.

For a while, when I was in high school, I used to watch *The Light of Day*. This was years before Jonathan played Evil Evan. In those days, I was much preoccupied with the fate of Sister Mary, a sweet young nun torn between Faith (in the person of Jesus Christ) and Passion (in the person of a severely smitten Jewish boy who was determined to lure her from the convent). What kept me watching was anxiety bled with a little bit of love: love for Sister Mary drew me in, while anxiety over her fate brought me back, day after day, especially after she went off to war-torn "San Carlos" to do good works and ended up being kidnapped by the sadistic guerrilla leader Pedro Santos. For weeks, I lived in suspense wondering whether Jeremy, her adoring suitor, would succeed in rescuing Mary before the malevolent Santos, with his Castro-like beard and cigar, gave in to lust and raped her. Every afternoon Santos's tobacco-scented breath puffed out over Mary's face; every afternoon, at the crucial instant, Chance stopped his hand on her breast. And then Chance took a day off: Jeremy saved Mary, but only after Santos had ravished her and vanished. Returning to "Montclair Heights," Mary left the convent and married Jeremy, whose child everyone took it for granted that she was carrying. Later, though, Santos turned up in "Montclair Heights." Despite everything that had happened, the former nun found herself powerfully attracted to the ex-guerrilla—at which point I left for college. Years passed. By the time I tuned in again, Jeremy was dead, Santos was out of the picture, Mary was blowsy, much divorced, and played by a different actress. For Evil Evan had ushered in a new era: *he* was Mary's son by Pedro Santos.

Of course, if I'd been tuning in all along—as, presumably, the woman in Speonk had—then perhaps this chain of events wouldn't have surprised me so much. After all, a soap opera is something you live with every day. What keeps you watching isn't, as with movies or novels, the assurance that a hostage taken at the beginning will be a hostage freed at the end. Instead, stories verge into one another. New plots rise from the ashes of old ones. Suffering is a principle: too much happiness foretells imminent catastrophe, just as minor fatigue bodes terminal illness. Time is elastic. Generally speaking, it conforms to time in the world—that is to say, Christmas comes for them when it comes for us, their springs and summers are shaped like ours. Only sometimes time compresses, too, and a single afternoon will take weeks to unfold. And sometimes time accelerates perversely so that a boy (Evan) graduates from high school eight years after his birth. And sometimes time seems not to exist at all.

The Light of Day, of course, goes on without Jonathan. It has been going on for forty-six years. I think of it the way I think of my life, as a narration without beginning or end. Oh, I know it began once, just as I know that someday it will have to end—all things do—yet this assurance is, finally, a haze for me, less a knowledge than a vagueness. The specificity of ending, that's what's so hard to get your mind around, the fact that one day, at some specific hour and in some specific place, this thing is going to happen. And it could happen anytime, anywhere. It could be tomorrow. It could be in Speonk.

Evil Evan took some people hostage, as I recall, in the last days of Jonathan's tenure. He took his lawyer and his lawyer's pregnant wife hostage. He paraded the wife around the courtroom, holding a gun to her abdomen.

This was just the sort of thing Evil Evan did, and that Jonathan claimed he could no longer tolerate. It drove him crazy, he said, having to point a gun at a pregnant woman's abdomen, even if he knew she wasn't really pregnant, that the gun was a prop, that the softness into which he was pressing its barrel was only a foam-rubber mold affixed to the inside of her dress.

"But isn't that just part of being an actor?" Naomi asked in the car, fishing in her purse for tollbooth tokens.

To which he replied: "It was a principle of my training that you have to become the character you play. And when you have to become Evil Evan five days a week, well, after a while it starts to make you nuts, you know what I'm saying? I mean, I would wake up in the morning, and think, 'Good, today I get to rape a fourteen-year-old. Cool.' Maybe some people can go, you know, 'This is just my job,' but not me."

We reached the city, and Naomi dropped Jonathan off at Second Avenue and Fifty-eighth Street; then we headed downtown together.

"Of course, there's more to that story than meets the eye," she said, once we were alone.

"Oh?"

She nodded. "One of those wasp-waisted space cadets he's

always going for. Works for Revlon or something. For the first six months they were together, she never watched *The Light of Day,* she was always working. Then one week she was home sick and decided to tune in. Wouldn't you know it? *That* was the week Evil Evan raped the fourteen-year-old."

"And his girlfriend didn't like it?"

"Are you kidding? She practically had a seizure. She kept saying that when she looked into his eyes she saw the eyes of a rapist, or some nonsense like that. I told him I thought it was idiotic, that he shouldn't take her seriously, but has Jonathan ever once listened to me where women are concerned? No. So he up and quits a perfectly decent job, gives up a great salary, just to prove to some bimbo that he's willing to make a sacrifice for her love."

"I had no idea being an actor could be so complicated," I said.

"It's not being an actor that's complicated," Naomi corrected. "It's Jonathan who makes things complicated—especially where his girlfriends are concerned."

We arrived at my building. I kissed Naomi on the cheek and stepped out of the car onto the curb. She drove off in what seemed to me an irritated fashion. Not that I cared: the truth is, I hardly know Naomi—she was just a friend of one of the girls I was sharing a beach house with that summer—and Jonathan—well, I only met him that once, that time in the car. They were just acquaintances, people who offered me a ride one weekend. Beyond what I picked up on the Long Island Expressway, I couldn't tell you much about Jonathan's life. I don't know where he grew up or went to school. (Naomi works for an Internet start-up, I believe.)

And yet, as the summer progressed, the story stayed with me. Perhaps it was the trucker with the tattoos who kept it alive, or my own memories of coffee before dawn in college, or else just the very idea of Speonk at two in the morning—an invented Speonk, the streets so silent that you could hear the thunk of the traffic light as it changed from yellow to red. Sometimes, when I tried to imagine what really happened to Jonathan, I wondered if he'd been in some kind of danger. This is the soap opera watcher in me. The soap opera watcher in me envisions the house into which the trucker led him as painted in the most ominous colors—arterial purples, the pale blues of suffocation—and filled with padlocked doors, rolls of rusty wire, rags soaking in gasoline. In this scenario, the trucker and his wife cannot even begin to distinguish Jonathan from Evil Evan. When he walks into their kitchen, she cries, "How could you do it? And to a woman in her condition!"

"It wasn't me," Jonathan answers meekly. "I swear to you, *I* didn't do it." All in vain. His fate is sealed: his mouth will be stuffed with rags, his wrists bound with rusty wire. And then, in that basement to which the padlocked door leads, he will be imprisoned, tortured, punished for deeds not his own . . .

Admittedly, the soap opera watcher in me is inclined to exaggeration.

A more realistic scenario, then: zoom in on a small, tidy, rural kitchen, the floor a blue-and-white linoleum checkerboard, the countertops corn-yellow Formica. Dishes dry on a rubber rack. Tin canisters marked FLOUR, SUGAR, and TEA are lined up next to the electric stove. There's a smell of pot roast and stale coffee. When the truck driver and his cousin bring Evan—Jonathan—inside, the wife stands from where she's been waiting at the breakfast table. Although she's still in her bathrobe, she's put on rouge, lipstick. She's wearing earrings. A Sara Lee pound cake defrosts on top of the refrigerator, where the cat can't get to it.

Jonathan sits down. He looks tired and tough and lost in his dirty white T-shirt. She stares at him, perhaps touches him, remarks at how much smaller he appears offscreen (I noticed this, too): not a villain, just a boy, a tough boy, tired and lost. He rests his head on his palm, and his head is next to the television set, the very television set on which, every weekday for two years, she's watched him, as if he really has stepped through the screen and come to life. Yet the truth is, he's been here all along: in her kitchen, in her house. In Speonk.

She asks him what it's like playing Evil Evan. He tells her that as of today, he's quit.

"But how can that be?" she asks. "The murder trial's not over yet."

"We always tape a few weeks ahead."

Her eyes widen. "So you mean that in a few weeks, Evan will be gone?"

"An inside tip—don't tell your friends, I'm sworn to secrecy on this—he's going to the slammer. The hoosegow."

The trucker's cousin laughs—probably at the word *hoosegow.*

"So now you're a little bit ahead of the game," Jonathan says.

The wife blushes. "Well, don't worry, your secret's safe with me. I won't tell a soul."

Jonathan would like to say that for all he cares, she can print the news in the *Speonk Gazette,* but he controls himself. Much better to give her the gratification of a secret.

She offers him a slice of pound cake; he says no, thank you. She offers him coffee; he accepts. It is late, the middle of the night; her husband and his cousin are shifting restlessly near the refrigerator, and Evil Evan is drinking coffee in her kitchen out of a mug that says, LIFE'S A BEACH. He drinks it in three gulps, puts down the mug. The truck driver suggests they'd better scoot if they want to get to Hampton Bays in time for his train. Jonathan has fulfilled his part of the bargain, and now the truck driver intends to do the same.

Jonathan stands; the wife stands. They look at each other for a moment. Then they say goodbye. The three men leave her, as men always do, alone with the television and the kitchen. Outside, she hears the truck's engine turn over as it pulls away, toward Hampton Bays and sunlight and the train that will take Evan away from Speonk, and out of her life for good.

Well, that's one way things could have turned out. But though this might be an end to Jonathan's story, it isn't the end to mine.

One Saturday, a few weeks after Naomi drove us to New York, I ran into her on the beach in Bridgehampton.

"Guess what?" she said, leaping up from the sand. "The other day, I looked up Speonk on a map, and it's only an hour from here—less in the middle of the night, when there wouldn't be traffic."

"So?"

"Well, doesn't that make it seem a little improbable?"

"What?"

"That Ben wouldn't pick him up."

"Pick up Jonathan? Maybe Ben was busy."

She rolled her eyes. "Are you kidding? He's one of Jonathan's best friends. But even if he did say no—which I find hard to believe—then why didn't Jonathan just call a taxi to take him to Hampton Bays?"

"Well, maybe taxis don't run that late in Speonk." I sat down on the edge of her towel.

"Fine. So why didn't he call me? He *knows* I would have picked him up."

I didn't want to get into the thorny question of why he might not have wanted to call Naomi.

"What are you saying?" I asked. "That he made up the whole story?"

"Not the *whole* story, necessarily. It's just, when you think about it, it's full of holes. For instance, this idea that he had no other choice but to hitchhike. Of course he had other choices! I've just listed them. And then the larger inconsistency, which is, how likely is it that some truck driver, some guy who spends all his time on the road, is going to recognize an actor from a soap opera?"

"Don't they usually drive at night?"

"Sure. But would *The Light of Day* really be up the alley of your average trucker?"

"Who says he was your average trucker?"

Naomi threw sand at me then. "Oh, be quiet, you're just playing devil's advocate," she said. "I can hear it in your voice, you're as dubious as I am. You're wondering, was Jonathan just making the whole thing up for the sake of giving a performance? You know, poor Jonathan, he couldn't bear playing the villain anymore, so he quits, and on his last day of work, look what happens. No matter where he travels, Evil Evan follows him. It's like something out of Stephen King."

"Or a soap opera."

"Exactly."

Making an excuse, I got up, and walked farther down the beach. Somehow I couldn't stomach any more of Naomi's suspiciousness—not at that moment. And yet I have to say this for her: with the tenacity that distinguishes certain very relentless and untrusting natures, she had managed to root out from Jonathan's story every questionable detail, every immoderate coincidence, laying those trophies before me the way a cat will lay out the remnants of its prey. And faced with such evidence, how could I not revise my own imagined version of what took place?

So: third variation.

Let's agree, at the very least, that Jonathan did end up in Speonk that night. Let's also agree that, either from necessity or by choice, he decided to hitchhike to Hampton Bays. A truck picks him up, only this time the driver is alone. No cousin tags along for the ride. The driver is beer-bellied, hairy-shouldered, wears a New York Knicks baseball cap. He grips the wheel so tightly his knuckles whiten, and the contemplation of those knuckles—the knowledge that this man could crush Jonathan's neck with his bare hands if he wanted—provokes a weird commingling of panic and arousal in Jonathan. His mouth waters. From the little green cardboard tree that dangles from the rearview mirror, there emanates a smell of men's rooms; of urinal cakes.

If the driver recognizes Jonathan, though, he doesn't let on. Instead he says, "Jerry," and holds his hand out sideways as he slows for a red light.

"Jonathan."

They shake. With an audible thunk, the light changes to green. The truck accelerates. "You know, if I take you straight to Hampton Bays, you'll just have to wait at the station," Jerry says. "Tell you what, why don't we go to my place? My wife will make us some coffee."

"Won't she be asleep?"

"Norma?" He laughs. "She never sleeps. Never goes to bed before three, and then she reads."

"Well, if you're sure—"

Without signaling, Jerry maneuvers the truck off the main drag and onto a narrow street lined with shingled houses. In most of them, the lights are off. A few more turns—left, right, left, Jonathan notes, in case he has to escape—and they pull into a graveled driveway bordered with lawn and geraniums. "Home, sweet home," Jerry says, switching off the ignition.

They climb out of the cab. The house is dark except for a yellowish light glimmering in one window. Taking a ring of keys from his belt, Jerry opens the door and shouts, "Norma!"

"In here."

They step through the front hall, where Jerry hangs his cap on a peg. A smell of pot roast and stale coffee lingers in the air. Pushing open a swing door, Jerry leads Jonathan into the kitchen, where a woman with long, badly dyed hair is sitting at the breakfast table, smoking and doing the *New York Times* crossword puzzle. Behind her is a padlocked door. In front of her sits a half-empty glass of orange juice and an ashtray in which a cigarette is smoldering. She is holding a pencil.

Lifting her eyes from the puzzle, she looks Jonathan over—not with surprise, exactly, though not with complacency, either; instead, her expression might best be described as one of slight botheration, enough to tell Jonathan that, though her husband may not be in the habit of bringing strangers home at two in the morning, neither is it unheard of for him to do so.

"Norma, this is Jonathan," Jerry says, and hoists himself up to sit on the corn-yellow countertop. "Jonathan, Norma."

"Hey."

"He was hitching near the station. Got the wrong train out of Jamaica. Has to get to Hampton Bays, but the next train don't leave for a couple of hours."

"Bummer."

"Make some coffee, will you?"

Obediently—but with evident impatience—Norma puts

down her pencil, gets up out of her chair, and walks to the stove. She has a big behind. She's wearing an old-fashioned lacy pink bathrobe, buttoned to the neck. Her age is difficult to read. Forty? Forty-five? Although she has the long hair of a girl, and she's painted her nails with glittery pink polish, nonetheless the skin around her throat is pliant and loose. There are tiny, colorless hairs on her cheeks. She reminds Jonathan of an over-the-hill Grateful Dead groupie he once saw interviewed on television—"rode hard and put up wet" was how Ben Brandt described her—and for that very reason, he finds her powerfully attractive, much more attractive, say, than Betsy, the pretty girlfriend for whose sake (at least in part) he quit his job. It's that slight air of tawdriness—the dyed hair, the glittery nails, and then the odd touch of the grandmotherly bathrobe: it all contributes to a fantasy he's working up, has been working up ever since Jerry invited him home. After all, he's no innocent, he's seen the ads in the back of the *Village Voice,* on Internet bulletin boards: COUPLE SEEKS SINGLE . . . INSATIABLE MOM CAN'T GET ENOUGH . . . GIVE IT TO MY WIFE WHILE I WATCH. Is this the real story, then, the real reason Jerry brought him here? And if so, will she go along with it? (Probably; to avoid trouble with her husband, he suspects, she's probably gone along with far worse things. Even so, her lack of interest is vivid, and, curiously enough, the knowledge that she would submit, if at all, reluctantly, only heightens his curiosity.)

And no one, not Betsy nor Naomi nor Ben, will ever know. For he goes unrecognized. That's the icing on the cake. Evil Evan is so far from here he might as well be dead.

Unless, of course, they *do* recognize him and are just pretending not to, so that they can spring something on him at a compromised moment.

The coffee is ready. Norma pours it into mugs and hands

one to Jerry, the other to Jonathan. "Thanks," he says. "Oh, 'Life's a Beach.' You know, I never got that joke before."

Norma says nothing. She sits down, grinds out her cigarette, and takes up her pencil.

"Any milk?" Jerry asks.

"Went sour."

A sound of gulping from behind Jonathan.

"Is that today's puzzle you're doing?"

Norma nods.

"I finished it on the train, so if you get stuck on anything, just let me know."

For the first time since his arrival, something akin to a smile passes over Norma's lips. "Okay, smarty-pants, so long as you're offering. Twenty-six across: Monster's home."

He grins. *"Loch,"* he says.

"Shit. Like Loch Ness." She erases. "I had *lair.* So that means twenty-six down is—Musical Lynn. *Loretta!"*

"I was born a coal miner's daughter," Jerry sings.

"Any others?"

She scans. "Thirty-seven down: Bygone queen."

"All right. How many letters have you got?"

"T-blank-blank-blank-I-N-A. At first I thought it might be *Titania*, but that doesn't fit."

"Tsarina."

"Tsarina." She writes in the word. "Which means that fifty-two across—Bleep—is . . . *Edit out!"*

"Why do you waste your time with these stupid puzzles?" Jerry asks. "Up all night, and doing what? Working on your novel? Nope. Puzzles."

"You're writing a novel?"

"I don't like to talk about it," Norma says. "He knows that. He knows I don't like to talk about it."

She returns to the crossword. Behind where she and Jona-

than are sitting, her husband chuckles a little. And how curious! Now the Grateful Dead groupie is, of all things, a novelist. She sits up at night doing crossword puzzles. Out of the
lips of her jokey husband emerge the words "Butcher Hol-
ler . . ."

Soon it will be time to go. Jerry will drive him to Hampton
Bays, where he will catch a train to Bridgehampton, where
Ben Brandt will pick him up: his own life. And then, in that
crowded summer rental on the wrong side of the Montauk
Highway, maybe he will tell his friends the story of Jerry and
Norma, or some variation on it, adding a twist to make it
more interesting and less incriminating. Months will go by,
and Betsy will or will not agree to marry him. Evil Evan will
recede, and the best part is, he will recede far faster than Jerry
and Norma. Far faster than Speonk.

Somewhere a bird starts singing. Only the song isn't coming from outside: it's the clock above the kitchen sink. Instead of numbers, each hour is marked by a different singing
bird: great horned owl for twelve, northern mockingbird for
one, black-capped chickadee . . .

Who's singing now? Northern cardinal. Three in the
morning.

"We'd better scoot if you're going to make your train,"
Jerry says, alighting from the countertop.

"Fine, just one more clue," Norma says. "Thirty-one
across: Arizona attraction."

"Petrified forest," Jonathan says.

"Petrified forest, of course." Feverishly she erases. "Good,
now I can finish the damn thing. Now, finally, I can finish the
damn thing and go to bed."

THE SCRUFF OF THE NECK

LILY'S GIRL, AUDREY, called Rose and asked if she could interview her; she was getting her master's degree in epidemiology, she said, and for her thesis she wanted to prepare a medical history of the entire family. "From soup to nuts" was how she put it. "And since you and Minna are the only ones of the brothers and sisters who are still alive, obviously it's worth the trip to Florida to talk to you."

"You'll want to see Minna, too, then?" Rose asked.

"Let me interview you first," Audrey said, and proposed that she come to tea at Rose's house the following Tuesday.

"Wonderful, dear. And you'll spend the night, won't you? Or a few nights."

But no, Audrey said, she was going to stay with her boyfriend's parents in Fort Lauderdale. "Oh, and if you could have your birth certificate and passport handy, plus any medical records—really, whatever you think might be relevant— that would be great. Also anything on your children. And grandchildren."

"I'll see what I can find."

Audrey hung up. This was on Friday; over the course of

the weekend Rose sifted through the boxes in the basement and the files at the back of the kitchen desk, trying to dig up material that Audrey might consider useful. Yet how could she know what Audrey might consider useful? She found vaccination certificates for two of the three children, some old passports, the insurance papers from when Burt had died. (Why had she saved all this stuff?) Also her marriage license. But would that be "relevant"? Rose had no idea, so she stuffed it along with everything else into a big manila folder.

It embarrassed her that she had no pictures of Audrey, or any memories by which to gauge what the girl looked like. The truth was, where her great-nieces and -nephews were concerned, Rose always felt a little at sea. When you are the youngest of eleven, nieces and nephews have a way not only of proliferating, but of sharing the same names, so that it becomes harder and harder to keep track of which David is which, or whether it was Ernie's Sarah or Laura's who had just graduated from law school. Some of them Rose had never met; Audrey she had met only once, when she was three years old. This was only in part circumstantial. Of all her sisters, Harriet, Audrey's grandmother, was the only one to whom Rose had never had much to say. To put it mildly, Harriet had always been eccentric, sitting on the porch on summer evenings and brushing out her long, dark hair to scandalize the neighbors. Later, for reasons that remained murky, she was thrown out of nursing school, then married a rabbi and gave birth to Lily, also a bit of a weirdo. Lily had been divorced more times than Rose cared to remember, had gone to India and changed her name to Anuradha, and stayed at the Betty Ford Center. She had only the one child; was it fair to say, then, based on her phone manner, that the girl took after her mother and grandmother in many ways?

Audrey arrived, as promised, on Tuesday. That morning, Rose woke up worried about tea. Generally speaking, tea wasn't part of her vocabulary; like Minna, she preferred coffee. Although Minna was about to turn ninety-six, she still had lunch every day at Ravelstein's, where she drank black coffee with her corned beef sandwich. She even drank coffee at supper. She had no patience for the cappuccinos and espressos and whatnot that you found at the new Starbucks, which she called Starburst, or sometimes Starbust; no, she preferred good old American coffee, she said, made in a stainless-steel pot. As for Rose, what little she knew of tea she had learned from *Masterpiece Theatre,* programs like *Upstairs, Downstairs,* on which much always seemed to be made over who poured. The details she tried to excavate from memory. At Publix she bought Peek Frean biscuits and cucumbers and Pepperidge Farm thin-sliced bread, as well as several varieties of tea: Queen Mary, Earl Grey, Prince of Wales. But then when she got home she realized that she didn't have any butter. Could you make cucumber sandwiches without butter? Would it be all right to add mayonnaise instead?

She cut the crusts off the bread, spread them with Hellman's Light Mayonnaise. From outside, barking sounded. She looked out the kitchen window and saw that Dinah, her puppy, was trying to kill the pool sweep again. Round and round Dinah went, chasing the little mechanical monster as it circled the pool, lunging at the water whenever it neared the periphery.

Rose rapped on the windowpane. "Dinah, no!" she scolded. But Dinah didn't stop. Catching the pool sweep between her teeth, she yanked it out of the water. "Dinah, no!" Rose repeated, hurrying out on the deck. "Bad girl! No!"

Dinah looked at her. From the pool sweep's underside, water jets sprayed the deck, the lawn chair, the silk dress Rose had put on for the occasion. "Oh, Dinah!" she said, extracting it from the dog's mouth. "Look what you've done. And now I'll have to change."

Then she picked Dinah up—as the dog lady on television had instructed—by the scruff of the neck. When they misbehave, this dog lady had said, just grab them by the scruff of the neck, the way their mothers did; that way they'll know you mean business.

Hem dripping, Rose carried Dinah inside. Dinah's belly was brindled, the fur on her vulva turned upward in a wet-kiss curl. With adoring eyes, eyes full of lamentation and contrition, she gazed up at Rose, who gazed back. "Oh, Dinah, why can't you learn?" she asked. "And to think that this dress cost more than you did!"

She was just undoing the buttons when the doorbell rang.

Audrey turned out to be a wisp of a thing, with short black hair and squinty eyes. A slender gold ring pierced her left nostril. She wore Groucho Marx glasses, a black turtleneck, black jeans, and carried a black backpack.

"Well, look at you," Rose said, kissing her on the cheek. "Little Audrey, all grown up."

Audrey flinched. Her shoulder blades, when Rose touched them, were bony; static electricity clung to her turtleneck. They stepped into the living room, and Rose sat her down on one of the recliners. From the kitchen she brought the tea things on a tray: the Peek Freans, the sandwiches, the cups and the sugar bowl and the milk pitcher. "You'll have to excuse my appearance," she said, "I've been having a little trouble with the puppy."

"You have a puppy?"

"A Wheaten terrier. Dinah. She's out in the yard now. You see, George—that's my oldest boy—gave her to me last autumn when your uncle Burt passed on. And she has this thing about the pool sweep. She loves to chase the pool sweep."

"What's a pool sweep?"

"Well, it's—how do you describe it? It's that little thing that circles round the pool and cleans it."

"I've never seen one of those."

"Newer pools don't have them. Ours is almost thirty years old, if you can believe it . . . oh, but I've forgotten to give you tea. And what kind would you like? As you can see, I've got 'em all. Earl Grey, Queen Mary, the whole royal family."

"Actually, I don't drink tea. Could I have a Diet Coke?"

"Of course. If I have any. I'll check. Otherwise it may have to be normal Coke."

"That's fine." Audrey was opening her backpack, arranging notebooks and binders and spreadsheets on the coffee table.

"Georgie's a stockbroker," Rose called from the kitchen. "He lives in New York. Oh good, here's some Coke. Anyway, he worries about me—too much, if you want my opinion. That's why he got me Dinah. At first I wasn't too happy about it, let me tell you. I mean, I've raised three boys, the last thing I needed was something else to take care of. But since then, Dinah and I, we've gotten to be good friends. And I must say, it's nice having something to shout at again!"

"My mother has a Rottweiler," Audrey said.

"Does she now?"

"For protection. I always say to her, Mom, with all those alarms and window grates, you've got nothing to worry about, you could be living in Fort Knox. Still, she says she can't sleep at night. So she bought this, like, killer dog."

Rose, popping open the Coke can, nodded gravely; sat across from her niece. "Cucumber sandwich?"

"No thanks."

"Cookie?"

Audrey was studying a spreadsheet. "Maybe later." She looked her aunt in the eye. "Well, Rose—do you mind if I just call you Rose?"

"You have to ask? We're family."

"Okay. So, Rose, like I told you, for my master's thesis I'm doing a medical history of the whole family, looking at which illnesses crop up most commonly, environmental factors, genetic predispositions—that sort of thing."

"What a wonderful idea. Your mother must be very proud of you."

"She's too out of it to be proud of anything I do . . . but never mind." Audrey opened her pen. "To begin with, I'd like to get the basic data on your branch of the family—you know, dates of birth, places of birth, that sort of thing."

"I got it all ready for you." Rose pushed the manila folder in Audrey's direction.

"And the full names of your children—let me make sure I have these right. George Robert, born July 7, 1954—"

"He's my oldest. Not married yet, but we're still hoping."

"Then Daniel Jeremy, born October 20, 1957."

"He's back in New Jersey. Tenafly. Teaches high school English. Got divorced last year, I'm still sorry about it, she was a lovely girl—"

"And finally Kevin Leon, born February 14, 1960."

"The baby of the family. They just moved to Singapore. The company sends him all over the place. First Germany, then France, and now—"

"And he's got kids, right?"

"That's right. His wife is Denyse—with a Y, not an I. The little ones are adorable. David Bernard and Sarah Rose. Would you like to see pictures? I've got pictures."

"That's okay. And all the documents are in here?" Audrey pointed to the manila folder.

"All there."

"May I take these with me and make photocopies? I'll bring them back, of course."

"Of course."

She scribbled. "So when did you move down to Florida?"

"It must have been . . . 1970? Could it have been 1970? Hard to believe, the time's gone by so fast. It's funny, most people assume that just because I'm an old lady, I must have retired here, but the fact is, we raised our kids in this house. Our boys all went to high school in West Palm."

"And Minna?"

"Oh, Minna was already here. Minna retired . . . it must have been sixty-five, sixty-six. She's been retired longer than you've been alive! But if you don't mind my asking, what have you found out so far? Anything about migraines? All my boys get terrible migraines."

"My data is really too preliminary to share. But I have prepared a survey"—she pushed some more sheets across the table—"which I wonder if you might fill out. Also your sons."

"And Minna?"

"Well, if she's—you know—clearheaded enough."

"Minna?" Rose laughed. "She's sharper than any of us. Oh, maybe she can't get around as easily as she used to, but she still drives, and she's got a mind like a steel trap. We should all be in such good shape at her age!"

"Good, then maybe you could give her a copy."

"But why don't you go see her yourself while you're here? She's just a little ways down the coast. And I'll tell you, it would make her day. She loves all the nieces and nephews, keeps up to date on all of you, I suppose because she never had children of her own."

Audrey coughed. Over her folder, she gave Rose a look of—what to call it? Curiosity? Pity? Some hybrid of the two?

"Yes, well, that was something else I wanted to talk to you about. I meant to wait until later, but since you've brought it up—"

"What, dear?"

"According to your birth certificate, you were born August 11, 1920, is that right?"

"That's right. A Leo."

"In Cape May, New Jersey."

Rose nodded. "You see, Momma wasn't feeling well that summer, and it was so hot that Poppa decided to send her away from Newark, so she went to stay at a hotel in Cape May. Minna went too—to take care of her."

"And when was Minna born?"

"When would that have been? 1902, 1903? 1902, I guess. Funny, isn't it, that of all eleven kids, only the two of us are left? Oldest and youngest. Like bookends."

Audrey pulled a stack of photocopies out of her briefcase. "Last year, I went to the hall of records in Newark," she said, "to see when all of you were born. And then, when I couldn't find your birth certificate, I asked my mother, and she told me about your being born in Cape May. So I went down to Cape May. It took me a while, but I tracked down the information."

"But, darling, you didn't have to go all the way to Cape May! You could have just called me!"

"Yes, I know. But I had another reason." She pointed at the photocopies.

"And what was that?"

"I'd better explain. As I'm sure you know, my grandmother was a major pack rat."

"Boy, do I. Harriet never threw anything away."

"Well, after the house was sold—your parents' house—she was the one who took charge of packing it up, on account of being the closest to home, and what was in the attic she just basically moved to her own attic. All those trunks and boxes, which no one ever opened. For years. My grandfather used to gripe about it, every now and then he'd threaten to burn it all, or have a sale, but Grandma wouldn't hear of it. And I suppose she had her reasons, because what Grandpa saw as just a fire hazard turned out to be a treasure trove for me, for my study. I mean, when I started going through those trunks last summer, I found everything: every doctor's bill, every dentist's bill, every medical record. Your high school grades. Your mother even made notes of all your illnesses, in a big black ledger. One for every year from when Minna was born until Grandma died."

"Momma was very meticulous."

"But here's the thing—that summer, the summer of 1920, there's just nothing."

"Well, as I said, she was in Cape May. And it was a hard pregnancy. She had to be in bed for most of it."

"And Minna went with her?"

"To take care of her. Poppa could only get away from the shop on weekends. You can ask her yourself when you see her, she remembers everything—the name of the hotel, what their room number was."

Audrey picked up the photocopies and started shuffling through them. "Have you ever seen these?" she asked, handing them to Rose.

"What are they?" Rose put on her reading glasses, which hung from a rope around her neck. "Let me see . . . Oh, doctor's bills."

"Dr. Homer M. Hayes, Cape May, New Jersey. An obstetrician."

"Oh, so this must have been the doctor that Momma saw when she was pregnant with me."

"But look at the top. Under patient's name, it doesn't say Effie Miller. It says Minna Miller. And not only on one—on all of them."

"Oh, it does, doesn't it?" Rose's hands fluttered, so that the papers made a slight noise, like birds passing overhead.

"There are bills here for ten different visits. All related to a pregnancy. And on every one of them the name is Minna Miller." Audrey leaned in closer, across the undrunk Coke and the Peek Freans. "Do you see?" she asked. "Do you understand why I had to talk to you?"

Rose played with her wedding ring. Glancing at one of the cucumber sandwiches, she observed that a little mayonnaise was dripping over the edges of the thin-sliced bread. She picked up the tea tray and carried it toward the kitchen.

"What's the matter?" Audrey asked, almost hungrily.

"It's nothing, dear," Rose said. "I think I hear Dinah, that's all. I think Dinah is crying to come in."

Once, in her youth, Rose had been thought a wild driver. Oh, how her mother had wailed whenever she'd gone off in her little roadster, in those years when it was considered shocking for a girl even to have a license! To Rose's mother driving was, quite simply, unladylike, the sort of thing you would have expected of Harriet. "But you let Minna drive!" Rose had countered.

"It's different in Minna's case," her mother had said. "Minna needs to drive to go to work." For Minna was an elementary school teacher, and the school at which she taught was out in the country, near New Vernon.

Fifty-some years later, Rose still drove—slowly. It was not that she was any less bold; rather, it seemed that the velocity of the world had increased while her own pace stayed the same, leaving her the object of impatient tailgating on the part of young women in station wagons: young women with children in the back seat, as she had had children in the back seat, not so long ago.

With Minna the problem was worse. She was always losing her car in the parking lot at Publix. That afternoon, just after Audrey left, she called Rose, and said, "I can't think where I've left it. I've been up and down every row. I can't think—"

"But, darling," Rose had said, "didn't you tie something to the antenna, like I told you the last time?"

"Yes I did. Only isn't that the joke? For the life of me I can't remember what."

"Dinah, no! Bad girl!" Rose hit the window, which shuddered. "Listen, Minna, don't worry. Just sit yourself down in the air-conditioning, and I'll be there in a jiff."

"As soon as you can. Otherwise the ice cream will melt. Oh, and Rose"—here Minna's voice grew soft, even coy—"I promise it will never happen again."

They hung up. Rose went into the garage. Really, Minna was getting to be a bit of a trial these days. When Rose was a girl, and Harriet had said something cruel to her, Minna always sat her in front of the mirror, brushed out her hair, and counseled, "This too shall pass." And usually Minna was right: the wrong did pass, though Rose never came to understand why Harriet hated her so much. Now she wondered if that hatred had passed through the generations, like the hook of the nose or of the lip, to Audrey. Audrey, like her grandmother, was clearly not the kind ever to let go of a grudge. Instead she would build a citadel from the wrongs that had been done her, and gain what sustenance she could from leeching other people's woes.

Who was the father, anyway? "My father," Rose said to herself, climbing into the Cadillac and lighting a cigarette.

For she couldn't remember Minna ever having had even a single boyfriend. She was the schoolteacher, the caregiver. And yet there must have been someone. Somewhere along the line, someone whose name was never mentioned, yet who had a name, a family with its own *meshugaas,* its own medical history to be charted by some enterprising niece. And where was that family? Was it big, with even more nieces and nephews for Rose to confuse? (Remembering that you could get a ticket for not wearing one, she put on her seat belt.) God, it was hot . . . Stupid to have stuck it out in south Florida for the summer, when in the old days she and Burt had always gotten away in August, gone north to the Cape. But Burt was dead, and she had Minna to attend to. Minna, quite simply, could not be left on her own.

Oh, what a foolish thing to do! And why had they done it? For it must have been a conspiracy. Not that anyone would have ever thought to question them, since as it stood Effie was pregnant all the time anyway, it made sense that she should be pregnant. And Minna . . . who would have ever guessed it of her? Never married. Up until today, Rose had wondered if she had ever even loved.

She pressed a button. With a creak, the garage door opened, admitting a light so harsh Rose had to squint against it. Where were her sunglasses? In her bag? She rummaged for a moment, found them at last, put them on (the world became pink), then, turning the key, felt the first gusts of hot breeze that presaged the air-conditioning hit her wrists. Lastly she switched on the cassette player—on the highway, Mozart calmed her—and looking over her shoulder, lurched backward, with a great shudder, onto Ixora Avenue.

Cautiously, even timidly, Rose made her way to the highway. Near a red light, a station wagon bore down on her, its driver, a young woman with children in the back seat, flashing her brights, making a face Rose could see quite plainly in the rearview mirror. Seconds pulsed by, the light changed, and she rose up onto the interstate; her tormentor passed her, disappearing into a haze of motion. Ten miles of blind panic now separated Rose from Minna, ten miles of off-ramps and merging lanes and terrifying low-slung vehicles with over-sized tires, windows tinted black, chain metal frames for the license tags. As if edges meant safety, she kept to the slow lane the whole way, sandwiched between a pair of trucks that let off plumes of exhaust but also offered, in their immensity, a measure of protection. Yet she was nothing as compared to Minna, who drove so slowly that she'd actually gotten a ticket for it. Yes, there was a speed limit on the other side too; you could get a ticket for going under it. Really, she had no business being behind a wheel, George said; she was a menace, and not only to herself. Only, who had the heart to stop her, when she valued her independence more than her life? For that was the thing everyone said about Minna: "She loves her independence!" Never asking anything of anybody, until lately.

Was that the reason, then? Would a child—would Rose—have compromised her beloved independence?

At last the turnoff neared. Where Minna lived was a world of old people. All the businesses catered to them. Clever entrepreneurs traded in urban nostalgia, peddling bagels with a schmear, take-out Chinese food spiced down to suit elderly stomachs. It always made Rose a little uneasy, coming here. After all, unlike her sister, she had moved to Florida as a vital woman of middle age. She had raised her boys in a nice neighborhood with frangipani and banyan trees, street games after school, and on Halloween so many trick-or-treaters they ended up having to give away the hard candy moldering on the piano.

Minna, on the other hand, had arrived already old. For three decades she'd been living in her one-bedroom apartment with its view of the Intracoastal, in a squat, modest building which had once shared the waterfront with no one, but over which, every year, more gleaming towers crouched, throwing shadows onto the patio, stealing the sun.

It was George's sensible opinion that Minna couldn't go on like this much longer. She could barely get herself dressed anymore. A nice old folks' home, he counseled, or one of those places where they *think* they're on their own, but there are nurses. And yet why was it that whenever George talked about putting Minna away, within seconds he invariably brought the conversation around to what he called Rose's own "situation"? "Why not sell the house?" he'd ask. "Now that you're on your own, it must be an awful lot to keep up with. Buy yourself a little condo instead."

The exit snuck up on her, as it always did. Alarmed by its sudden appearance, she cut across three lanes of traffic, enraging a truck, which honked and startled her. Off the highway a red light gave her a moment to collect her thoughts. Back when she and Burt had first moved here, farmland had shouldered the interstate on both sides. But now everywhere she looked there were warehouses, and warehousey strip malls, and supermarkets, including the Publix where Minna had lost the car. From where she waited, Rose surveyed its parking lot, stretching all the way to the cyclone fence that blocked off the highway.

Finally the light changed. She turned right, pulled up to the curb in front of the market and, leaving the engine running, hurried through the doors to find Minna. There she sat, slumped on a bench by the telephone. Her white hair fell over her forehead in a wave. She was wearing a striped jersey and stretch blue jeans. Even though she was asleep, one of her hands lolled protectively over the handle of a cart brimming with groceries. And what on earth made her think she needed all that stuff? It would only go to waste.

"Darling, I'm here," Rose said, patting Minna's shoulder, at which point Minna's eyes opened.

"Oh, Rose! I must have dropped off." She hoisted herself to her feet; made to take hold of the grocery cart.

"No, I'll get it," Rose said, and pushed her away with a gesture so violent that Minna's hands flew instinctively to her face.

"Darling, what a relief it is to see you," Minna said, once they were safe in Rose's car. "You can't imagine how vulnerable I felt, sitting there by myself, with all that food. People stared."

"It's all right, I'm here now."

"A man stared . . . a long time. I was afraid."

"Only I do think that in the future you might consider asking Mrs. Lopez—"

"And then I thought, what would I have done if you hadn't been home? Sat here until the market closed, or you came back?"

"Nonsense, you would have called Mrs. Lopez and she would have fetched you."

"But her car's in the shop. She takes the bus."

"Well then, I'm sure the police would have helped." (In fact, if George had had his way, she wouldn't have rescued Minna at all. Instead she would have left her to stew in her own juices, learn her lesson the hard way.) "Anyway, now we need to concentrate on finding your car. Where do you think you left it?"

"I'm sure it was on the left. And not too far back."

"You didn't happen to write down the row number, did you?"

"I didn't think I needed to. Because I'd tied the whatcha-macallit to the antenna. The whosiwhatsit. And I thought . . . Oh, look! Yes, I remember now, it was a dog toy. A little rubber blowfish, with spikes all over—look, there's one!"

"But, Minna, that's a Toyota. You drive a Ford."

They turned right. To Rose's surprise, practically every car in the parking lot had something tied to its antenna: stuffed dolls, balloons, brightly tinted clothespins. It was inevitable that there should be repetition, which was why so many anxious-looking old men and women were now pushing their carts through the heat, eyes open for signs of home, trying to stave off the terror of being lost. None of them was as lucky as Minna, with Rose at the ready to rescue her.

"Honey, forgive me for asking, but you do have your keys, don't you?"

"Yes, of course. That's the first thing I checked."

"Good. And you did lock up—"

"Of course I locked up! What do you take me for?"

"Nothing, darling, I just thought it was worth making sure—" Suddenly Rose braked. "There," she said. "There it is."

"Oh, thank God!" Tears welled in Minna's old eyes. "I didn't want to say anything, but the truth was, I was scared."

"I know," said Rose. For Minna's car had been stolen before. It had been stolen because she had left the keys in the ignition and forgotten to lock the door. Another time she *had* locked the door, but left the engine running. Both times Rose was summoned.

With a great effort, Minna climbed out of her sister's car and got into her own.

Minna's progress was glacial. It took them nearly twenty minutes to get back to her apartment building, which was three-quarters of a mile from the Publix. "Thanks, honey," she said when they finally pulled into the parking lot. "Say, you want to come in for a minute? Have a cup of coffee?"

"Of course I'll come in." Rose popped the trunk. She got out of the car, picked up a bag of groceries.

"Be careful. Don't hurt yourself."

"What choice do I have? I can't leave this stuff to rot."

The apartment was on the ground floor. "Sit down," Minna said once they were inside, and she was easing herself into the lounger in front of the television. "Take a load off. You want some ice cream?"

"No thanks." Rose unpacked.

"I got chocolate marshmallow. Your favorite."

"No, I wouldn't care—Minna, what on earth do you need with three gallons of ice cream?"

"Someone might drop by."

"But no one ever drops by! When was the last time in twenty years that anyone dropped by? And look—you've got three in the freezer already. That's six gallons."

"But Georgie loves ice cream."

"Georgie lives in New York now. He only comes down twice a year." She put the ice cream away. "Honey, you've really got to start using your head, otherwise—"

"Or that Audrey. Lily's girl. What if she drops by? You said she was coming this week."

Rose closed the freezer. "Yes, Audrey might. It's interesting, she's doing a medical history of the family. For her thesis. She seems very bright."

"Lily's always been a strange one, hasn't she?"

"Takes after Harriet."

"Momma was very hard on Harriet. Especially after she got thrown out of nursing school."

"Momma always seemed to resent all of us girls for being girls."

"You can say that again."

Rose sat down across from Minna. "You know, Audrey's dug up the most incredible stuff for her study," she said. "For instance, in Harriet's attic, she found some old ledgers where Momma wrote down every time one of us got sick. Plus all the medical reports, the doctors' bills . . ."

"Momma was very organized. It's a pity women couldn't go to work in those days. She would have made a great CEO. She was much smarter than Poppa. Poor Poppa. Without her, he would have run the store into the ground."

"Yes, Minna, but as I was saying, Audrey found all the old medical bills, even from Cape May."

"You mean when you were born?"

"I've always wanted to know more about that summer."

"Well, Momma was sick. She had terrible morning sickness to start with, plus she had bleeding, so the doctor said she needed to stay in bed until it was time. And with all the kids, and the heat—it was murderous that summer—there was no use in her staying home. So we went to Cape May."

"To a hotel."

"Not much fun for me, I can tell you! Just a girl, and cooped up in that room all day with Momma."

"And was Poppa there?"

"He came when he could. But basically it was just the two of us. Momma and me. I tell you, we sure got on each other's nerves! Talk about cabin fever. And of course she was nervous, knowing that Poppa was running the store by himself. He couldn't keep books very well, not to mention the women coming in all the time. Momma was never easy in the head when she couldn't keep an eye on him."

"And then she had me?"

"We stayed on a few days more so she could recuperate. Then we went home."

"But, Minna, honey"—Rose leaned closer—"those bills that Audrey dug up, there's something funny about them. The name on them isn't Momma's, it's yours."

"Mine?"

"I mean, you're listed as the patient."

"Oh, then they must be bills from a different doctor. I remember I had a terrible flu—"

"No, they're from the obstetrician. Dr. Homer Hayes."

"Then he must have gotten our names mixed up."

Rose blinked. Minna's eyes were focused on the switched-off television, the gray amplitude of which reflected only her own face. She stared at herself as it she were a program.

Rose got up. She walked to the kitchen, where she pulled some bowls out of the cupboard.

"If you don't mind, I think I will have that ice cream now," she said.

"Have all you want. There's loads."

"And you?"

"Sure I will. Chocolate marshmallow."

The ice cream hadn't been in the freezer long enough to harden up after the wait at the supermarket. With a wet plopping noise it fell from the spoon into the dishes, which were chipped at the edges, patterned with butterflies. Rose carried them back into the living room.

"Minna—" She handed her the ice cream. "What Audrey said, it doesn't make any difference. Once, maybe. Not now."

"I did have the worst flu that summer. I could hardly get out of bed."

"We're none the worse for it," Rose said. "None the better, but none the worse." Then she sat down with her ice cream, and they ate. The sun was warm, until a cloud blocked it, throwing shadows against the television. And how curious—in that darkened moment, Minna looked to Rose like no one so much as Dinah, when she had picked her up by the scruff of the neck. Eyes wide, she gazed at Rose, helpless and inscrutable and oddly tranquil. Then the cloud passed. Light returned, revealing a greasy fingerprint on the edge of the screen, a fissure of thread where one of the curtains had been mended.

"Oh, honey, your hair's a mess. Let me brush it."

"It's all right."

"No, let me brush it," Rose insisted. And she picked up a brush from the tray table by the television; pulled her chair alongside Minna's lounger. "You used to do this for me, when I was little."

"Ow!"

"Sorry, did I pull too hard?"

"It's okay. I did, didn't I? Whenever Harriet made you cry."

White hairs, long and fine, collected on the bristles. "You know, I always wanted to have a little girl," Rose said. "Just my luck I should end up with three boys."

"Momma was hoping for a boy," Minna said. "She was always hoping for a boy. But I wanted a little girl, too."

THE LIST

SUBJ: **The List**
DATE: Monday, July 17, 2000, 2:43:51 PM
FROM: ivorystuds@entropy.net
TO: jkwitt@wellspring.edu

Dear Jeff,

I thought you might get a kick out of the attached list of gay/lesbian pianists from the past two centuries, which Willard Pearson and I have been putting together in our spare time. Do you know Willard, by the way? Since 1995 he's directed the piano program at St. Blaise College in New Hampshire; he's also the former president of the Paderewski society, and editor of the society's journal. The list began as a simple exchange of gossip but gradually grew to epic proportions as each of us added names and solicited information from friends. You'll notice at the bottom there's a section called "On the Fence," featuring pianists about whom we've heard rumors but received no corroborating evidence. Any additions you might like to make would be most welcome.

Re your biography of Bulthaup: although I continue to read and enjoy the ms., I feel I must warn you that by emphasizing the sexual side of his relationship with his manager, you risk an upheaval of negative response. Many orthodox admirers will accuse you of "outing" B. just to sell copies, claiming that his sexuality was irrelevant to his playing etc. My feeling so far (I'm on Chapter 11) is that in Chapter 9 you tread on particularly shaky ground by suggesting that B.'s sexual confusion influenced his performance style. Are you trying to appease the "queer studies" crowd here? Or has your publisher been pressuring you to give the book a "gay" angle, in order to guarantee review attention?

While I know that you need my collection of photos, programs, etc., for research purposes and to reproduce, I'm sure you'll understand that I could not possibly permit you to use this precious archival material if I did not feel that the project was one with which I was in unwavering accord—i.e., one that presents B. in the proper light. We'll have to wait until I've seen your revisions before I make a decision. Please remember that I have a responsibility to B.'s heirs as well as to history.

Hugs,
Tim

P.S. Am I ever going to get to hear your voice? Or see your face? Do you ever come up to San Francisco? :)

▪

SUBJ: **Re: The List**
DATE: Monday, July 17, 2000, 4:41:32 PM
FROM: jkwitt@wellspring.edu
TO: ivorystuds@entropy.net

Dear Tim,
    Thanks very much for your e-mail of earlier this after-

noon, as well as for "the list," which (not surprisingly) I've spent the last several minutes perusing. You and Pearson (whom I don't know personally but who once published a letter of mine in the *Paderewski Journal*) have certainly done your homework! Let's get Bulthaup out of the way before I proceed, however.

First of all, I want to say that I really appreciate your warnings about the risks implicit in my frank discussion of B.'s homosexuality. As I'm sure you know, one of the great difficulties inherent in any biographical project is that of balancing the short view with the long view. It's all too easy to lose perspective, until you can no longer tell what you might have overstated. And, as I'm not one of those writers who balks at the possibility that his ideas might ever be less than perfectly worked out, might I ask you a favor? As you read, could you note in the margins those passages where you feel I overdo the gay thing? I can then use your suggestions as a guideline in editing the book.

Let me state from the outset, however, that if I lay stress here to the "gay angle," as you call it, it is for none of the reasons you propose. Indeed, I bristle at the implication that I would ever write to appease anyone, queer studies professors or publishers or even you. On the contrary, I'm simply doing the biographer's job, which is to portray the subject's life as it was lived, and not as other people (including Bulthaup himself) might want it to be portrayed. Bear in mind that if Fabia Bulthaup were still alive, she'd have lawyers breathing down my neck to stop me from even mentioning his affair with Cesare, though this was common knowledge not only in New York and Paris, but in the Bulthaup household.

Now, an important question: I know you well enough to know that you would never advocate the suppression of material that would be crucial to an accurate rendering of the man's life and career. And yet you express worry lest my book should fail to show B. in the "proper light." Well, what is the proper light? If what bothers you is my referring to the possibility of a homosexual aesthetic of performance, as epitomized by Bulthaup's playing, please remember that it was Bulthaup himself who first suggested that idea, in a letter to Cesare (now published). If I take my cue from anyone, it's from him. Believe me, I've labored for many hours over this point, and have really come to believe in my argument: not only Bulthaup's interpretations, but his choice of music, program organization, obsession with lighting, etc., reveal what he himself called (I did not invent this) an "invert's preoccupations." If this part of the book provokes controversy, well, what interesting argument doesn't provoke controversy? And I would rather be attacked for saying something challenging than cosseted for having been a good boy.

As for the photos, programs, etc.—obviously I realize that you own this material, and that it is yours to do with it as you see fit. I also understand that to a great degree, your livelihood depends on the material maintaining its value on the antiquarian market. And yet I hope you will bear in mind as you make your decision that in asking you to let me reproduce some of this stuff, my motive is neither to reduce its commercial value nor to misrepresent Bulthaup; instead it is simply to make B. the human being more accessible—more "real," if you will—to an audience of admirers that has rarely seen his private side. (In this regard the photos are of far greater value than the programs.) What I'm saying is that I want to use the photos *in order* to show Bulthaup in the proper light, and that, though I hope and trust we can come to an agreement, I'm not prepared to betray my instincts in order to obtain them.

On to the list: what a curious document! Although many

of the names came as no surprise to me, some, in particular [omission], quite took me aback. I mean, so far as [omission] is concerned, all you ever hear is that she's always been something of a *femme fatale*, with many (male) lovers. What I find hard to believe, in other words, is not that she had a taste for lesbianism, but that she had time for it.

For your "On the Fence" section, let me add two names. Years ago the horrible Crispin Fishwick told me that [omission] made eyes at him backstage during the Levintritt competition. He is hardly reliable, however. (Did I mention that he has the lowest body temperature of any human being with whom I've ever had the misfortune to share a bed? Literally a "cold Fishwick." Ha-ha.) The second name I would suggest is that of [omission]—this based on nothing except an intuition I felt when I heard him play Szymanowski last year.

All best,
Jeff

▪

SUBJ: **Re: Re: The List**
DATE: Wednesday, July 19, 2000, 7:12:02 AM
FROM: ivorystuds@entropy.net
TO: jkwitt@wellspring.edu

Dear Jeff,

Thanks for your thorough reply to my earlier e-mail. You've given me a lot of food for thought, and it will take me several days to digest it all! For the moment, though, rest assured that of course I will note in the margins of the ms. those moments where you overdo "the gay thing," as you call it.

Re [omission]: back in the late seventies when I was living

with Andy Mangold in New York City, and she was married to [omission], they were part of that swinging Studio 54 crowd. Andy and I were sort of on the fringe of all that. In those days both she and [omission] were pretty AC/DC (you'll see that he's on the list too), and I know for a fact that she had an affair with [omission], who was just starting her film career then. After that ended she took up with [omission], had a child, etc. But for a while there she was a card-carrying glamour-dyke.

I can't write much as I'm just back from a music memorabilia swap meet in Montreal, where I picked up a nice autographed Bulthaup program from 1932. On the way back I stopped off at St. Blaise to have lunch with Willard Pearson. I'm afraid that when I told him I'd shared the list with you he went into an absolute tizzy, as apparently he's just finished reading the manuscript of your book, which he got from Greg Samuels when he was visiting the Meerschaum Institute last week, and has concluded that you are a relentless gossip, not to be trusted, etc. Now his demented worry is that out of some zealous desire to "out" everyone on the list, you'll not only distribute it far and wide but make sure everyone you show it to knows that he was responsible for it, resulting in the ruin of his career, blah-blah-blah. I wouldn't worry about this too much. Willard is an hysterical queen of the old school, which means it doesn't take much to get his panties into a wad. And as he gets older, he just gets worse. In any event, by the end of lunch I'd managed to calm him down, reassure him that you would never send the list to anyone, and restore at least a little of his trust in me.

Better run—I have to take the dog for a walk.

Hugs,
Tim

▪

SUBJ: **Re: Re: Re: The List**
DATE: Wednesday, July 19, 2000, 9:43:22 AM
FROM: jkwitt@wellspring.edu
TO: ivorystuds@entropy.net

Dear Tim,

I can't pretend it doesn't disturb me that Willard Pearson has formed such a low opinion of me. Please reassure him that I have no intention—indeed, have never had any intention—of sharing his list with anyone. In fact I've already erased it from my hard disk.

I must also confess that his attitude toward the list itself perplexes me almost as much as his attitude toward my book. I mean, why is this such a big deal to him? Does he really imagine that if the list got out, it would provoke anything more than a yawn? Things like this circulate all the time. Nor is the world of the piano one in which news of this sort would "ruin" a career—not anymore. Maybe it's generational, but I simply fail to see why the matter has assumed, in his mind, such epic proportions, or why, if he's so worried about his professional colleagues finding out that he's queer, he put the list together in the first place.

I wish Greg Samuels hadn't shown my book to him. I sent him the ms. in confidence. Indeed, aside from a few friends here at Wellspring, you and Samuels are the only people who've seen the thing so far (and a rough thing it is at this stage, too). Nor is this the sort of behavior I would have expected from Samuels, who has always struck me as upright almost to a fault—if anything, too straight an arrow.

Fondly,
Jeff

■

SUBJ: **Greg Samuels**
DATE: Wednesday, July 19, 2000, 10:36:12 AM
FROM: ivorystuds@entropy.net
TO: jkwitt@wellspring.edu

Dear Jeff,

Greg is a very intelligent man, and a talented musician in his own right. I wouldn't worry too much about the fact that he gave your book to Willard: they are old friends, and I'm sure Greg felt he could trust Willard with it. I've known Greg for years, ever since he was an aspirant in his own right and used to come sometimes to parties at Lenny's apartment. He was very good-looking as a youth, and I remember that once when some old pouf made a pass at him, he nearly had a stroke—he was so naive, he didn't know what homosexuality was.

Fortunately he's loosened up a lot over the years, and though his home life's pretty starchy—you know, perfect wife, 3.5 kids, suburban house—he no longer bats an eyelash when the rest of us act outlandishly. At first, when he was hired to direct the Meerschaum, I was dubious—I didn't think he had the scholarly qualifications—but since then he's surprised me by doing a superb job.

Hugs,
Tim

▪

SUBJ: **Re: Greg Samuels**
DATE: Wednesday, July 19, 2000, 10:52:00 AM
FROM: jkwitt@wellspring.edu
TO: ivorystuds@entropy.net

Dear Tim,

While I appreciate the testimonial to Greg Samuels's good heart, I'm still very upset and angry that he would share the manuscript with *anyone* without first asking my permission. That kind of behavior, in my view, is inexcusable in a professional.

Fondly,
J.

·

SUBJ: **No Subject**
DATE: Wednesday, July 19, 2000, 11:45:31 AM
FROM: jkwitt@wellspring.edu
TO: gregory_samuels@meerschaum.org

Dear Mr. Samuels,

This morning I received an e-mail from Tim Kruger, who tells me that last week you gave a copy of the manuscript of my Otto Bulthaup biography to Willard Pearson. Needless to say, this came as something of a shock. When I asked you to read the manuscript, and you kindly agreed to do so, I thought it went without saying that the draft in question was meant for your eyes only. Instead it appears that you have been casually making photocopies and distributing them to all and sundry, which in my view amounts not only to a breach of civility, but of professional ethics. After all, this is only a working draft, and hence not intended for public consumption.

I believe you owe me, at the very least, an explanation.

Yours sincerely,
Jeffrey K. Witt
Assistant Professor of the Humanities
Wellspring University

·

SUBJ: **Re: No Subject**
DATE: Wednesday, July 19, 2000, 12:32:12 PM
FROM: gregory_samuels@meerschaum.org
TO: jkwitt@wellspring.edu

Dear Mr. Witt,

Thank you for your e-mail of earlier this morning. Despite whatever Mr. Kruger may have told you concerning Mr. Pearson, I can assure you that the charges you have made against me are completely unfounded. While Mr. Pearson did visit my office last Tuesday for the purposes of research, and while he did ask about your manuscript, which was sitting on my desk, aside from verifying that you had sent it to me for comment, I never discussed the matter with him, nor offered him the opportunity to look at anything more than the title page. At a certain point during our conversation, it is true, I was obliged to leave my office for approximately three to three and one half minutes, during which time Mr. Pearson might possibly have thumbed through the pages in question. Unless he is a devotee of Evelyn Wood, however, I cannot see how he would have been able to read the entire book in that brief span of time; nor did the pages appear to have been disturbed in any way during the period I was away from my desk.

I am not, nor have I ever been, in the habit of distributing photocopies of manuscripts sent to me in confidence to "all and sundry." Indeed, I have shared your manuscript with no one, not even my wife.

Let me suggest that in future you apprise yourself of the facts before sending e-mails of this sort, or at the very least make inquiries before making accusations.

Sincerely, Gregory C. Samuels, Director,
The Hilma Meerschaum Institute for Research on the Piano

▪

SUBJ: **Re: Re: No Subject**
DATE: Wednesday, July 19, 2000, 12:57:01 PM
FROM: jkwitt@wellspring.edu
TO: gregory_samuels@meerschaum.org

Dear Mr. Samuels,

Thank you very much for your prompt reply to my e-mail, and please accept my apologies if in it I seemed to cast aspersions on your character. Unfortunately, I took it for granted that what Mr. Kruger reported to me regarding Mr. Pearson was true. Obviously I was mistaken. Either Mr. Kruger was misinformed by Mr. Pearson, or he misunderstood what Mr. Pearson said. I am very sorry that I jumped to conclusions, and trust that this unfortunate misunderstanding will not affect our future relationship.

Yours sincerely,
Jeffrey K. Witt
Assistant Professor of the Humanities
Wellspring University

·

SUBJ: **Fwd: Re: No Subject**
DATE: Wednesday, July 19, 2000, 3:44:12 PM
FROM: jkwitt@wellspring.edu
TO: ivorystuds@entropy.net

Dear Tim,

Please find enclosed a copy of a letter I just received from Greg Samuels, to whom I wrote after you told me that he had shared my ms. with Willard Pearson. If Samuels is to be believed, then Willard Pearson must have gotten the ms. from another source—Might he have read your copy? Or perhaps he only pretended to have read the manuscript. Yet if that were the case, what would have led him to assume that I was such a gossip?

Any illumination you could provide would be much appreciated.

Jeff

·

SUBJ: **No Subject**
DATE: Thursday, July 20, 2000, 6:49:31 AM
FROM: ivorystuds@entropy.net
TO: jkwitt@wellspring.edu

Dear Jeff,

You should not have written to Greg Samuels. Now, as a result of your interference, my friendship with Willard—a friendship of twenty years' standing—is over. Greg wrote to Willard, who wrote to me. The fragile peace we had brokered was destroyed as he accused me of betraying his confidence not once but twice—the second time by telling you that he had read Greg's copy of your book. Now he fears that Greg will never trust him again. He also considers your hotheadedness with Greg further evidence that you are a dangerous person so far as the list is concerned. Which is to say nothing of Greg's annoyance with me!

Under the circumstances, you will understand that I can no longer possibly allow you to use my Bulthaup material, no matter what revisions you make. I shall be sending the ms. back to you shortly.

Tim

·

SUBJ: **Tim Kruger**
DATE: Friday, July 21, 2000, 2:14:03 PM
FROM: jkwitt@wellspring.edu
TO: willard.e.pearson@music.stblaise.edu

Dear Professor Pearson,

We have not met. I am the Bulthaup biographer with whom Tim Kruger recently elected to share a certain list that you and he had compiled—a decision that has provoked all sorts of ill will, and led, at least from what I gather, to the dissolution of your long friendship. Now I find myself in the unenviable position of suddenly being *persona non grata* with three colleagues none of whom I have ever met. Tim blames me for wrecking his friendship with you, Greg Samuels is affronted that I accused him of behaving irresponsibly, and you consider me an untrustworthy gossip—and all this thanks to a list I never asked to see, read with only the mildest interest, and erased from my hard drive no more than half an hour after receiving it.

What has happened? Initially I approached Tim Kruger only because mutual friends had told me he owned interesting photos of Bulthaup that I could find nowhere else. But now, because of the list, Tim has virtually prohibited me from ever seeing, much less using, any of his material. In addition, I appear to have offended Greg Samuels by complaining that he had shown you my manuscript. But if Greg did not give you a copy, then who did?

I hope that in writing to you this way I am not simply deepening the hole in which I find myself. My goals are simple: I want to get along with people, and I want my book to be described accurately.

Yours sincerely,
Jeff Witt

SUBJ: **Re: Tim Kruger**
DATE: Saturday, July 22, 2000, 8:59:47 AM
FROM: willard.e.pearson@music.stblaise.edu
TO: jkwitt@wellspring.edu

Dear Mr. Witt,

Your letter saddened me. Obviously much about this case has been misrepresented to you, most notably the part I play. I shall try to clarify things as best I can.

To begin at the beginning, it is true that about sixteen years ago Tim Kruger and I began compiling a list, mostly for our own amusement, of gay and lesbian pianists. This game had its origins in an age considerably less lenient in these matters than our own, and during which homosexual pianists assumed that exposure would lead to the decimation of their careers. In his capacity as a premier antiquarian in the field of the piano, and in mine as President of the Paderewski Society, Tim and I were privy to certain information few other people possessed, and we began to exchange knowledge. Soon the list had grown into a document of considerable size, and when e-mail came along, the labor of its tracking and honing was greatly eased.

I must emphasize, however, that from the moment of its inception, the list was a private document. Rarely would Tim and I share it with anyone, and if one of us did, he would always ask the other's permission first. This is why his decision to send you the list took me aback: he had neglected to ask me first whether I approved.

On Tuesday, July 11, it is true, I did go to visit Greg Samuels at the Meerschaum Institute. We spent twenty minutes or so talking in his office, and in the course of our conversation I did notice the manuscript of a Bulthaup biography on his desk. As I am quite interested in Bulthaup, I inquired of Greg as to its provenance. In reply he told me who you were, and that you had sent him the book because you wanted his advice on the project. *At no time, however, did he offer to give me a copy of the manuscript, nor did I at any point ask for one, or even thumb through his.*

On to the following week: on his way back from a swap meet in Camden, Tim Kruger stopped by St. Blaise, where we had lunch at the faculty club. As we were beginning our first course, I mentioned my recent visit to the Meerschaum Institute, at which point we discussed Greg Samuels for some minutes, our conversation inevitably leading to your Bulthaup project, about which I inquired as to his familiarity. Immediately Tim became flustered and said (I am sorry to have to repeat this) that indeed he did know of the book, that you and he had of late established what he called an "e-mail intimacy" and that he considered you to be the worst kind of gossip, a "gay radical" whose only real interest was in outing Bulthaup. In his view, you were absolutely the wrong person to write such a book, which ought to have been penned by another friend of his, a psychiatrist, since only a psychiatrist could possibly understand Bulthaup's "childlike" nature. I listened carefully, expressing amazement and consternation at the appropriate intervals, until our entrees arrived. At this point Tim "broke down," and announced that he had a confession to make: driven to recklessness by what he called the "romantic intensity" of your e-mail rapport, he had sent you the list. Naturally I was surprised, and after questioning the wisdom of sharing the list with someone he himself had just described as a gossip, asked him to explain his actions. In response he blurted out apologies, insisted that he would never forgive himself, and asked me if I could find it in my heart to forgive him. I told him that I could, but that I would appreciate it if he would write to you, urging you not to show the list to anyone. He agreed.

That was the last I heard of the case until this past Wednesday, when to my amazement I received an outraged e-mail from Greg Samuels, accusing me of lying and threatening to take legal action if I did not immediately retract the charge that he had given me a copy of your book. He also sent me your original e-mail to him. Deeply consternated, I wrote immediately to Tim, who telephoned by way of reply, insisting pitifully that he had never told you that I had got the manuscript from Greg, that you had invented the connection in order to destroy our friendship, etc. I did not believe him, and told him so in no uncertain terms. As you may have guessed by now, this is by no means the first time that I have found myself in this kind of muddle thanks to Tim. By nature he is a machinator—he cannot help himself—and as I have learned over the course of many years on this planet, a machinator's most dangerous skill is his capacity to seduce others into doing his dirty work for him. Once Tim has one ensnared, in other words, one will often find oneself behaving in much the same way that he does, without even realizing that one is doing it. Sincerity and honesty become well nigh impossible. He had led me down this ugly path too often, and this time I resolved no longer to tolerate such behavior, and to end our friendship.

That, then, is what happened. I'm very sorry that Tim decided to involve you in such an unpleasant, if trivial, episode, and even more, sorry that you suffered over the case as you so obviously did: it is clear that you are a man of conscience, and to the sort of tactics Tim employs, unfortunately, those of conscience are particularly susceptible. It was not until I received your e-mail, however, that his motives in enacting such a petty drama became clear to me. As you know, Tim is both by profession and character an antiquarian: that is to say, he sees his own value mostly in terms of the things he possesses.

By expressing a desire to use his material, you flattered him, yet you also set off an old fear that no one was interested in him for himself, only for what he owned, etc. This was why he set up so many hoops for you to jump through in order to win his trust. And yet I'm fairly certain that in the end he had no intention of giving you the photos, for fear that once you had them, you would lose all interest in him.

Well, that is the whole sorry story. Try not to let it bother you too much. So far as the photos themselves go, I have never seen them. No doubt they exist, no doubt they are fascinating, and yet with Tim it's often hard to distinguish between truth and bluff. He could have a trove, he could have a single snapshot.

All best,
Willard Pearson

•

SUBJ: **Re: Re: Tim Kruger**
DATE: Saturday, July 22, 2000, 4:03:42 PM
FROM: jkwitt@wellspring.edu
TO: willard.e.pearson@music.stblaise.edu

Dear Willard (if I may),

Your letter came as a great surprise to me. Yes, I am comforted to know that all of this was less my fault than I thought at first. Still, the whole affair has left such a bitter aftertaste in my mouth that I can't help but wonder if, in interpreting Bulthaup's life as I have, I might simply be displaying the same will to misapprehend that you ascribe to Tim. Perhaps the book really is just souped-up gossip, as he claimed.

It hadn't previously occurred to me that Tim might have

any emotional investment in our relationship—after all, he has no idea what I look like, has never heard my voice, etc.— yet going over his e-mails in light of your observations, I see that I might have been missing the key element all along.

I will continue to trudge along with the biography, albeit sorrowfully, the wiser for having suffered.

Yours,
Jeff

•

SUBJ: **Bulthaup**
DATE: Monday, October 23, 2000, 4:01:27 AM
FROM: ivorystuds@entropy.net
TO: jkwitt@wellspring.edu

Dear Jeff,

How long it's been since I've heard from you! Are you well? I've been thinking about you since last week, when I happened to be at the Meerschaum Institute, sitting with Greg Samuels in his office. There on the desk was the ms. of that new collection of essays on Schumann and the "queer musicology." When I asked Greg about it, he pushed it my way and said I could have it, that it was "garbage," etc. Which set me to wondering whether he and Willard might have been lying all along about what they did with *your* ms.

And speaking of your book, the other day I saw an announcement of its forthcoming publication. Congratulations! I see that it's now scheduled to come out in April—plenty of time to include some of my material, if you're still interested. Looking back, I realize I may have been a bit liverish about the list business . . .

Will you be up in these parts any time soon? If so, perhaps we could meet for lunch and discuss the issues involved. It would be a great pleasure finally to meet you. And your book will only be the poorer if it does not include the pictures in my files.

Hugs,
Tim

HEAPED EARTH

To CELEBRATE her husband's latest movie, a biography of
Franz Liszt starring the much-admired John Ray, Jr., Lilia
Wardwell decided to throw a party. The studio had high
hopes that the film might win the Oscar that year; *Ben-Hur*
had won the year before, and the word was that this time
something more intimate might take the prize, so a party was
just the thing. The theme would be Romanticism. A pianist,
done up in Liszt's soutane, would play wonderful music, while
waiters in nineteenth-century livery circulated with trays of
hors d'oeuvres. Also, in addition to the usual Hollywood
crowd, she would invite Stravinsky and his wife, Vera.

She called her husband at the studio, and said, "Frank, I
need a pianist for the party. Any ideas?"

"I'll see what I can do," he answered. As it happened,
there *was* a pianist around the studio, an immigrant called
Kusnezov who, people said, could play any song without the
music, just by hearing it hummed. Whenever a piano scene
was required, it was Kusnezov's hands that were filmed; in
the Liszt movie his hands were substituted for those of John
Ray, Jr.

From the associate producer, Wardwell got Kusnezov's number. He expected he would have to do some prodding, as in his experience artist types tended to be sensitive. Instead Kusnezov proved to be extremely cordial and, having first inquired with delicacy as to his fee, agreed instantly to the job—providing, if it was no inconvenience, that he be paid in advance, and in cash. From this Wardwell deduced that he either gambled, drank, or had an ex-wife pressing him for alimony.

At seven o'clock on the evening of the party Kusnezov arrived at the Wardwells' house and knocked, as instructed, at the service entrance. In the kitchen a dozen or so waiters were fighting their way into tight suits from the studio's costume bank, while the cook and her assistants spooned caviar onto toast points, and cut sandwiches into the shapes of playing card suits, and emptied canned hearts of palms onto silver platters. Having first explained who he was to a man in butler's livery, Kusnezov waited quietly by the refrigerator until Mrs. Wardwell appeared. She was a woman of heft, with a shelflike bosom and béchamel-colored hair. Her perfume commingled perversely with the cooking smells. "Mr. Kusnezov, so glad to meet you," she said, offering a moisturized hand, and gave him the once-over. His appearance worried her. After all, though he was wearing the requisite soutane, Kusnezov—it could not be denied—was old. When he leaned forward to kiss her hand, his breath smelled of liquor. Also Liszt (and John Ray, Jr.) had those wonderful, Samson-like locks, whereas Kusnezov was mostly bald, with just a few watery hairs brushed forward over his pate; hardly what she'd envisioned when she'd planned the party.

Still, she was determined to be game and, clasping his hand in hers, took him into the living room, which was harp-shaped, sweeping, with ribbed walls. "I'm told the acoustics here are sublime," she said, leading him across the polished floor to the piano. Most of the furniture—Scandinavian, of light wood and leather—had been pushed up against the walls. As for the glossy white piano, it stood on a platform before a row of louvered floor-to-ceiling windows, through the glass of which Kusnezov could see a blue swimming pool refracting the sunset, a barbecue pit, an array of houses in crisp shades of pink and green spilling down the hills toward an ocean you could still make out in those days before smog.

They stepped up onto the platform. "I trust our humble instrument will be to your liking," Mrs. Wardwell said, positioning herself beside the piano like a soprano. "Do sit. It's a Steinway, of course. My husband wanted a cheaper brand, but I said, 'Frank, Steinway is the instrument of the immortals.'"

"And do you play yourself?" Kusnezov asked, adjusting, with a finicky backward motion of the hands, the height of the white leather stool.

"Not seriously, I'm afraid. Still, I do enjoy tinkling out a bit of Chopin now and then . . . Oh, I had the tuner up this morning."

Having first wiped his hands, which were slippery with her moisturizer, onto his handkerchief, Kusnezov sat down and played a scale.

"A lovely tone," he said. "Not too bright."

"Fine. As for the music, as I'm sure my husband explained, it should be romantic, in keeping with the film. Still, this is a party, so we don't want everyone getting down in the dumps, do we?"

"No, madame."

"So nothing dreary. I would be most grateful."

He bowed his head.

"Oh, haven't you brought any music?"

"There is no need, madame."

"Of course you're welcome to use any of *our* scores. My daughter Elise can turn pages."

"There is no need, madame."

"Fine." She rubbed her hands together. "Well, the guests should be arriving in a half an hour or so. Oh, would you like a drink? Burt"—she signaled the bartender—"get Mr. Kusnezov a drink. What will you have?"

"A whiskey and soda. Straight up."

"A whiskey and soda, Burt. And now if you'll excuse me, I must check on things in the kitchen."

He nodded. She left. Burt brought Kusnezov his drink, which he guzzled fast. Smiling, Burt mixed him a second one.

The doorbell rang. The man in butler's livery admitted a group of five into the foyer—all dear friends of Mrs. Wardwell whom she had asked to come early, to "break the ice." Sitting at the piano, Kusnezov played some Chopin waltzes. The next guest to arrive was Lee Remick. And then Mrs. Wardwell strode in, and Mr. Wardwell, who had been drinking alone in his study, and their daughter Elise, who scowled through thick glasses. Everyone except Elise chatted amiably as Mrs. Wardwell allowed her gaze occasionally to rest with approval upon the figure of Kusnezov, who had moved from the waltzes to Liszt's late evocation of the fountains at the Villa d'Este.

After forty minutes, he took a break. Burt mixed him a third whiskey and soda. In the meantime John Ray, Jr., had arrived, an event which had provoked the assembled to burst into a round of applause. Square-jawed, from Texas, the young actor had large hands and thick, blond hair that to his regret, he had recently been forced to cut in preparation for his next role, a navy lieutenant. Although his official escort for the evening was a lesbian starlet named Lorna Baskin, he had made a secret arrangement to rendezvous at the party with his lover of the moment, the young professor of musicology at UCLA who had served as musical advisor for the Liszt movie. As instructed, the professor came alone, and late. Kusnezov was by now taking his second break. Most of the guests—Hollywood socialites and actors, though alas no Stravinskys—were out on the patio. In the living room a group of studio executives took advantage of the lull to share Cuban cigars and cut deals. As for Kusnezov, he was leaning against the bar, talking with Burt about the dog races.

The professor asked Burt for a screwdriver. He was a Bostonian of thirty-five, new in southern California, having taken his position at UCLA only the year before. In the weirdly artificial atmosphere of the party he appeared himself to be in costume, with his bow tie and eastern tweeds. His face melancholic (for he did not see his lover), he peered out the door at the humming crowd, before strolling over to examine the piano. After a few minutes Kusnezov stepped past him and took his place again. They nodded at each other.

Kusnezov started to play—a Chopin nocturne in C minor that, as it happened, was one of the professor's favorites. He sat down to listen. All at once, and quickly, the music carried him away from that ample California living room with its ribbed walls, and into a small house, a winter house, where a coal fire was burning. There was grief in the air, not fresh, but a few years old, its presence vague as the smell of cooking. No one dared address it. No one dared acknowledge the sprite of memory that danced in the heavy, soot-thickened air. Then the professor smiled, for now he felt sure of something he had long suspected: that Chopin had written this nocturne for a sister who had died in childhood. In Kusnezov's hands, the supposition became a certainty.

Burt was silent. Even the executives fell silent. As for the professor, he was remembering a poem by Oscar Wilde, written also in memory of a sister dead in childhood, a sister buried:

Tread lightly, she is near
  Under the snow,
Speak gently, she can hear
  The daisies grow.

From the patio John Ray, Jr., entered the room. He was talking to John Wayne. Their loud conversation dimmed only once they recognized that people were listening to the music, at which point they stopped and stood by the door, smiling respectfully.

The professor looked at John Ray, Jr. John Ray, Jr., looked over the professor.

Peace, peace, she cannot hear
  Lyre or sonnet,
All my life's buried here,
  Heap earth upon it.

The prelude ended. No one applauded. Once again, Kusnezov got up and got a drink, as did John Ray, Jr., John Wayne, and the professor. The lovers did not acknowledge each other.

Only once the two actors had returned to the patio did the professor dare approach Kusnezov. His eyes revealed his knowledge—that he had heard; that he had recognized.

"That was magnificent," he said.

"Yes, it was," Kusnezov answered simply.

"May I ask you a question?" The professor stepped closer. "Who *are* you?"

"Who *was* I? you mean. That is the apposite point."

"You mean before the war . . ."

Kusnezov shook his head. "The war is not to blame. I came to live in this country thirty years ago."

"Then what happened?"

"What happened? What happened?" The pianist laughed. And meanwhile Jane Russell had come into the room, Mrs. Wardwell had come into the room, bringing with her a loud, invasive odor of perfume. She shot Kusnezov a glance, the meaning of which was obvious: *Get back to work, and no more of the depressing stuff.*

"I must go," he said to the professor. And putting down his empty glass, he returned to the piano.

The Marble Quilt

Via in Selci

"Do you know of anyplace the professor might have gone to eat beans?"

I look down at the *maresciallo*'s hands, spread languidly across the gunmetal surface of the desk. His nails are neatly pared. He wears a gold wedding ring; a brilliant gold chain-link bracelet is draped loosely over the bones of his wrist. To his left, on the edge of the desk, sits one of his deputies. To his right, another of his deputies takes down my statement on an old computer, the letters pulsing green against a black background. Other *carabinieri* come and go, listen for a few minutes, light cigarettes or snap the tops of Coke cans. All of them are Roman, in their early thirties or younger, with glossy dark hair and thick wrists. This is the homicide division, and I am here to give testimony.

"Beans?" I repeat.

"Yes, beans."

"Well, I know Tom was very fond of the Obitorio—the 'morgue'—that pizzeria down on Viale Trastevere, next to McDonald's. Of course, *obitorio* is just the nickname he gave it, because of the tables. They're made of marble, so . . ."

"Oh, of course. The pizzas are very good there."

"They also serve beans. It's one of their specialties."

The *maresciallo's* deputy types; reads aloud, "The professor often ate at a pizzeria on Viale Trastevere that he called the 'morgue,' because of the marble tables. It was known for its beans."

"Is that all right with you?" the *maresciallo* says.

"Yes, that's fine," I say.

More than once, during this interview, I've asked questions about Tom's murder, and been told, ever so politely, that I am here to provide information, not solicit it. Nonetheless, some of the *maresciallo's* questions reveal things. For instance: Did Tom make a habit of drinking red wine? Had he ever mentioned a trip to Tunisia? Where might he have gone to eat beans?

Not necessarily things I need, or want, to know.

Other questions merely perplex me, add to the air of confusion and hopelessness that surrounds the investigation.

"When you visited him in his apartment, did he ever ask you to take off your shoes?"

"Did he ever make reference to someone called Ludovico?"

"Do you know if he had friends on Borgo Sant'Angelo?"

"No," I answer. Repeatedly, no.

They've assured me, from the very start, that I'm not a suspect. After all, I have my alibi. When Tom was murdered, I was nowhere near his apartment; I was with some American businessmen, giving them a tour of the Vatican museum.

Still, alibis can be fabricated. Friends will lie.

"Did he ever mention an article he was writing about the floors at San Clemente?"

Actually, the article about the floors at San Clemente he did mention. It was part of his new life, his Italian life, in which I played, at best, a marginal role. In this life Tom taught English, and wrote the occasional travel piece, and devoted much of his time to exploring some of the more arcane corners of Roman history; thus his fascination with church floors, in which hand-cut pieces of marble—hexagons and triangles, circles and diamonds and teardrops—were arranged into precise geometries. Speckled deep red porphyry, green *serpentino*, butterscotch-colored *giallo antico*: "like the squares of a quilt," he once told me. "Only instead of cloth, the quilt is made of marble. A marble quilt."

"Not only San Clemente," I tell the *maresciallo*. "Also Santa Maria in Cosmedin, and San Giovanni in Laterano, and Santa Maria Maggiore."

His deputy types; reads. "The professor spoke to me of an article he was writing about the floors of Roman churches."

"He had been living in Rome for three years, is that correct?"

"Yes."

"Obviously your Italian is fluent."

"It's my job. I'm an interpreter."

"Of course. My compliments. In your view—that is, speaking as an authority on language—did the professor speak a good Italian?"

"Not bad," I say, "considering that he only started studying once he arrived here."

"Yet his mother was from Italy."

"She was born in Naples."

"Actually in Caserta. But that is very close to Naples. In your view, was the professor's Italian sufficiently fluent that he would never have misunderstood what another person was telling him?"

"Misunderstood?"

"That is to say, might he have misunderstood what another person said to him, if the other person were speaking Italian?"

"He might have."

The *maresciallo* cracks his knuckles. Then he removes his ring and polishes it with his shirtsleeve. Then he takes a cigarette from a pack lying open on the desk. "Do you smoke?"

"No, thank you."

He lights the cigarette.

"How often do you come to Rome?"

"Two or three times a year."

"For work?"

"Usually. But sometimes just for pleasure."

"Did you ever come specifically to visit the professor?"

"A few times."

"And the last time?"

"I was working."

"Where were you working?"

"PepsiCo was hosting a conference for its European executives."

"Why didn't you stay with the professor? You did on other occasions."

"There was no need. A hotel room was provided for me."

"And if a hotel room hadn't been provided for you?"

"I might have stayed with Tom. But probably not."

"Why not?"

"Well, his apartment was very far out from where I was working. Also, when you used to live with someone—when for years you shared a bed with someone—it can feel awkward, sleeping on the living room sofa. It can feel . . . wrong."

His deputy—the one sitting on the edge of the desk—smiles in sympathy. Clearly he knows of what I speak.

"How long did you live with the professor?"

"We lived together for ten years, five years ago."

"In San Francisco?"

"Yes."

"And now you live in Düsseldorf."

"Yes."

He opens a folder; examines what appears to be a list of questions; writes a note to himself.

"When you did stay with the professor—on the sofa—did he ever make advances toward you?"

"Good heavens, no! We were well beyond that."

"Did he ever bring someone home to share his bed?"

"Of course not! Tom didn't do that sort of thing."

The *maresciallo* raises his eyebrows. I wince.

"What I mean," I correct, "is that he never *admitted* to doing that sort of thing. Certainly he would never have brought anyone home when he had a friend staying. He claimed to live like a monk."

The deputy at the computer types; reads, "When I came to Rome, it was usually for work, in which case I stayed at a hotel. When I came for pleasure, I sometimes stayed with the professor, which made me uncomfortable as a consequence of our having once lived together, in San Francisco. The professor never made advances toward me, however, nor was I concerned that he might bring someone home to share his bed, because he never admitted to doing that sort of thing, and in my opinion, would never have done that sort of thing when he had a friend visiting. He told me he lived like a monk."

"Change the last line," the *maresciallo* says. "I don't like 'He told me.' Change it to 'He claimed.'"

"He claimed to live like a monk," the deputy repeats.

I wonder if in America cops would ever be so fastidious about their prose style.

Oh, what a nasty business an autopsy must be! Not that there was ever a worry about preserving "the integrity of the body," or any of that New Agey nonsense we used to hear in San Francisco—not in this case, since by the time the police broke down the door and found it, Tom's body had very little in the way of integrity left. He was tied to the kitchen table. His skull had been smashed in. He had been rotting for seven days.

By then, of course, I was back in Düsseldorf. During the last forty-eight hours before my flight, I must have called him a dozen times. And a dozen more times from Düsseldorf. Always his answering machine picked up. The *carabinieri* listened to the messages, then got my number out of his Filofax. They were very nice. They never said I *had* to come back to Rome—only that if I were willing to, it would be a great help to their investigation. Otherwise the German police could interview me by proxy.

Naturally I agreed to come back.

Tom's San Francisco friends, those couples whose children he had baby-sat and whose dinner parties he had catered, started calling me. Over the phone they spoke cautiously of the need to "protect Tom's reputation." Obviously they'd seen the newspaper articles, the ones in which his Rome friends, the correspondents, made pretty obvious what everyone took for granted anyway: that he had been done in by a hustler, some Romanian or Albanian he'd picked up at the station and brought home. Sex, then a beating, or perhaps sex that included a beating, followed by a blunt object smashed against his skull. (Was it perhaps the obelisk of *semesanto*, the red brecciated with chunks of white, like pieces of fat in a salami?)

And then, somewhere in those hours, the red wine. And the shoes. And the beans.

Did I mention that his nose had been broken—*before* he was killed?

With his San Francisco friends, it wasn't a question of what they themselves believed; it was a question of what they wanted other people to believe: a matter, it seemed, less of protecting Tom's reputation than their own. After all, they had trusted him with their children. To have it revealed that Tom had been conning them the whole time, that in truth he was no different from any other faggot—this would have been too embarrassing. So they decided to take the line that the police and the journalists were wrong; worse, that they were homophobic, to assume that just because Tom had been beaten and bludgeoned to death, his killer had to be some lowlife he'd dragged in off the street. "Maybe those others," his friend Gina told me over the phone, referring to the twenty-two homosexual men who have been murdered in Rome over the last decade, "but not Tom." To Gina, the important thing seemed to be that his name never be added to that statistic; that the number remain twenty-two.

"It had to be something else. What if he surprised a burglar?"

"But nothing was taken."

"Or maybe it was someone he was having an affair with. A lover."

So was it better to have been murdered by a lover, I wondered, by someone you trusted, than by an immigrant you had picked up in the men's room at the train station?

That mysterious men's room, where the urinals were divided by glass partitions—glass, of all things.

Tom told me that. Not that he'd ever been there himself, he added: it was only from his friend Pepe, who frequented such places, that he garnered this intelligence. Pepe, according to Tom, spent much of his time in the park on the Monte Caprino. That kind of park. Only once had Tom accompanied him there, under duress, after a boring lunch party. He noticed the plants, not the loiterers. "Oh, that's spleenwort—*asplenium filicinophyta!*" he told Pepe. "Wait here while I go home and get my Japanese pruning shears." And Pepe waited, and Tom went home, and came back with his Japanese pruning shears. For a cutting.

Soon a rumor began to circulate in San Francisco that he had been having an affair with a fellow English teacher, and that very likely it was this teacher who had murdered him. A lover's quarrel.

If this was true, I could well understand the teacher's motives. Back when I lived with Tom, I too found myself tempted, on more than one occasion, to pick up a blunt object; to smash in his skull; to break his nose.

Oh, he could be such a hypocrite! And he met a hypocrite's just end. Like the hypochondriac who finally gets something fatal. In the angry weeks right after I heard the news, when Gina and her husband, Tony, and all sorts of other people were calling every night to talk about "damage control" (they actually used that phrase), a few times—just to horrify them—I said, "Come on, folks. What do you really think? Don't you really think he got what he deserved?"

Wool Street

A few months before he died, I went back to San Francisco. I went to look at the house we used to own together. High on a

San Francisco hilltop, the fog woolly, rolling across the sky in grand, sluggish banks. And this was appropriate, because the street on which we had lived was called Wool Street.

Back then, the house was yellow. Now it was white. Pristine. There were Jaguars and Acuras and Jeeps parked along the curb: not the battered pickup trucks and Volkswagen Beetles of our day. For when we lived there, Bernal Heights was a run-down neighborhood, even a bad neighborhood. At that point, of course, I couldn't have afforded in a million years to buy back our old home. Now that San Francisco was the dot-com capital of the world, even a funny, creaky little house like ours, with no backyard and a crumbling foundation, went for $700,000 or $800,000. Or more.

A strange sensation, to be priced out of a place you once thought of as yours. But then again, one of the lessons of marble—one of the lessons Tom taught me—is that ownership of any kind is a dream.

Were any of them still around, our old neighbors? Walking across the street, I peered at a letterbox: LOPEZ, it said. But it should have said, COOPER.

Where was Dominic Cooper, whom I barely knew, but who sometimes waved to me, walking past with his dog? An Old English sheepdog, the fur on her head pulled back into a topknot so that it wouldn't get into her eyes.

Dead, I supposed. Most of them were, our neighbors, either because, a dozen years ago, they were already old, or because they were faggots.

Bad faggots.

Tom and I were not bad faggots, so we remained alive. For the moment.

Tom was the good faggot. He wrote children's books that never got published. (Not getting them published—this was an essential part of being the good faggot.) He rolled his own pasta, and volunteered at an AIDS hospice, and never went to any of the bars or sex clubs for which San Francisco was infamous—oh no! Instead he lived with me. We had matching gold rings. We told people we'd met at a party in New York, when really I'd seen his dick before I ever saw his face, emerging inquisitively from under the partition between two stalls in the men's room at Bloomingdale's.

Most of Tom's friends were young marrieds. They trusted their children with him. Not only that, they made a fuss over how much they trusted their children with him. "Tom's so good with kids!" they'd say. "He's Justin/Samuel/Max's favorite babysitter. When we go away, Justin/Samuel/Max *loves* spending the weekend with Tom."

In other words, not a child molester. To leave their little boys with Tom was to make a sally into that favorite West Coast game of More Liberal Than Thou. It was to flaunt their tolerance in the same way that a few years later, when they got rich, they would flaunt their immunity to greed. Not BMWs, not Manolo Blahnik pumps. Instead Birkenstocks, SUVs, and several million in stock options.

It goes without saying that they never asked Tom to babysit their *daughters*. What would have been the point of that?

He was godfather to something like eleven little boys, at least three of whom were named after him.

And now all those Justins and Samuels and Maxes—yes, and Toms—they must be teenagers. I wonder if they remember the June mornings when he would take them to watch the Gay Pride parade. Hoist them onto his shoulders. Their parents alongside, smiling at the drag queens done up as Carol Burnett or Debbie Reynolds.

And of course, when the coalition from the North American Man/Boy Love Association marched by, all those clerkish men in suits and ties, what did his friends think? They never said a word. Instead they kept their eyes averted, until the NAMBLA guys had filed past, and there were safe, funny drag queens again.

Our house on Wool Street could not have been more unassuming. Like a child's drawing of a house, Tom used to say. It was situated as close to nowhere as it is probably possible to get, on a neutral hill near a characterless intersection somewhere in the midst of that vast anonymity of streets no tourist ever drives, and that San Franciscans call the Mission.

I worked as an editor for a leftist magazine that was published by a foundation: a slick magazine to which rich people subscribed out of guilt, but did not read. Tom ran a catering business, and was devoted to the domestic. He could spend weeks searching for just the right toilet brush to match the bathroom fixtures. When I finished showering in the mornings, he'd sometimes wait until he thought I wasn't looking, and then stealthily adjust the towels so that they draped in just the right way.

Once the discovery of a food stain on the bedspread made him freeze in the middle of a kiss, mutter, "I'll just be a second," and pad off naked to the kitchen for spot remover.

You see, this was San Francisco in the late eighties, and many of the people we knew had died.

Two of our neighbors had died. And a Greek man who ran a deli. And the editor of the magazine I worked for. Even our doctor had died.

So I suppose that was why we bought our little house, our "crypto-dream-house," as Tom used to call it, quoting Elizabeth Bishop. By establishing and guarding this shelter, he must have hoped he could protect us both from the stained sheets and fouled toilets and soggy mattresses that are the necessary accessories of death.

Later, when I saw the photographs of Saddam Hussein's atom bomb–proof bunker, with its marble bathrooms and carpeting and candelabrums, I thought, yes, of course—something along those lines.

People in San Francisco talked a lot in those days about "grief management." Now I look back, and it seems to me that grief was managing *us* all that time: grief, the puppeteer, cool behind the curtain.

When, I wondered, would grief pull off its mask, switch on the light, burst into the room in troops, like cops at a stakeout?

I thought it was going to happen one night in 1988. We were getting dressed for the opera when the telephone rang. It was Tom's friend Caroline, and she was calling to tell him that Ernie, with whom he had once lived for half a dozen years, had died an hour earlier.

"Vincent," he said to me, putting the phone down. Nothing more, but I knew. I was in the middle of tying my tie, and I remember that I stopped, the tie hanging half-looped around my neck, like a noose, and without saying a word I walked over to Tom and held him, tightly, and then we just stood like that, me holding him and his body shaking, but he never cried, or said a word. And then we let go of each other; I finished tying my tie. And we went to the opera.

The opera that night was a concert version of *Dido and Aeneas*. A famed soprano stood before us, resplendent in feathers and white satin, and sang Dido's deathbed aria:

When I am laid, laid in earth,
Let my wrongs create
No trouble, no trouble, in thy breast;
Remember me, remember me,
But ah, forget my fate!

So grief sang, in her feathery gown. Bejeweled grief. *Couture* grief. And it seemed that she was looking at us as she sang, and what were we, after all, but two well-heeled faggots in the last decade of a century we had no assurance we would see the end of?

Whose fate, in any case, would doubtless be forgotten?

How can it be that I've neglected to say what he looked like? That is, what he looked like when he was still alive.

Well, he looked like . . . the good faggot. Handsome, in a neutered sort of way. He always clipped the hairs out of his nose. His skin was unblemished, his nails tidy as the *maresciallo*'s.

He was not tall. Gray streaks ran through his black hair—thick, dark hair, a fringe benefit of Italian blood. Whereas I was going bald early.

Of course, the thing about Italian men is that often, no matter how handsome they are in youth, they age very badly. I suppose I should have been alerted to this likelihood the one time I met Tom's father, who was a second-generation immigrant from Sicily. Although he wasn't yet seventy, he had a face like a shar-pei's. His teeth were yellow from smoking. Moles bloomed on his cheeks. Yet his eyes, his mouth, even his nose—these were Tom's.

It was only after we broke up that his looks really started to go—as if inheritance, after waiting in the wings for decades, had suddenly decided to step forward and stake its claim: I gave this to you, I take this from you. The blessing and curse of the genes.

A year had passed during which we had not seen each other—he had just moved to Rome, I had just moved to Düsseldorf—when out of the blue, I got an assignment to work a film festival in Rome. So naturally I called and told

him I was coming. He insisted on meeting me at the airport.
When I stepped off the plane, a jowly little man ran up to me,
holding a bouquet of violets.

I blinked. Could this be Tom? Since we'd last seen each
other he'd gained what looked like forty pounds. His hair had
thinned in front, and to compensate, he'd grown it long in the
back. He had a ratty beard.

A few days later, while I was waiting to meet him near
Torre Argentina, I got to talking with an old lady who came
there to feed the stray cats. It seemed that she was one of a
group of women—*gattaie,* they were called—who had set up a
makeshift cat clinic down among the ruins, a sort of squat-
ter's hospital. The city was trying to evict them, she said, because many of the cats had feline AIDS and people were
afraid of catching it. ("A ludicrous notion," she added, "since
they are separate diseases. But Italians are not very interested
in facts.")

A cat approached—fat and white, blind in one eye. She
picked him up and handed him to me. "We call him Nelson,"
she said, "after the admiral."

I smiled at Nelson. His blind eye was clouded and milky,
like a piece of Carrara marble. I stroked his neck and he
purred. Then Tom appeared, waving at me from across the
street. I put Nelson down. "My friend is here," I told the
woman.

She peered. "Is that him? He's very ugly," she observed, in
that mild, uninflected tone that a Roman adopts when he
informs you—meaning no offense—that you've gotten quite
a bit fatter since the last time you saw each other.

Bidding her goodbye, I hurried to meet him. "Sorry I'm
late," he said. "I got held up by one of my students. Pierluigi."
He groaned. "Those double names—Pierluigi, Piergiorgio—
they'll get you every time."

"Handsome?"

"*Mamma mia.* And to make matters even worse, a Fascist. I mean, a major Fascist. 'The man I most admire in the world is Jean-Marie Le Pen,' he wrote in his paper. So naturally I failed him. And then his father called. And then . . ."

"What?"

"Well . . . it was all very tiresome."

We turned a corner, and went into a trattoria. In Rome all social occasions with Tom took place in restaurants. "I only just found this one last week," he said. "It's got the best pasta and chickpeas."

The trattoria was stuffy, narrow. We were led to a back table, far from any window. Tom ordered for us—pasta and chickpeas, naturally—and soon enough two bowls of soup arrived, carried by a handsome young waiter with whom he appeared to be on a first-name basis. The first name, in this case, being Enzo.

"Taste that rosemary," he said, his eyes on Enzo's back.

I tasted. Believe me, I know something about cooking, and no rosemary had ever come near that soup.

After a while, the trattoria got busy. A crowd had gathered in the foyer, businessmen and neighborhood shopkeepers, all waiting for tables to open up, while Tom, with a kind of obstinate disregard, remained rooted to his chair even though we had long since finished our meal. The coffee came. He took a long time stirring in his sugar, then asked me about Düsseldorf. Did I have much of a social life there? Were my friends American or German? What was the food like?

Something of a social life, I answered. I had both German and American friends. The food was . . . German.

And my apartment?

I leaned back. I was wondering when he was going to work up the courage to ask the question that was obviously on

his mind—that is, was I "seeing" anyone in Düsseldorf—
when Enzo appeared, and asked very sheepishly if we might
mind paying up and getting out. As we could see, people were
waiting.

Tom's neck stiffened. "What? You're asking us to leave?"

"I'm sorry, *signore,* but as you see—"

"That's hardly the way to encourage a regular customer,
Enzo. Why, for all you know I might be a journalist, about to
write a review of your trattoria for an important American
newspaper!"

Enzo spread out his hands. "*Signore,* what can I do? How
can I vindicate myself?"

Tom smiled. He pointed to his cheek. "A kiss," he said.

Straightening his back, Enzo laughed, as if in disbelief.
Then he looked over his shoulder. Then he bent down and
kissed Tom, very quickly, on the cheek.

"Might he have misunderstood what another person said
to him, if the other person were speaking Italian?"

Of course, his claims to have no interest in "that sort of
thing" begged the important question of what he was doing
in that men's room in the first place.

"Well," he said, "you know that whenever I'm in New York
I always go to Bloomingdale's. And I was shopping for sheets,
when nature called. Normally I would never have stayed,
once I'd realized that it was *that* kind of men's room. But then
your socks caught my eye."

"My socks?"

"They were all I could see under the door to the stall. Blue
and red argyle. I liked them."

"So that was the only reason you went into the next stall?
Because you liked my socks?"

"I suppose."

"And if it hadn't been for my socks?"

"I would have left. You know I can't bear that sort of atmosphere."

"But wait a minute . . . that means that our whole relationship—our whole history together—owes to the fact that you liked my socks."

"I guess you could put it that way," Tom said. "Not that I ever would."

It is worth noting that when we had this conversation, we were looking at china. We seemed always to have our most important conversations while looking at china; even that first afternoon, after the men's room, it was to the china department that we drifted, and in the china department that we told each other our names.

"Oh, this is nice," Tom said. "Hand-painted, too."

Because the carnality that had started everything seemed suddenly so remote, I glanced at his crotch.

"The measure of a man," I began.

He blushed. "Oh, please. Do you like Aynsley?"

"I'd like to do more with you. Preferably without a wall between us."

He picked up a teacup. "I know a place in London where you can get this stuff dirt cheap. Seconds, of course. Tiny flaws."

"I'd like to kiss you for about a month."

He smiled with pleasure, looked over his shoulder. "Ssh," he said. "People will hear you."

Spode. Wedgwood. Royal Doulton.

We had our picture taken together. Tom framed a copy, and put it on the desk in the kitchen, the one on which he worked out the menus for the dinners he catered, and wrote the children's books he could never get published.

His devotion amazed me. Nineteen manuscripts, hundreds of rejection letters, and still he persevered, claiming that he derived enough satisfaction from the mere act of writing, and enough pride from the pleasure the books gave to the children he knew.

For they all read his books in manuscript, those Justins and Sams and Maxes. Their mothers read them too. "Those New York publishers are absolutely crazy not to take these," Gina said once. "If they did, they'd make a fortune."

But not even his friend Mary, whose brother worked at Simon and Schuster, ever offered to help him.

He asked her once. I don't know how, but somehow he mustered the wherewithal to ask her. If she could mention him to her brother, mention his books . . .

Mary's mouth tightened. "But my brother works in the marketing department," she said. "Probably he doesn't know anyone in children's books."

That *probably*. It gave everything away. The truth was, she wanted him in his place.

Caterer. Babysitter. Giver of kitchen wisdom. Have I mentioned marriage counselor? If Tom had come into his own, he might no longer have been available.

"Tom, you're so wise!" How often I heard those words, spoken by his weeping married friends. Sitting in our living room, they would sob and vent. Stories would dribble out, of stains and threats and temptations.

And Tom would hand over the box of tissues, pour the tea, and proceed to give the shrewd and reasoned advice for which he was famous.

He was good at it, too. He kept more than one spouse from straying. Unfortunately, it was never his own.

Via in Selci

I'm starting to relax now, to fall into the rhythm of interrogation. Already I've been here for three hours. Once we've gone out for coffee—me, the *maresciallo,* and his deputies. We walked down Via in Selci to Via Cavour, to a bar on the corner, where all three of them bought cigarettes. We ordered espressos. As is the masculine fashion in Italy, the *carabinieri* drank theirs Arabic-fashion, out of shot glasses.

Afterward, they fought over who would pick up the bill. The *maresciallo* won, which probably explains why he is the *maresciallo.* Then we returned to the *caserma.* It was just after eleven o'clock in the morning, the sky cloudless and blue, a perfect backdrop for the Colosseum rising above rooftops. I remembered Tom taking me on one of his typically brisk tours around its periphery. As was his habit, he had pointed out unusual details: the flowers growing in the cracks, the birds who had built nests in the little holes pocking the ancient stone.

"Lovers used to come here for trysts," he'd said. "Remember 'Roman Fever'? Malaria—from the Italian, *mal aria.* Bad air."

Last night, the Colosseum was lit up with bright yellow spotlights. I asked the *maresciallo* why.

"They're lit every time a death sentence is commuted somewhere in the world," he said.

"Whereas in Italy," I said, "even if you find the person who killed Tom, you couldn't sentence him to death."

"Would you want us to?"

"No! I've always thought the death penalty was barbaric."

"You are more civilized than most of your countrymen," the *maresciallo* said.

■

At the *caserma,* he waves to the guard in his bulletproof cubicle, then leads me down a badly lit corridor, past two empty holding cells, up a staircase, through a storage room, and back into his office. Once again, he takes his place at the gunmetal desk. His deputies, however, change positions. The one who had been typing sits on the corner of the desk. The one who had been sitting on the corner of the desk prepares to type.

"So where were we?" he says, opening his pack of cigarettes. "Oh, yes. You were saying that the professor would never have brought someone home with him when he had a guest staying."

"At least he never did when I was staying there."

"Please forgive me if this is an intrusive question, but when you and he lived together, were you faithful to each other?"

"He was faithful to me."

"As far as you know."

"That much I know."

"Would you describe him as jealous?"

"I made sure he never had occasion to be jealous."

The *maresciallo* smiles. Like his colleagues, he is broad-shouldered and hairy-chested, the first three buttons of his shirt undone to show off the gold chain around his neck. When I first arrived here, I felt anthropological, as if I were a member of some tribe whose habits the experts interviewing him found fascinating but bizarre. In Italy examples of the "out" homosexual are still rare. Much more common is what one might call the *situational* homosexual, the man who, though he might go now and again to the park on the Monte Caprino, or even to the bar just up Via in Selci from the *caserma,* would never in a million years identify himself as a *frocio.* Perhaps the *maresciallo* himself went around that block a few times, when he was doing his military service, before he got married . . . Yet the idea that Tom and I, beyond youth and very publicly, should have chosen to make this thing the center of our lives—even to forge a sort of marriage—this was the part I feared the *carabinieri* would never get their minds around.

The surprise, however, is that the hours we've spent together have revealed unsuspected common ground. If nothing else, the *carabinieri* recognized that my life wasn't really all that different from theirs. For instance, the reluctance to sleep on the sofa of someone with whom you once shared a bed—that they could understand. Or the sly evasions of the disloyal spouse.

"Let's move on to another matter," the *maresciallo* says, lighting another cigarette. "Did the professor ever speak to you of a friend called Pepe?"

"A few times."

"Do you know his last name?"

"I never met him. I only heard about him."

"Did he ever happen to say how he met Pepe?"

"I think they were neighbors when Tom first moved to Rome."

"When he was living in Monti."

"Exactly."

"How old is Pepe? Do you know what he looks like? Have you ever seen a photograph of him?"

"I haven't. I'm sorry."

"Do you know if the professor ever had sexual relations with Pepe?"

"The way he talked about him, it seems unlikely. My impression was that they just went out together. That they were friends."

The deputy reads: "The professor had an acquaintance called Pepe, who had been his neighbor when he first moved to Rome and was living in the Monti area. As far as I know, he never had sexual relations with Pepe, though they went out together."

"Might Pepe have been a person the professor approached if he hoped to procure a sexual partner for money?"

"It's possible."

"Was the professor in the habit of offering money in exchange for sex?"

"Certainly not when we lived together. In Rome . . . well, if he was, he never said anything about it."

"Did he ever speak of anyone to whom he was attracted? A student, perhaps?"

I think for a moment. Then I remember our lunch. *Taste that rosemary* . . .

"There was a waiter," I say. "His name was Enzo. He worked at a trattoria—Da Giuseppina, I think it was called—near Torre Argentina."

"But not a student."

"Come to think of it, he did mention a student. Piergiorgio, Piervincenzo: one of those compound names. Tom said he was very good-looking. The only problem was that he was a Fascist."

"And the professor was a Communist."

"He was a Democrat, yes."

The deputy reads: "The professor expressed attraction to a waiter called Enzo, who worked at the Trattoria da Giuseppina, as well as to a student with a compound name, beginning with 'Pier.' However, they were of divergent political views."

"Anyone else?"

"Only the Dying Gaul."

"The Dying Gaul?"

"Tom always claimed to have a crush on the Dying Gaul," I say.

■

When did it start, his passion for marble? Certainly there was no evidence of it in our San Francisco days. I don't remember anything about marble from our San Francisco days. Back then Tom had other passions: cooking, chiefly. He also collected baseball cards. Though this may have been more for the sake of his many godsons.

As for me, I went to night school. Foreign language courses. I was lucky; fluency came naturally to me. For most people new languages are buffeting, even brutal oceans. I dived into them without hesitation. Although timid in English, I found my voice when speaking these stepmother tongues, deriving a gastronome's pleasure from words: *tendresse, Zitronen, geniale.*

Already I spoke French, German, and Italian. Now, three nights a week, I studied Russian and Japanese. Later, just for the hell of it, I convinced a woman I knew from Bilbao to give me lessons in Basque. "Vincent is so intellectually curious," Tom would say at his dinner parties. My studying, my lessons with the woman from Bilbao, became his amusing excuse for my being out on the evenings when he gave dinner parties.

The marble, though—it must have come after we broke up, when he was first living in Rome, in that tiny apartment on Via del Boschetto. Not yet the big, dreary apartment in the Olympic Village, in which he was killed. For the moment, his plans were too uncertain to justify furniture. After all, he had moved to Rome on the spur of the moment, in the immediate wake of my deciding to move to Düsseldorf. Tit for tat; or maybe he left in order to feel that he wasn't being left.

In Rome, he let two furnished rooms from a widow who lived on Via Frattina. Like many Romans, she owned pockets of real estate all over the city, none of which she occupied. Instead she rented the apartments she owned in order to pay for the apartment she rented. Recently she had sold her beach house in Fregene, the furniture from which had been moved into Tom's bow tie–shaped flat. Old seaside junk: a rattan sofa with matching armchairs, the wicker uncurling; a wrought-iron dining table with four wobbly chairs; a bed with a headboard shaped like a wave, topped by a crest of white foam.

There was always a smell of salt air in that apartment, which was odd, since it was very dark, its attic windows giving only onto rooftops and balconies and other attic windows. No water, no fishing boats. If you took the pillows off the armchairs, grains of sand scattered onto the floor.

I remember one afternoon we were taking a stroll through the Forum. It had been raining, and the ground was muddy. Tom was talking about the different kinds of marble that the Romans quarried. "That's *africano,*" he said, pointing to a paving stone that lay propped against a rusty fence, in tall grass. "Look how it glows, after the rain. As if it's been polished."

I looked. In the gray light, the stony masses that made up the slab glistened green and red and a white like lard. Nearby lay a column, cream veined with purple-brown. It made me think of fudge-swirl ice cream.

"*Pavonazzetto,*" Tom said. "And that one there, that's *rosso antico.* Not porphyry. You can tell because the red isn't speckled. Porphyry is always speckled. It's the caviar of marbles."

"*Marmo come lardo,*" I said, my eyes still on the *africano.* "It's like a poem."

Tom had his eyes on the path in front of us. "If you look carefully, sometimes you see glints of things," he said. "Especially after the rain, the stuff comes up like mushrooms. For instance—there." And he stopped. "You have to use your toe," he added, digging in the mud with his boot.

The path winked. He stepped back.

"Make sure no one's watching," he whispered.

I glanced over my shoulder. In the distance a German family was photographing itself. "Be my lookout," Tom said, and pulled a screwdriver from his jacket pocket. Then he bent down and jabbed at the mud.

The German family put away its cameras and walked toward us. "Tom," I said.

"It's okay," he said, stuffing something into his pocket.

"Well, what did you find?"

"We'll see in a minute."

We turned off the path, into a copse of umbrella pines, where Tom took out his treasure. At first I thought it was an ordinary rock, until he scraped the dirt off with his nails. It was the color of red wine, spotted like a duck's egg.

"See?" he said. "Porphyry."

He put it back in his pocket.

"But isn't it illegal to take things out of the Forum?"

"A little crumb like this? Who'll even notice? Anyway, the real crime would be *not* to take it. To leave it there to crumble into tinier and tinier pieces, under the tread of all these tourist feet. Instead of which—think of it this way—I'm saving a piece of history." He took my arm, which one could do in Italy. "Besides, no one ever really *owns* marble. It'll outlive us all. All I'm doing is giving it a home for a few years. Protection from the elements."

How many excuses he had! Nor were most of them unconvincing. After all, as he went on to show me that day, the Forum was already overflowing with relics, more than anyone had the money or resources to catalogue, much less display. In ditches left over from old archaeological digs, in makeshift "temporary" warehouses set up decades ago and never dismantled, bins of marble fragments lay untouched, unsifted. Cats meandered past them, slept on them, peed on them. He was right. What did a little chip like that matter?

A few nights later, though, returning to his apartment after some touring of my own, I tripped over something as I came through the door. The paving stone—the enormous one of *africano*—was sitting on his living room floor.

"How on earth did you get it out?" I asked.

He winked. "I used my toe," he said.

He started to acquire larger and larger pieces. Some of these, he told me, he had bought from a dealer he knew, while others he had won at poker games hosted by his friend Adua. Although by profession Adua was a doctor, her real passion—her only passion—was for marble. "You think I've got good stuff!" Tom said. "Wait until you see what Adua has stashed away!"

I met Adua only a few times. She was a small, heavy-hipped woman in her mid-forties. Her hair was dark, crudely cut. She lived alone, Tom told me, and was a sort of theoretical lesbian, though she had no lovers of whom he was aware. All her friends were men, fellow *marmisti*, or marble collectors. I called them the marble thieves. Around Tom, at least, Adua spoke of little else save her collection.

One morning she took us for a drive along the Via Appia Antica. The air was muggy that day. Outside her apartment building in Monte Verdi, where we met, she opened the trunk of her battered Fiat so that we could put our coats away. An immense block of serpentine sat next to the spare tire, half-covered in plastic.

"From the Temple of Heliogabolus," Adua said.

"Where did you get it?"

"I won it," she said. "The only problem is, I haven't figured out how to get it up the stairs."

"In the old days, at Hadrian's Villa," Tom said in the car, "you could find incredible stuff. All the marble, it was just piled up in these caves the archaeologists had dug out. The caves had metal doors on them, but they were never locked. You could walk in and help yourself."

"And now?"

"Oh, everything's padlocked. I suppose they got wind of what Adua was up to."

He winked. Adua tousled what hair he had left. By now we were out of the city, driving through the *campagna,* a flat landscape of sunflowers and hayricks. Big villas passed us, their high walls studded with hunks of broken glass bottle.

We came to some ruins—old arches and bits of aqueduct. Behind a tall fence, fields of grass and wheat spread out. In the distance I could see sheep grazing against a silhouette of buildings, one of which I recognized as St. Peter's.

Adua parked the car. We got out. It was raining, which should have clued me in on what they had in mind. With a kind of medical authority, as if it were a gland to be palpated, she felt at the metal fence. A sign was tacked to it, explaining in bureaucratic Italian that this was an archaeological zone: no trespassing.

"I think we can get over it," Adua said, fitting her foot into one of the wire squares of the fence. Yet when she hoisted herself up, the fence sagged. She started again. "Push my ass," she commanded, and we did. She hauled herself over, dropping abruptly onto the other side.

Tom went next, then I. As I fell, my jeans caught on the fence, which ripped a hole in them.

"Don't worry," Tom said. "Torn jeans are fashionable this year."

I looked back at the fence. How were we ever going to get back over it? I wondered. Meanwhile, Tom and Adua had set off toward St. Peter's. I followed them. For several minutes we trekked through mud and grass. Very far out, so far that you could no longer see the car, the ground started yielding up marble. The rain had moistened it, making it easier to see. I hadn't noticed before, but both Tom and Adua were carrying backpacks. Very quickly, they began gathering up their booty. "Look, this one's perfect!" Tom said, digging out a hexagonal paving stone.

"Oh, *cipollina*," Adua said, as she yanked a column fragment from the mud. "Look, the surface is striated, like a slice of onion."

After about twenty minutes—by now their backpacks were nearly full—a dog appeared. She was a very friendly, very dirty, brown and white sheepdog. I patted her head. Next some sheep rounded a hillock, accompanied by an old man carrying a stick. All of them gazed at us.

Immediately, Tom and Adua put down their backpacks.

"Good morning," Adua said to the old man. "Are these your sheep?"

"They are."

"What are you raising them for? Ricotta?"

"Ricotta, pecorino."

She smiled confidingly. "It's not too easy now, finding a really fresh ricotta in Rome. Not like in the old days."

"Everything was better then," the shepherd agreed.

Rather disingenuously, I thought, Adua touched Tom on the shoulder and pointed toward the skyline. "Perhaps you can help us," she said to the shepherd. "I've brought my American friends here so that they could get a view of the city from a distance, and we were wondering if that building was St. Peter's."

"Yes, it's St. Peter's," the shepherd answered. "And that one's San Paolo fuori le Mura."

"Of course! I didn't recognize it from here."

The shepherd now proceeded to give us a telescopic tour of the great Roman monuments. Adua asked him how long he had been working these fields. All his life, he said. Seventy-eight years.

"Well, we'd best be heading back," she said after a few minutes, and offered her hand. "It's been a pleasure."

"Arrivederla, signora," the shepherd said, moving away with his dog.

Adua and Tom picked up their backpacks, and we started moving back toward the fence.

"Incredible, isn't it?" Tom said. "Sheep and shepherds—yet we're still inside the city limits."

"I hope he didn't notice what you were up to," I said.

Adua laughed. "Don't worry," she said. "He's not interested in marble. He's only interested in his ricotta."

After that, Tom became a fixture at Adua's poker games. The other players, he told me, were "lunatics" like him. He had "gotten the disease." He sent me letters in Düsseldorf describing his winnings: a slab of *giallo antico* from Ostia, some perfect tesserae of green *serpentino* from the baths of Caracalla. "Adua's had a lot of her pieces put into the floor of her apartment, like tiles," he said. "Only she keeps them covered with a carpet. She lives in terror of the *carabinieri* coming after her."

Via del Boschetto, he told me, was getting too expensive, so he had decided to sublet the apartment of a friend of Pepe's, on Via Bulgaria, in the Olympic Village. "Far out from the center, but the place is huge, and has a terrace. And compared to Via del Boschetto, I'm paying nothing. Practically nothing."

"But isn't it a problem getting to work?"

"Why? The fifty-three bus stops right outside my door."

I visited him only twice on Via Bulgaria. Even by the grim standards of the Roman *periferia,* the Olympic Village was ugly to the point of inspiring a kind of interior desolation:

what Eastern Europe must have looked like before the wall came down. Long ago the habitations of 1960s athletes (designed, no doubt, according to sound principles of architectural rationality) had been converted into public housing: long, low rows of apartment blocks, constructed from umber-colored brick and raised up on pylons. A bramble of antennas sprouted on the roofs, and though there was space beneath the pylons for plenty of shops, almost all were vacant, only the most basic—a tobacconist, a grocery store, a pharmacy— having proved capable of flourishing in such meager soil.

Most of Tom's neighbors were elderly. They trod up and down the pedestrian walkways, daughters of seventy leading mothers of ninety. On the door of the pharmacy, to which he took me the first day, a placard announced, AVAILABLE HERE: INCONTINENCE DIAPERS.

As a language, Italian tends to eschew the sort of polite euphemisms in which English glories. Yet Tom, who in San Francisco had always displayed such a need for cheer, here seemed immune to the dreariness of his surroundings. Indeed, as he led me across the so-called park, clotted with weeds and littered with hypodermics, or down dark streets that, because the city had designated this the official zone for driving lessons and driving tests, were always filled with cars screeching to a halt, irritated instructors slamming their feet on auxiliary brakes, he exulted. "This is the real Rome," he said. "You want to eat the way the Romans eat, you want to eat *abbacchio* cooked the Roman way? This is where you'll find it."

As for his apartment—well, as he had promised, it *was* large. Essentially it consisted of a corridor off of which three square rooms opened. The floors were terrazzo, the walls a blinding white, the ceilings lit by naked bulbs. Because he had as yet had no time to shop, there was little in the way of furniture: a table (the one he was tied to) and two chairs in the kitchen, a foldout sofa in the living room, an ugly laminate armoire and a mattress in the bedroom. No lamps, no pictures, none of the decorative frippery to which he had been so devoted in San Francisco. Instead the apartment was dark, especially on those mornings when the *scirocco* swept down the long, quiet streets, spattering every outdoor surface with Saharan sand. Most of the marble he kept hidden in the armoire, and took out only when he wanted to show it off.

No doubt the apartment's strangest feature, however, was its door, which was padded, covered in what looked like red leather, and buttoned like a chesterfield. It would not have looked amiss in an asylum. Nor would any loud noise—for instance, a scream, or glass breaking—have been likely to penetrate that door. For what reason, I wondered, had Pepe's friend had it installed?

His new apartment made me frightened for Tom, much more frightened, even, than I'd been the day I'd gotten off the plane and he'd walked up to me, so changed that I barely recognized him. Everything about the move seemed contrary to his spirit—or perhaps I should say, contrary to the spirit he had displayed when we lived together. And why did he need so badly to save money? We had just sold the house, so he had some cash. Was it because he was spending everything he earned on marble? Or on something else?

It occurs to me, sitting in the *caserma*, that perhaps I ought to mention the poker games to the *maresciallo*. Only if I do, I might get Adua in trouble—assuming they haven't already found her. No doubt *her* number was in Tom's Filofax.

So did they just show up at her door, leading her, for an instant, to believe that her day of reckoning had come at last, and that her marble was to be confiscated? That she was to be fined, jailed, ruined? Probably. Until they explained the real reason for their visit. Tom was dead.

Something else I hadn't thought of: after the murder, when the *carabinieri* searched his flat, they must have found the paving stone. The one in *africano.* Not to mention the obelisk—a poker game winning. And God knows what other contraband.

Oh, how complicated it's all getting! Such a proliferation of motives! If Gina knew, she'd be thrilled. Yes, she'd say, it had to be one of those marble thieves. An intrigue. Killed for the sake of some *cipollina rossa.* Or a fragment of *frutticoloso,* so called because its many component colors suggest a basket of fruit, and, according to Adua, the rarest of the rare.

If they ask me, I'll tell them. I'll tell them everything I know. As long as they don't ask me, though, I'm keeping my mouth shut. This was something I learned to do in San Francisco, when I was cheating all the time on Tom: always tell the truth, but never volunteer anything.

Wool Street

Would things have gone better for us if we'd behaved like all the other faggots we knew, and had what was known as an "open" relationship? If Tom had been the sort of man who, upon surprising his lover in bed with someone else, didn't get mad, but got undressed . . . well, would we be living on Wool Street still? Sitting on a fortune in real estate? Still together? Tom still alive?

No, no. The scenario's too simplistic. For just as easily as it might have liberated me, the knowledge that Tom, too, was getting up to "that sort of thing" could have provoked in me a jealousy equal to his own. Or the lifting of the onus might have defused the thrill of adultery altogether. When transgression is divorced from subterfuge, the illicit becomes banal. The pleasure of cheating, it's in the scam, not the pay-off—right?

So I took his loyalty for a ride. He never found out. Discord overwhelmed us, and we parted.

Oh, everything went so wildly, so perversely out of kilter! None of this was supposed to happen: not the Olympic Village, not Düsseldorf, not the patrol car nosing its way stealthily around the corner of Wool Street as I stand gawking at the house we used to own. For suddenly I'm there again—no longer in the *caserma* at all. The policeman slows, lowers his sunglasses. And what am I but a loiterer, a ne'er-do-well, just the sort of rabble he's paid to scare away?

Of course, if I wanted to, I could explain my presence to him. "I used to live here," I could say. "This neighborhood used to be my neighborhood. I used to shop at the grocery store on the corner." But I don't want to. Instead I smile, walk back across the street, and climb into my rental car. Switch on the ignition. Drive away.

It's all my fault. I squandered what I should have cherished. I took for granted Tom's reliability, the fact that every day, at every hour of the day, I knew where to find him: mornings in the kitchen, writing or cooking; from noon to one, the gym; afternoons back in the kitchen, or baby-sitting. More crucially, on those rare occasions when he veered from his routine, he always made a point of calling to tell me. "I'll be at Gina's until three-thirty," he'd say. "Then I'm going grocery shopping. Then I have to meet Mrs. Roxburgh to plan a lunch. I should be home by seven, unless I hit traffic—"

"That's fine," I'd say.

"Let me give you the number at Mrs. Roxburgh's," he'd say.

"That's all right. I don't need it," I'd say.

"I just don't want you to worry," he'd say.

·

As for me, I gave him no outward cause for anxiety. I kept all my ducks in a row. Only sometimes I'd call half an hour before one of his dinner parties and say that I couldn't come. "I forgot that we have a test this week. My Urdu class."

How feeble was the noise he made on these occasions, disappointment thudding in the echo chamber of purported indifference.

Sometimes I wondered if he ever got suspicious. I rather hoped he might. I rather hoped he'd make inquiries, and discover that indeed, an Urdu class *was* being offered at San Francisco State on Thursday evenings. For my deceptions were artful. I knew Tom well enough to know that once he found out the course existed, he would never check whether I was actually enrolled in it. Instead, shame at having distrusted me in the first place would swamp him, inducing that superfluity of regret that in his case almost always took the form of an urge to bake: something creamy and sticky, which I would find waiting for me when I got home.

It was on these nights—sitting in our kitchen in the aftermath of some carnal misdeed—that I would experience most deeply the giddy relief of the liar. Nor is this delight so remote, in the end, from artistic ecstasy, the pleasure of seeing a well-crafted thing work well.

All my ducks in a row.

Or perhaps I have it wrong, and it was Tom who was playing *me* for the fool. Perhaps, the whole time, he too was getting up to "that sort of thing"; in which case his pledges of fidelity, his insistence on keeping me abreast of his many activities— all this was as much a needless vaudeville as my Thursday night Urdu class.

Needless—unless what he needed was to feel that he was getting away with something.

I tried to remain faithful, if not to him, then to his fear, to his largely unspoken conviction that only by being "good" might we hope to avoid the sort of fate so many others had suffered. For he seemed to perceive our coming together as a covenant, the terms of which required us to give up, in exchange for health, the very life implied by the place where we had come together. Only by retreating from a septic world, as the storytellers in the *Decameron* had done, might we save ourselves, save each other.

According to this way of thinking, to look for sex outside your marriage was not merely to betray the person you loved, but to bring rabies into England—as if a vow of loyalty were the same thing as a vaccination.

In lying there is often this lie: that we do it to protect other people.

Keeping him in the dark was never very difficult, I think in part because, without even being aware of it, he wanted to be kept in the dark. Also, the combination of my language classes and Tom's devotion to his friends' children left me with large amounts of time for which I wasn't accountable, especially on those weekends when he would volunteer to baby-sit for some couple who were going off to Lake Tahoe to save their marriage. He'd move himself into their house, sleep in their bed, and take care of their kids.

During those weekends, what seemed most important to him was that he establish, with those Justins and Samuels and Maxes, the very camaraderie of boys from which, as a boy, he had been excluded, thanks largely to his inability to throw a ball, his high voice, in short, his stubborn adherence to all the classic attributes of the good faggot. For despite the cruelty that had marred his childhood, still, he longed to be treated as a boy by boys, which was why, even as he baked, he collected baseball cards, and was always trying to get me to go to the park with him to play catch.

Now he was not so much the adult to whom children looked up as the secret playmate whose grown-up bearing and possessions (a credit card, a driver's license) brought certain enviable and forbidden attractions within reach. With Tom, his young charges could eat the things they weren't supposed to eat, see the movies they weren't supposed to see. In this regard Tom fit perfectly the clinical profile of the pedophile . . . except that he was not a pedophile. Sexuality had nothing to do with it; to him those boys were not emblems, they were not "the boy" whose allure must wither as he himself blooms. Instead he loved them simply and individually, as well as loving the ease with which they loved him, their love reliable and pure of complication, and remote from the bristly, fitful love of adult for adult.

And yet in the background, there always lurked a certain unease, a skittishness on Tom's part to match the volubility with which his friends avowed their trust in him.

For instance, I remember a dinner once—it was an occasion dinner, though I can't recall which occasion: Thanksgiving, perhaps. Tom had done all the cooking, of course. There were children, and two or three of the couples, and only one other queer: his former boyfriend Ernie, whom he had invited only because he was alone, and dying. Visibly dying.

I mean, you could see the patches of foundation make-up that he had rubbed onto his face to hide the KS lesions.

A husband—this was Tony, who was married to Gina; typically, he worked in the computer industry—was talking about his boyhood. About all the "macho crap" he'd had to put up with, coming of age in the fifties. Of late Tony had joined a men's group, the members of which went on camping trips, and danced around a wood fire, and wept together over paternal cruelties.

"When Justin grows up," he said, "I want him to be at peace in his masculinity. That way he'll be a better father than I am. A better husband, too."

Gina picked up her napkin and dabbed at the corner of her eyes. Reaching across the table, she squeezed his hand.

A silence fell. I remember there was a big bowl of tangerines and walnuts in the center of the table. Ernie took a walnut and cracked it between his teeth. "All well and good," he said, "but what if Justin grows up to be queer?"

Tony, who was taking a gulp from his wineglass, spluttered onto the tablecloth, then looked anxiously toward his son, who was playing with Lego blocks.

He appeared to regard Justin's fixation on the Lego blocks with relief.

"You see?" Ernie said. "The very idea terrifies you. And yet who's to say he won't grow up to be queer? I did. Tom did."

"Ernie, please," Tom said.

"Look, I understand your point, and I respect it," Tony said, "only in the case of Justin, it seems fairly obvious—"

"Why, because he plays baseball? I played baseball. For Christ's sake, I was pitcher on the varsity team."

"What Tony means," Gina interjected, "is that we just want our son to grow up to be happy and well adjusted. To be a good partner and a good parent."

"So you're saying you won't mind if he turns out to be queer?"

"Please keep your voice down."

"Well, that proves my point. Suddenly *queer*'s a dirty word. And if that's how things are in your house, then no matter what Justin does, he's fucked for life. For all your sanctimonious good intentions, you're making it clear that you expect him to grow up a certain way. In a sense you're ordering him to."

"Justin, why don't you go to the other room?" Tony said. "The grown-ups need private time."

"No," said Justin.

By now Tom was nearly apoplectic. He hated it, he told me later, when his dinners were spoiled. And what had spoiled this one?

"Conflict," he replied, plunging a steel pan into scalding dishwater.

"But Ernie only said what he felt."

"He didn't have to be so confrontational. He offended Tony."

"Tony offended him."

"Tony didn't mean to offend anyone. A guy like that, it's not easy for him to open up. For once he was feeling at ease, like he could really say what was on his mind. Now he'll always be on his guard with us."

"He offended me," I added after a moment.

"I just don't see why Ernie had to be so holier-than-thou. It's as if he thinks being sick means he isn't obliged to be civil."

"Was he being uncivil?"

"He should have watched his language. Also, his timing was terrible. He upset everybody, especially the children."

"The children weren't listening."

"How do you know?" Tom asked.

What seemed imperative to him, during those years, was a certain kind of forgetting: to do one's duty, to pay one's dues, and then at the end of the day to return to a place from which illness—even the mention of illness—was effectively barred.

And because sex was for him so intimately bound up with illness, this had to be a place from which sex, too, was barred—virtually barred.

So once a week—it seemed to be part of that bargain he had struck, altruism in exchange for a life sentence—he volunteered at the AIDS hospice that his friend Caroline ran. Sometimes I accompanied him. I liked the hospice, which was in many ways far more cheerful than our own crypto-dream-bunker. It was located in a small, sunny house at the end of a cul-de-sac around which children rode their bicycles with unusual ferocity. We would bring food, and if it was spring, fresh flowers—irises and tulips—and I remember that one morning Tom was arranging the flowers in vases, when one of the patients called out, "Caroline, could you come here for a moment? I think John just died." Caroline went, and it was true: John had died. No one seemed overly upset. The police were summoned. They did not, as I'd heard they had early in the epidemic, when no one knew anything, pull a gun on the corpse. ("If you'd feel better about it, you can tie him up," the distraught widower is reputed to have remarked on one of these occasions; "it wouldn't be the first time.") A doctor arrived to sign the death certificate, an ambulance to take away the body. Quiet prayers were said, and lunch was made.

"Around here," Caroline said, "death is never an emergency. The only emergency is pain."

We stayed for lunch—corn chowder, chicken with almonds, chocolate pudding. Comfort food, all made by Tom. Then the roommate of the man who'd died called Caroline over to his bedside and whispered something to her. "He wants to speak to you," she said.

"Who? Me?" asked Tom. "Why?"

"I don't know."

We walked over to the man's bed. He had a tube in his nose. He could barely lift his head.

There was a chair next to the bed, and Tom sat down in it.

The man lifted his lips to Tom's ear. "Don't you remember me?" he asked.

"I'm sorry," Tom said. "I . . ."

"I'm a friend of Ernie's. Keith Musgrave. Don't you remember that weekend in Lake Tahoe? We rented a cabin— you and Ernie and Steven and I. Four boys and only one bed."

Tom blushed. "Oh, of course. How are you?"

"How am I?"

"Sorry," Tom said, "I didn't mean . . ."

"It's okay. So how's Ernie doing these days? Are you two still in touch?"

"Ernie? Oh, well, he's . . . passed on. Just a few weeks ago."

"Ah. So I'll be seeing him soon." Keith looked up. "Or on second thought . . ." And he looked down.

Tom stood. "I'm afraid we have to go," he said. "It's certainly been a pleasure."

"The pleasure was all mine," Keith answered, turning to look out the window. And we headed out the door.

It had started raining by the time we left the hospice. I remember Tom's silence in the car, his pale and vulnerable profile: chiseled sideburn, protruding nose, watermelon-colored lips. His hand gripping the wheel. One half-obscured, blinking brown eye focused, urgently, on the road. We had no plans for the rest of the weekend, and I was desperately trying to think some up, running in my head through an ever shorter list of friends on whom we could still count for company . . . but Mary's baby was sick, and Gina and Tony were at Disneyland, and Joan's best friend was dying. Suddenly a car made an illegal left turn in front of us, Tom honked the horn,

smashed on the brakes, we skidded in the rain and nearly col-
lided with a 94 bus. "Fuck," he said, in a voice that suggested
he was sorry we hadn't, then, righting the car, lugged us back
into traffic.

"Was the problem that you didn't recognize him?" I asked.

"Who?"

"Keith."

"Oh, him. No, at first I didn't."

I stretched my arms behind my head. "So I guess it
mustn't have been a very good weekend."

"And what's that supposed to mean?"

"Nothing. Just . . . that if it had been a good weekend,
you'd have remembered it."

"We didn't do anything unsafe, okay?"

"What does that have to do with anything?"

"Well, clearly that's what you're wondering . . . and if that's
the case, you can rest assured. I've been completely up front
with you so far as my history is concerned. You've got nothing
to worry about."

"Of course I've got nothing to worry about. We never
have sex."

"Oh, so we're back to that again—"

"We're not back to anything."

"Why won't I just have the test and be done with it."

"I never mentioned the test. You brought up the test. All
of this is in your head, not mine."

We arrived home. The rain had gotten worse. I remember
that I was correcting proofs, and Tom was sitting at his desk,
drawing endless concentric circles with a protractor, when I
felt a drop of water hit my head and, looking up, saw a patch
of paint on the ceiling bulging like a tumor, rainwater collect-
ing underneath. Tom noticed it the same moment I did, a
pregnancy gathering there, and then before we could do or
say anything the fragile membrane broke, and water fell to

the floor, as before a birth. He jumped up, grabbed a box of tissues, and dropped to his knees before the spreading gray stain on the carpet.

"Call a plumber!" he screamed, but I just watched as he piled tissues on top of tissues to soak up the water.

"But, Tom, a plumber can't—"

"Are you just going to stand there? Aren't you going to help at all?"

"Okay, okay."

"You don't need to use that tone of voice. There's really no justification for that tone of voice. And bring some paper towels."

I went into the kitchen, where we kept the phone books. I called a plumber, though I could not fathom what he was supposed to do. In crisp tones, he informed me that a weekend visit would cost $55 off the bat, plus $35 an hour, plus parts. "Whatever," I said, hung up, and went back into the living room, where Tom was still crouching over his soggy pile of tissues.

"I've called the plumber. He's on his way."

"You're so slow. Three minutes I've been waiting here for you to bring me paper towels. And now that I think about it, it's probably been three minutes every day since we started living together—at least. That's twenty-one minutes a week, eighty-four minutes a month, over a thousand minutes a year. Which means that in ten years, I've lost a hundred and sixty days—something like five months—just waiting for you. Now give me the damn paper towels."

"I forgot the paper towels."

Tom looked up at me. I sat on the sofa.

"I can't stay here anymore," I said. "I'm going crazy. You're driving me crazy."

"Are you saying you're leaving me?" he asked, his voice low, as if he'd been expecting it.

"Not you. This." I pointed to the rug, to the sopping pile of tissues.

"I knew you'd do this one day," Tom said. "You're a coward. You think you can run away from pain. Soon enough you'll find out, though. No one can."

He quieted, and I turned to watch where the rain was falling against the window, so thickly sheeted that for a moment it seemed to be flowing upward.

"Just don't expect me to be waiting for you when you come back," Tom said. He was rubbing his hands together, gathering the white clots of tissue into a ball.

"I wouldn't expect that."

Suddenly our voices were calm, we were talking like normal human beings. "Where are you planning to go, anyway?" he asked, as casually as if I were a friend planning a vacation.

"I thought Düsseldorf."

"Düsseldorf!"

"There's a job in Düsseldorf. I saw it posted at school. For an interpreter."

"Oh, that sounds grand! Now I know why you were taking all those language courses."

I hadn't known myself until then.

He threw a vase at me. I remember feeling a certain detached curiosity, because no one had ever thrown anything at me before, and the vase was the same color as the water, and suddenly, everywhere, there were pieces of vase, and water, and flowers.

I put on my jacket, even though my shirt was soaked with the stinking water the flowers had been rotting in. "Vincent!" I heard him call as I went out the door, but his voice was distant already, as if I'd never see him again. I got into my car. He was standing by the window, looking out at me. Silent. The heavy rain against the glass made him look as if he were melting.

Via in Selci

Is it only thanks to what happened afterward—to that shadowing of motive with which retrospect tints the past—that I remember Tom, the last time I saw him, as somehow both sullen and brazen, withdrawn and at the same moment broken-bottle sharp, as if he had decided to throw off once and for all that wadding of gentility in which most of our intercourse sheathed itself? Not surprisingly, the occasion was dinner. The Morgue. Across a marble table the metaphorical ironies of which would only become apparent later on, we peered at each other—or rather, I peered at him and he peered over my head, over my shoulder, at a new waiter who had started the day before. Since the episode with Enzo and the pasta and chickpeas—not surprisingly, he had never gone back to Trattoria da Giuseppina—this matter of Tom and waiters had become a source of worry, and not only to me but, I learned later, to all his Roman friends. "Look at those forearms," he said, and I did—hairy and dark, the requisite gold bracelet slung low on the wrist. The hands that gave us our pizzas were blunt-fingered, with clean, moon-colored nails.

"Noontime shadow," Tom said.

"Noontime what?"

"That type would never make it to five o'clock."

It was typical of his jokes. "He looks like Tony," I said.

"Does he?" Tom put on his glasses, which of late he'd taken to wearing on a cord around his neck. "No, he doesn't. He doesn't look anything like Tony."

We ate our pizzas quickly, and without saying much. Later, I would try to explain to the *carabinieri* the peculiar impression I took with me as we left the pizzeria, of something having changed in Tom . . . and yet my Italian wasn't up to explaining just what that something was. Now I've had time to consider the matter, and I think I can fairly say that what had changed was his attitude toward love. Somehow it was both harder and sharper than it had once been, vulnerable and rapacious at once, like a can with a rusty edge. When we'd lived together, I'd often thought that Tom perceived love the way dogs did, that the idea was for us to be a warm lap in which he and I could curl up; love, in other words, as sleep. Only I hadn't played along. I'd left, and in doing so robbed the crypto-dream-house of its lazy, cozy, dull, lovely dream.

All this I try to tell the *maresciallo* and his typing deputy, who takes down every word. Even so, I fail, at least in my own mind, to get the idea across in all its raggedness. Any student of language knows that limit. They are silent while I speak, and I speak for a long time. Then I stop speaking. The deputy stops typing. "Yes," he says.

The other deputy coughs; interrupts. "Excuse me," he says, "but may I ask if the professor ever expressed any resentment, after you left him?"

I shake my head. "Not a word. He never rebuked me, or threatened me, never even tried to convince me to come back. In fact, the only thing he said was that he respected the choice I had made, and wanted to do everything he could to make sure we stayed friends."

The deputy types: Tom's nobility, his humility, glow green against that black screen. And yet even as I extol him, I'm doubting myself. After all, for whom else but me could he have been performing the last night at the Morgue, when he stared so brazenly at the waiter? Not merely undressing him with his eyes, but tearing into him with his eyes, the rusty edge of his eyes—as if to say, because of you, Vincent, I am brought this low. This is my revenge. There is no better way to hurt someone else than by hurting yourself.

The interview is almost over. Across from me, the *maresciallo* regards his folder; says, "Bah-bah-bah"; drums his fingers against the desk. "Let me see if there's anything else . . . Oh yes, the waiter at the Morgue. What did he look like?"

"Well, he was tall. Dark."

"The classic Mediterranean?"

"I suppose you could say so."

"Thin?" interjects the typing deputy.

"No, quite well built."

"Hairy?"

"Quite."

"Hairy like me," the *maresciallo* asks, "or like my colleague?" And he points to the deputy at the corner of the desk.

I glance from one chest to the other. Both men have the first several buttons of their shirts undone, and both have abundantly, one might even say exuberantly hairy chests . . . which Tom, it was true, always admired. I don't have a hairy chest. In fact, I wasn't his type at all, nor was he mine.

And yet I don't go along with the pornographic joke, I don't, as Tom, in his last days, might have done, say, "Well, I'm not sure. Perhaps if you took your shirts off . . ." For Tom is dead, and I must not be nearly so bad a faggot as I have pretended, for I simply tell the *maresciallo,* "I would have to say hairy like your colleague," and then look away, as if it's no business of mine.

The *maresciallo* gets up from his chair. "Thank you," he says. "I believe we're finished now."

"Are we?"

"All that's left is to print out your statement. You can read it and see if there's anything you'd like to change or delete . . . or add. Then you need merely to sign the document and you're free to go."

"But who killed him?"

He laughs. "If we knew that, we wouldn't have dragged you here from Düsseldorf, now would we?"

Pages spit out of a printer and are handed to me.

"My name is Vincent Burke," I read, "and I first met Thomas Carlomusto in New York in 1985 . . ."

The story of our lives, then. Yet who would have guessed it would have been written here, and in such exceptionally elegant Italian?

After the interview's over—after I've signed the statement, shaken the hands of all three *carabinieri,* and been treated, against my will, to yet another coffee—I walk through the Forum to the Colosseum, and then down Via San Giovanni in Laterano, until I reach the church of San Clemente. The church has just reopened. No one's there except for a young seminarian, perhaps an assistant to the sacristan, who has come to remove the guttered candles. Through the gloomy church light he looks at me; across pews and frescoes and acres of marble, those intricate floors by which Tom was so bewitched.

Was it him, then? He could not resemble the *maresciallo* less: a beanpole of a boy, with narrow shoulders, squinting eyes, a fat nose out of which hairs grow. Like a grotesque figure in some Renaissance painting . . . and yet, as he gathers the dead candles, he gazes at me, and his gaze is unwavering.

Was that what got Tom, then: the allure of the uniform? The rough belt loosened, and then, all at once, his mouth inside the cassock, sucking in the odor of wool and sweat?

The seminarian's hands clutching his head, like a bobbing pregnancy?

Well, it's possible. Anything's possible. It could have been the Fascist student, or an offended waiter, or a marble thief. Or a Romanian hustler—an *extracommunitario*—picked up at the station men's room, the one with the glass partitions. Or a fellow English teacher. Or it could have been me. Really, there's no reason at all why it couldn't have been me.

You'll never know. The case will never be solved. In a few months the folder with Tom's name on it will be shut, taken off the *maresciallo*'s desk, and deposited in that storage room through which I was led on the way to his office. Filed away with others of its kind.

Twenty-two others, to be precise.

I approach the seminarian. *"Buon giorno,"* he says.

"Buon giorno," I say, and feed a 500-lire coin into a black metal slot. There is an echoey clangor as it hits the dark bottom of the collection box. Then I take a fresh candle and light it; set it down amid all the other votives; form my lips around Tom's name.

I walk away. I have no idea if the seminarian is watching me, if he is lifting a monstrance or an obelisk to smash against my skull. Instead I have my eyes on the floor. These Escher-like interlardings of color really do create the most peculiar illusion of depth . . . and yet if you fell into them, they would break your nose. You couldn't lift it off, once you'd been spread out on that table, and the marble quilt had been drawn over your eyes.